FIREFIGHTER SEA DRAGON

FIRE & RESCUE SHIFTERS 4

ZOE CHANT

Copyright Zoe Chant 2017
All Rights Reserved

🌸 Created with Vellum

The Fire & Rescue Shifters series

Firefighter Dragon
Firefighter Pegasus
Firefighter Griffin
Firefighter Sea Dragon
The Master Shark's Mate
Firefighter Unicorn

Fire & Rescue Shifters Collection 1
(contains Firefighter Dragon, Firefighter Pegasus, and Firefighter Griffin)

All books in the Fire & Rescue Shifters series are standalone romances, each focusing on a new couple, with no cliff-hangers. They can be read in any order. However, characters from previous books reappear in later stories, so reading in series order is recommended for maximum enjoyment!

CHAPTER 1

*J*ohn Doe would never understand human ways.

For sea dragons, mating was simple. If you were fortunate enough to find your one true mate, then you immediately consummated the union. Joining minds and souls was a simple matter of uniting bodies in ecstasy. Nothing more was needed.

Apparently, for humans, tiny paper boxes of pink candies were also required.

"They're wedding favors, not incendiary devices, John," Griff said with a small smile. The griffin shifter's uncannily keen eyesight had obviously caught John's hesitation. "You don't need to handle the chocolates so gingerly. They aren't going to explode."

"I do not wish to make a mistake." With infinite care, John lowered the minuscule morsel into the waiting nest of tissue paper. "I would not wish to be the cause of any flaw in your strange human mating ritual."

Next to him, his comrade Chase let out a muffled snort. The pegasus shifter's dextrous hands never paused in tying gold and silver ribbons around the boxes, but his shoulders shook with suppressed laughter. He and Griff shared a quick, private glance across the table.

John was well used to that particular silent communication

amongst his fellow firefighters. It indicated that, once again, he had failed to grasp some fine point of human culture.

Life at the bottom of the sea had been so much simpler.

"I'm already mated to Hayley," Griff said to John, the laughter lines around his warm golden eyes crinkling with amusement. "The wedding is just a formality. You know that, right?"

"You have devoted six months of unstinting effort to this 'formality,' my oath-brother." John narrowed his own eyes, concentrating on picking up the next chocolate without accidentally squishing it. "And though I am unfamiliar with your mating rituals, I am *very* familiar with your peculiar human habit of saying one thing and meaning another. I choose to pay attention to your actions rather than your words. And your actions tell me that everything about tomorrow must be perfect."

Chase cocked an eyebrow at Griff, grinning. "He's got a point."

Griff tilted his shaggy blond head a little in wry acknowledgement. "Well, I appreciate the concern, but given that the wedding is tomorrow, we're going to have to speed up a bit. Don't worry John, it's not going to be ruined if a few of the favors are a bit rushed."

"If you ask me, it wouldn't be ruined if there were no wedding favors at all," Hugh muttered from the other end of the table.

The white-haired paramedic had been assigned the duty of attaching decorative plant matter—*flowers,* John reminded himself of the strange human concept—to the assembled favor boxes. It was a critical task, requiring great delicacy of touch. From Hugh's scowl, which deepened further with every box, he did not fully appreciate the honor of his role.

"Hugh also has a point," Chase said, casting a rather mournful look over at the pile of chocolates and cardboard still waiting to be turned into elegant table decorations. "Griff, I think I speak for everyone here when I say that we, as your fellow firefighters and dearest friends, had greatly anticipated spending the evening before your wedding toasting your future happiness with your family's finest Scotch. Not doing arts and crafts. Are these *really* necessary?"

"Yes," Griff said amiably. "For one thing, this is keeping all you bastards too busy to scheme to get me drunk tonight."

"Why would we seek to impair your physical state before such an important event?" John asked, bewildered, as Chase and Hugh spluttered in protest.

"I know *you* wouldn't." Griff bumped John's shoulder with his own affectionately. "But trust me, it's another inexplicable human custom for the groom's friends to try to ensure he's nursing a hangover down the aisle."

Hugh glared at Chase. "I *told* you he'd spot your scheme, and find a way to avoid it."

"I have no idea what you're talking about," Chase said, with great dignity. "And in any case, it was your idea in the first place."

"So you do not truly require these items, oath-brother? This was just a diversionary tactic?" John dropped the box he'd been unsuccessfully trying to fold, a wave of relief sweeping over him. "I must admit, that makes much more sense. I could not believe that even humans were peculiar enough to have a tradition of giving uselessly tiny portions of foodstuffs to guests as gifts, *after* the end of a meal."

Griff's mouth quirked up. "Ah, no, actually that is a real tradition. And I do genuinely need these. Hayley saw them at a wedding fair and loved them, but ended up deciding they were too expensive. So I thought I'd surprise her. Which means I really do need help."

"Tempted as I am to leave you to deal with the consequences of your too-clever scheme, Connie would never let me live it down if I abandoned these half-finished. She's taking her role as Matron of Honor rather seriously." Chase let out a long-suffering sigh, picking up another box. "The things we do for our mates."

"The things *you* poor sods do for *your* mates," Hugh corrected, pushing his chair back from the table. "This just makes me hope even more fervently that I never meet mine. Come on, John, let's go get a drink."

Yes, whined John's inner human. *This is a boring, pointless task. We aren't even any good at it. No one would mind if we went and enjoyed ourselves.*

With the ease of long practice, John suppressed his inner human's whispers. No matter the soft, two-legged creature that shared his soul, he was a *sea dragon*. He was above such selfish, hedonistic instincts.

He lifted his chin. "I cannot abandon my oath-brother in his hour of need. You must go if you feel so moved, but I shall stay until the bitter end."

Hugh looked hard at him for a moment, then dropped back into his chair with a groan. "For someone who claims to be honor-bound to only tell the truth, you are suspiciously good at manipulating people. No wonder the weather does what you tell it to do."

"I do not manipulate either water or people," John said, truthfully. "I simply speak. It is up to the listener to decide what to do in response."

"I should have managed to inoculate myself against your more-noble-than-thou attitude by now." Despite his surly words, Hugh picked up another flower and started to weave it into the next box. "You're a bloody bad influence, you know that?"

"Truly, you don't need to stay and help with this, John," Griff said. He jerked a thumb at Chase and Hugh. "I may need to keep these reprobates out of trouble, but that's no reason for you to be roped in as well. You've already done more than enough for me and Hayley. You should go, get some rest. We can handle this."

John's back stiffened. Only a coward would flee the field while his brothers-in-arms still fought. To suggest that he should do so…well, if Griff had been a sea dragon, John would have been demanding a duel to satisfy the insult to his honor.

He forced his muscles to relax. Humans could not be expected to understand proper etiquette, he reminded himself for the thousandth time. Griff didn't mean any offense.

"I owe you my life, oath-brother," he said, as levelly as he could. "Honor compels me to stand by your side in the face of any threat."

Griff blinked. "I'd hardly call table decorations a threat."

"I would," Chase murmured as he wrestled with ribbons.

John tried to simplify the concept, as though addressing a very young child barely past first molt. "You said that accomplishing this task would please your mate. I am your oath-brother, which means I am sworn to guard your treasure as if it were my own. Your mate's happiness is your greatest treasure, is it not?"

"When you put it like that…" Griff let out a long breath, shaking his head a little. "Well, I just hope I can return the favor one day."

It was John's turn to blink. "I do not follow."

"I mean, help you with *your* mate," Griff said, as though that explained anything.

"My mate?"

"Sea dragons do have mates, don't they?" Chase asked curiously.

"Of course we do," John said. "But I am a Knight-Poet of the First Water."

Hugh glanced up, his white eyebrows rising. "I know you're sworn to celibacy, but I didn't realize you'd be bound by that even if you found your mate."

John was rather startled that Hugh knew about *that* knightly vow. It was one that he'd never felt the need to share with any of his colleagues. Nonetheless, it was clear that even Hugh didn't understand the real meaning of the vow.

"The situation would never arise," he said. "I *have* no mate. No sea dragon knight does. Before we take vows, we must scour the seas, singing for our mate. I did so myself, circling the globe thrice round, and each time was met with nothing but silence."

Griff's brow furrowed. "But you just searched underwater. What if your mate isn't a sea shifter?"

"That does not happen with us," John said. "Sea dragons only mate sea dragons. None of us have ever found a mate among humans, or even other shifters. We are too different."

"So you've contacted literally every sea dragon in existence, and know that none of them are your mate?" Chase's usually merry face wore an unusually somber expression. "You poor bastard."

"Oh, it is not a matter for sorrow," John reassured him. "Only those without mates are permitted to become knights. I could swear myself to the service of the Pearl Throne, in the knowledge that my loyalties could never be divided between love and duty. Rest assured, I am well content."

Griff and Chase didn't look convinced by this, but then, they were mated. John supposed that they could not help but pity those who did not share that fortunate state. Hugh, on the other hand, seemed delighted by the revelation.

"I *knew* there was a reason I liked you," he said, reaching up to clap John's shoulder. "Nice to know there'll always be at least one other unmated person in the team."

"Your people too have a similar tradition, shield-brother?" John asked, curious.

He still did not know what sort of shifter the paramedic actually was. He'd never wanted to ask directly, for fear of breaking some unwritten human rule of courtesy.

"You could say that." Hugh transferred his attention back to the wedding favors. "But enough chit-chat. By my count, we've got at least a hundred of these things to go."

The fire crew went back to their tasks. John couldn't help but notice that Griff and Chase were still casting him rather pitying glances.

It was irksome. He was the Walker-Above-Wave, Emissary to the Land from the Pearl Throne, Knight-Poet of the First Water, Sworn Seeker of the Emperor-in-Absence, and Firefighter for the East Sussex Fire and Rescue Service! He was not accustomed to being *pitied*.

John set his shoulders, shrugging off their misplaced concern. He reached for the next box, vowing to prove his worth to his colleagues. Though this was not his accustomed arena of battle, he was determined to prevail.

If only these dry-beached things weren't so small!

When he'd been a child, John had been taught that sea dragons were the noblest and most magnificent of the draconic breeds. He hadn't fully appreciated the truth of that until, as an adult, he'd first stepped onto land. Even among his fellow shifters on Alpha Fire Team —none of them small men by human standards—he *towered*.

Now, even more than usual, he felt like a whale trying to school with minnows. His sword-calloused fingers dwarfed the delicate candies. He might as well have tried to manipulate individual grains of sand in his claws.

When he finally managed to get three candies correctly placed and aligned, John felt as elated as the first time he'd bested a colossal squid. Unfortunately, swept up by his triumph, he slightly misjudged the amount of force required to close the box's lid.

Again.

Chase flicked squashed chocolate off the sleeve of his suit. "I don't mean to insult John's sensitive honor, but is there *nothing* else he could do?"

Griff sighed. "John, you really don't have to-"

"I cannot leave my comrades-in-arms to face a foe unaided, oath-brother." He looked down at the sad little pile of crumpled cardboard. "No matter how…singularly unsuited I may be to this particular fight."

Chase's expression brightened in a way that signaled that the pegasus shifter had just been struck by an absolutely *terrible* idea. "You just said that your first loyalty always has to be to the Pearl Throne, right?"

"Yes," John said, cautiously. He had learned to be deeply wary when Chase adopted that particular innocent look.

"And the whole reason you came out of the sea in the first place was to search for your missing sea dragon king, right?"

Why did humans have to be so *imprecise*? "If you are referring to the Pearl Emperor, King of Atlantis, Ruler over all Shifters of the Sea, Commander of Waves and-"

"Yes, yes, him." Chase cut off the list of titles with a maddeningly discourteous flip of his hand. "Anyway, you're supposed to be searching Britain for him, aren't you? Going off and questioning all the major rivers and lakes and stuff?"

"When I am not otherwise occupied using my skills to assist in the fight against fire and flame, yes." Not for the first time, John was completely mystified by the currents of the pegasus shifter's thoughts. "How is this relevant?"

Chase gestured in the direction of the window, at the dark waters of the wide lake beyond. "Well, have you searched *here* yet?"

Even through the intervening layer of glass, John could still hear the water calling to him, a siren song promising freedom and space. To swim, to stretch into his true form, unbounded by walls or gravity…he longed for it so fiercely that his first instinct was to deny Chase's argument, purely on the grounds that to agree would be to indulge his own desires.

But still…

"My vow as Seeker takes precedence over my duty to my oath-brother, it is true," he said, slowly. "And this part of Britain is new to me. I had thought to pursue my quest tomorrow, after the mating ceremony. But if I truly cannot be of service with the current task…"

"Oh, no, you should definitely go now," Chase said. His expression was solemn, but the wicked glint in his eyes betrayed some hidden amusement. "Go on. Go for a swim. A nice long swim."

Griff stared at Chase in dawning comprehension. "*Oh* no. No, no, no."

John looked at Griff in concern. "Is there some problem with that of which I am not aware?"

"No problem," Hugh said, a slow smirk spreading across his own face. "Absolutely no problem at all. In fact, I can't think of a more appropriate place for you to go for a dip."

John couldn't help casting a wistful look out at the tranquil waters. "It does indeed seem to be a most inviting and hospitable lake. And I must admit, I have been feeling somewhat stifled, this far from the ocean."

Griff buried his face in his hands. "You want to go for a swim. In sea dragon form. In *Loch Ness*."

Chase and Hugh were both tight-lipped and shaking with repressed laughter. Griff raised his head in order to shoot the pair a dirty glare, which only appeared to increase their mirth.

Even for humans, this was most peculiar behavior.

"Am I missing something?" John asked.

"Never mind," Griff said to him with a resigned sigh. "Go on, then. Just for God's sake, don't let anyone *see* you."

Peals of laughter followed John out, undercut by Griff's muttered curses. John closed the door behind him, shaking his head.

"Humans," he said out loud, to the uncaring clouds and the unconcerned waters below. "I shall never understand them."

Neither the clouds nor the lake answered, not that he had expected them to. Water did not listen to the graceless human tongue.

But all water was one water, and if you spoke with the language of the sea…

His blood rose with anticipation as he strode away from the hotel, passing out of the harsh glare of unnatural human lights and into the more welcoming embrace of moon and star. He followed the curve of the lake shore, the quiet song of the water becoming clearer the further he went from the noise of the human world.

Finding a quiet spot out of the view of any window or passing car, he loosened the buttons of his shirt, shrugging out of the constraining fabric. The irritating pants and even more irritating shoes quickly followed. Chase had complained ceaselessly about the cold and damp ever since they had arrived in Scotland yesterday, but to John the night breeze felt pleasantly warm and welcoming. He was always too hot on land, accustomed as he was to the sunless depths of the Atlantic ocean.

The night breeze caressed his skin, whispering echoes of distant clouds. Despite his eagerness, he made himself take the time to carefully fold his clothes. He had only a handful of human garments, since they'd all had to be personally tailored for him. Even clerks at specialist shops for humans of unusual size had blanched when he'd ducked through their doorways.

He could have shifted with his clothes on, of course—all mythic shifters could. But he'd discovered that although his human clothes could survive his shifting, they fared less well with his swimming. Wherever it was they went when he transformed, it didn't keep them dry, and he'd shifted back on more than one occasion to discover himself clad in bedraggled, ruined garments. Human clothes were not nearly as practical as his own people's traditional garb in that respect.

He hid the hated human clothes in the shadow of a water-smoothed boulder, and finally, *finally*, he was ready.

The lake whispered welcome as he waded out into it. As soon as it was deep enough, he dove, striking out away from the shore with swift, powerful strokes. Even in this feeble form, he could have kept pace with a seal, let alone any human swimmer. But it was still slow, so slow, compared to the supple speed of his true self.

The water rolled curiously over his skin, exploring his hard planes and long limbs, murmuring with surprise. Its song echoed in his veins, carried by the tides of his blood: *All seas are one sea, and all water is one water. You are of the flow, and yet apart. What are you?*

He sang back, as best he could with tiny human lungs and a tongue like a beached fish: *All seas are one sea, and the salt lies hidden under my skin. Patience. I will show you.*

Bearing in mind Griff's warning, he swam until the lights of the hotel were pinpricks in the night, and the lake yawned deep and dark beneath his fragile human feet. Like all mythic shifters, John could prevent humans from seeing him in dragon form...but he couldn't prevent humans from noticing the effect he had on his surroundings.

When he was certain that he was far enough out that the wave wouldn't attract attention, he shifted.

His own true body was incalculably vast compared to his tiny shifted, human form. A shock wave of displaced water exploded outward in all directions. The entire lake leaped, calling out in a mighty cry of delight and recognition.

Opening his jaws wide, he was at last able to proudly proclaim his name, his *true* name, every mighty chord and rippling arpeggio of it. The sound of it shook the water, and the lake trembled in awe.

The lake embraced him like a long-lost lover. It wasn't the saltwater of the ocean, but it was still a taste of home. He luxuriated in it, weightless, stretching out every coil and claw to fullest extent.

I am born of water, and borne by water, and to water I return! he sang, and the lake picked up the melody and joined him in joy.

He could have happily spent hours there, swimming and singing and listening to the lake's tales of season and sky...but his duty called him.

Do you know my song? he queried the lake. *Do you know my shape? Did an even greater one ever grace your depths, a secret power amongst your swift-darting fish?*

He'd asked this many times over the past two years, to many different waters. He had swum the fractal coastline of Britain and queried its bays and harbors. He'd called out to lakes both smaller and greater than this one. He'd even ventured into the oily, metallic waters of the great Thames river, and shouted his question over the crash and clamor of London.

Every time he'd received the same answer: *No.*

And this time was no different.

No, said Loch Ness.

His heart sank within his chest...and then thudded in shock as currents curled coyly around him. Despite the lake's denial, it *did* know something. There was a secret here, concealed in its depths.

And it was debating with itself whether to tell him.

Please! he cried out to it. *The heart of the sea lies empty, and my heart is empty too. If you know what I seek, if you can fill that void, tell me!*

The waters of Loch Ness whispered and swirled around him for a long moment, eddies breaking apart and reforming like the thoughts of a divided mind.

Then it said, simply: *Come.*

CHAPTER 2

Neridia couldn't believe it, but so far, the first date was turning out to be a total success.

Maybe all that work will actually pay off!

She'd left nothing to chance this time. After a long string of disastrous dates with the freaks and perverts who were attracted to her own online profile, she'd gone fishing for herself.

She'd scoured the profiles of every man within a hundred miles. She ignored their pictures—except to weed out the ones who were clearly far too good-looking for someone like her—and concentrated on their words. She'd created spreadsheets to analyze their professed interests and backgrounds and dreams, comparing them against her own.

Out of a sea of disappointment, she'd found Dave.

He came from the Loch Ness area, just like her. He liked classic Hollywood movies and gardening and long hikes through the Highlands, just like her. He dreamed of having two kids and a dog one day, just like her. He was even Scottish-Chinese, so he'd understand the challenges of growing up looking a little different from most of the other people around.

To top it off, he was a park warden! There couldn't be a more perfect match for a conservationist. They were clearly made for each other.

And there wasn't the slightest chance that he would ever, in a million years, message *her*.

So Neridia had screwed up her courage, tweaked one *tiny* fact on her own profile... and messaged him.

As she'd hoped, they'd instantly hit it off. Now, after two months of increasingly flirtatious online conversations, here he was, sitting in a romantic little pub on the north shore of Loch Ness. With her. And, to all appearances, having just as good a time as she was.

Neridia pinched herself again, just to make sure she wasn't dreaming.

"I wish we'd done this sooner." Dave wagged a finger at her teasingly. "I warn you, I'm not going to let you find excuses to delay our next date for another two months. No matter how busy you may be."

Neridia shifted a little in her chair, a stab of guilt twisting her stomach. She was glad that her dark skin hid the blush rising in her cheeks.

Despite what she'd told Dave, she hadn't been busy at all. It had been the same quiet, lonely routine as always—long, solitary treks cataloging evidence of deer activity for her job, followed by long, solitary evenings back in her small lakeside cottage. She could have gone out to meet Dave at any time.

Except, of course, that then he would have *seen* her. And that would have been the last she'd have seen of him.

"Oh, w-well, there's been a lot of work to do, what with the proposal to reintroduce wolves into the area," she said, her words sounding unconvincing even to her own ears.

She'd never been a good liar. Dave was looking at her a bit funny, as if he could tell something was up. Seeking to distract him, she placed her hand on his, smiling across the table at him.

"I'm glad we got to know each other first, before we met in person." *That* was perfectly true. "Don't you think there's something to be said for discovering who a person is on the inside before getting distracted by what they look like on the outside?"

Dave's furrowed brow smoothed. "*Oh.* And your profile picture only showed your face…Neridia, did you deliberately delay meeting me because you thought I wouldn't be interested once I saw all of you?"

She flinched, unable to meet his eyes. "I've…had some bad experiences."

"Then those guys were idiots." She looked up in surprise, and discovered that he was smiling at her. "You're stunning. Maybe some fools can't appreciate a curvy woman, but *I* certainly do."

"U-uh, um." She was tongue-tied by mingled fear and hope, simultaneously marveling at how perfect he was and utterly terrified that she was about to mess it all up.

I'm never going to get a better opportunity to broach the subject.

"It, I, well…" She let go of his hand, before he could notice how much her own palm was sweating. "Um. It wasn't my weight that I was worried about."

Dave's forehead wrinkled in confusion. "What do you mean?"

She'd made sure to arrive at the pub a full hour before they were due to meet, to ensure that she'd be safely seated behind a table before he arrived. He'd clearly been a bit surprised that she'd stayed sitting down when he'd walked up, but better to be thought a bit odd or old-fashioned rather than revealing her secret too soon.

I have to do it. I can't stay sitting down for the rest of my life. He'd be bound to notice eventually.

"Your glass is empty," she said, striving for a casual tone and no doubt failing miserably. "I'll go get the next round, shall I?"

She took a deep breath, steeling her nerves.

Then she stood up.

Dave recoiled as hard as if she'd just tasered him. "*Holy fucking shit!*"

She'd changed one tiny detail on her online dating profile. Just one number, one single digit. She'd told herself that it was okay, that men did it all the time.

Of course, they were usually adjusting their heights in the opposite direction.

Still, it wasn't like she'd claimed to be *short*. Dave should have been prepared for her to be taller than him. Five foot six inches was pretty tall for a woman, after all.

From Dave's expression, *six* foot six inches clearly went past "tall" and into "monstrous."

The raw dismay and revulsion in his previously friendly face rocked her back on her heels like a shotgun blast to the heart. She stumbled as she caught the backs of her knees on a neighboring table. Off-balance, she flung a hand out to catch herself, and only succeeded in upending the entire table with an almighty crash of breaking glass. The gang of men who'd been seated around it surged to their feet with startled curses.

"Hey, bastard-!" The angry voice stopped dead as the speaker got an eyeful of her unmistakably female curves. "Jesus Christ, the circus must be in town."

"Nah, it's just one of them lads what pretend to be lasses," slurred another drunk. Neridia yelped, batting his hand away as he made a grab for her breasts. "I'll prove it. Burst them balloons down the front of that dress."

"Whatever it is, it spilled my drink," growled a heavyset man who barely came up to Neridia's elbow. "*Nobody* spills my drink."

Neridia cast a frantic glance at Dave, but he was still staring up at her in frozen shock. He didn't make the slightest move to help her as the pack of men closed in.

Turning on her heel, she fled, driven as much by that blank look of rejection as by the gang of angry drunks looking for revenge. Her stupid, oversized elbows and feet knocked into more tables and chairs as she stumbled for the door. Angry exclamations rose around her, turning into startled gasps as people craned their necks to gawp up at her.

She burst out into the night air and ran blindly down the street, hot tears of humiliation spilling from the corners of her eyes. She didn't know where she was going, or care. All that mattered was getting away.

I should never have come. I should never have dared to hope.

I should know better by now.

This was why she never went anywhere, outside of her tiny home village where everyone already knew her. She hated being at the center of attention. She hated the way her size dragged every surrounding eye to her. She hated hearing the whispered and not-so-whispered comments rise in her wake.

Maybe it would have been tolerable if she'd been supermodel-skinny to go with the supermodel height. But a ridiculously tall, *fat* woman of color? The sort of comments she attracted weren't ones of admiration. She was too big in every way. She occupied too much space just by existing.

Her lungs were burning in her chest. She was forced to stop, gasping for breath. Looking around, she realized that she'd unconsciously fled straight to the lake shore. Loch Ness spread out before her, vast and serene under the glimmering stars.

Stepping off the path, she picked her way down closer to the water. The lake's surface seemed curiously agitated tonight, even though there was no wind. Small waves lapped over the rocks, their gentle murmur washing away some of the hurt in her heart.

She'd lived next to Loch Ness all her life, and its lonely shores had always been a place of refuge. She liked the unapologetic bigness of it, and the way it made her feel small in comparison. It was vast and wild, and yet no one could deny that it was beautiful.

She had so many happy memories of standing by the lake at night, just like this. Feeling so totally at home, surrounded by beauty and love, with the waters sparkling in front of her and a large, strong hand engulfing her own...

Neridia's hand crept up to her neck, closing around the pendant she always wore. The single, large pearl felt warm to the touch, heated by her own body. If she closed her eyes, she could almost imagine it pulsed with a life of its own, like a steady, protective heartbeat.

"Miss you, Dad," she whispered, tears prickling her eyes again.

"Oi!"

Neridia leaped at the shout, letting go of the pearl. Whipping round, to her horror she recognized the five men whose drinks she'd spilled in the pub.

There was nowhere to run. Heart hammering, Neridia could only back away as they came stumbling and swearing down the rocky slope of the lakeshore toward her.

Her left foot splashed down into cold water. For a split second, she had a mad urge to turn and dive, anything to avoid the pack of men...

Water may look pretty, my Neridia, her father had always said when she'd been little, usually while pulling her back from trying to toddle straight into the loch. *But you must never forget that it is also deadly. Don't allow it to lure you into its trap.*

There was no escape that way. And though she was big, she wasn't a fighter. She didn't stand a chance against so many men.

"Oi, freak show!" one of them called out again, with the loud aggression of a very drunk man spoiling for a fight. "You ruined our night!"

"I-I'm so sorry." Neridia's mouth was dry with fear. "It was an accident."

"Apologies won't buy us a fresh round." Another man thrust out his hand, palm open. "Twenty pounds. Each."

Neridia reached for her purse, only to realize that she'd forgotten it in her headlong flight from the scene of her humiliation. Water swirled around her ankles, waves rising higher even though she hadn't moved. It was as if the lake itself was responding to her distress, the previously calm waters becoming more and more agitated.

"I, I left my money behind in the pub," she said, trying to keep her voice calm, as if they were all just having a perfectly civilized discussion. "But of course I'll pay you. If we just all go back-"

"Do you take us for fools?" The spokesman for the group knotted his fists, scowling at her. "You think we're going to let you just stroll back into public and scream for help? No, you pay us here. *Now.*"

"I can't!" Neridia flung out her hands so that they could see she wasn't lying. "Look, see, I don't have anything!"

The man's eyes narrowed. "What about that pretty trinket round your neck, eh?"

Neridia's hands flew protectively to her pendant. "No. You can't have that."

"Fuck me, it's a real pearl then?" One of the other men let out an impressed whistle. "What's something like that worth?"

"I think it's worth five spilled beers," the spokesman said. "Hand it over, and we'll call it quits."

"No!" Neridia would have backed away from him even further, but the water was up to her knees now. She didn't dare go any deeper. "Please, don't. It was a present from my late father. It was his final gift to me before he died."

"I see. Means something to you, does it?" The man's face twisted with gleeful malice. "Good."

Without warning, he lunged for her. Neridia tried to evade him, but two of the other men cut her off. In seconds, they had her pinned, rough hands closing on her wrists and forcing her arms down. The spokesman snatched the pearl pendant from around her neck, easily breaking the thin golden chain.

"*No!*" With the strength of desperation, Neridia twisted free of the men restraining her. "Give that back!"

The man dangled the pendant from his fist, taunting her with it. "Come and get it."

"Your challenge," said a deep voice, impossibly, from *behind* her, "is acceptable."

Neridia whirled, and found herself staring at a man as he rose out of the lake. Water streamed from his immense shoulders and bare, muscular back. He didn't stand up fully, but halted in a kneeling position, head bowed respectfully. His long hair shadowed his face, droplets of water glinting like diamonds in the narrow dreadlocks.

"My lady," he said to her, completely ignoring the gang of men goggling at him from the shore. "Forgive my intrusion, but I cannot help but notice that you appear to be in need of a champion. If you would allow me the honor?"

Neridia stared at him, utterly lost for words.

Whoever he was, he appeared to take this as assent. He raised his head, his features still in shadow, and looked across at Neridia's would-be attackers.

"I am the Walker-Above-Wave." His voice rang out like a church bell, sending shivers through every bone in Neridia's body. "Emissary to the Land from the Pearl Throne, Knight-Poet of the First Water, Sworn Seeker of the Emperor-in-Absence, and Firefighter for the East Sussex Fire and Rescue Service. You appear to have a treasure which does not belong to you. I strongly advise that you return it."

As one, all five drunks gaped at him.

"You what?" one of them said at last.

"I am the Walker-Above-Wave," the man began again, speaking more slowly this time as though he'd just revised his estimate of their intelligence sharply downward. "Emissary to the-"

"You're fucking mental, is what you are." The man still clutching Neridia's pearl rallied, knotting his free fist. "Piss off, fishboy. This is none of your business."

"As I now have the great honor of being the noble lady's Champion in this matter, I believe that you will find that it is." There was an odd, musical quality to his voice. Neridia couldn't quite place his accent. "Do you wish to withdraw your challenge?"

The spokesman set his feet in an aggressive stance. "There's five of us and one of you, fucker."

"Ah." The man nodded gravely, his mane of dreadlocks shifting over his massive shoulders. "Yes, that is an inconvenience. I too have other matters to which I must attend tonight. Though it is unorthodox, in the interests of concluding this disagreement swiftly, I would be pleased to duel you all simultaneously rather than sequentially."

"Whazzat mean?" one of the drunks said, looking at the leader for translation.

The spokesman's scowl deepened, as if he thought the stranger was mocking them all. "It means he wants to get his fucking thick head kicked in. Get him!"

It happened so quickly, Neridia could barely follow the stranger's movements. One second, he was kneeling at her feet; the next, he'd surged past her, a solid wall of muscle interposed between her and the gang. The first two drunks to reach him were met with a blur of motion that sent them staggering back as if they'd run straight into a cliff face.

That was enough to give the rest pause. The stranger settled back into a poised, balanced stance, hands held loose and relaxed. Despite the fact that he was facing off against a pack of angry drunk men while wearing nothing more than a pair of swimming briefs, he seemed for all the world to be enjoying himself. He was even *humming*, a strange but unmistakably cheerful tune.

The gang closed in again, more cautiously this time. Neridia noticed that the leader was hanging back a little, letting his friends throw the first punches. She didn't like the cold, calculating expression on his face. She wanted to shout a warning to her strange champion, but didn't dare interrupt his concentration.

Still humming, the stranger blocked every would-be attack with his left arm while returning powerful blows with his right. Yelps and shocked curses filled the air. In short order, one man was staggering back clutching a broken nose; another wheezed helplessly on his knees, all the breath driven out of him by a seemingly casual fist to his stomach.

One of the remaining men evidently decided that he didn't want a drink *that* badly, and started backing away. The stranger's humming sharpened, like a violin crossed with a wolf's snarl. He lunged after the retreating man, one enormous hand closing over the back of his neck.

"Only a coward seeks to retreat from a challenge honorably met." The stranger straightened, lifting the man clean off the ground without any apparent effort whatsoever. "But if you insist, allow me to assist you."

He spun, as if throwing a discus, and released his grip. The unfortunate man was sent hurtling through the air, limbs flailing.

Open-mouthed, Neridia followed the drunk's trajectory. He splashed down into the shallows a good fifteen feet away.

Most of the other men retreated in a hurry, scrambling over each other in their haste to get out of the stranger's reach. Only their leader remained, still holding Neridia's pearl.

Except now, in his other hand, he was also holding a knife.

The stranger's humming cut off abruptly. He went very still, focused on the blade. The man holding it grinned with vicious satisfaction.

"Not so tough now, are you?" he taunted, making the knife weave like a snake about to strike. He definitely knew how to use it. "That's changed your tune, hasn't it?"

"Yes," the stranger replied, clear contempt ringing in every word. "I sang for the joy of challenge, and there is no challenge here now. Only the tedious task of exterminating vermin."

The man's face darkened as he worked out the insult. He paused for a second, mouth half-open as if trying to come up with a witty retort.

"Motherfucker," he spat, and lunged.

Neridia shrieked, instinctively surging forward. She had no idea what she'd intended to do—grab his arm? Try to distract him? Protect her champion by getting stabbed herself?—but as it turned out, the stranger needed no assistance. He calmly sidestepped the attack, the knife missing his bare chest by mere inches. Grabbing the man's arm, he gave it a sharp twist.

The leader screamed, the knife falling away from a suddenly limp hand. He sagged, only the stranger's grasp keeping him upright.

"I can only break your bones," the stranger told him, without any hint of pity or remorse. "And bones quickly heal. You have broken your own honor, and from that injury, there is no recovery. Go, and live with your shame, all the remaining days of your worthless existence."

The stranger plucked Neridia's pearl from the leader's other hand, then tossed the man aside like a piece of garbage. The leader staggered back, curled over his broken arm. The other men grabbed him, hustling him away with nervous backward glances.

The stranger stared after them until they'd disappeared from sight, then turned, holding out his hand. Neridia's pearl gleamed in his broad palm.

"My lady," he said, and the voice which had been so fierce mere moments ago was now as soft and gentle as the ripples murmuring against the shore. "Thank you for the honor. I believe this is yours."

Still feeling as if this was all some sort of dream, Neridia was already reaching out for her pendant. As her fingers brushed his skin, a jolt went through her. It was like a static shock, except a hundred times more powerful...and pleasurable. She gasped, her head jerking up.

For the first time, their eyes met.

"Yours," the man repeated, his musical voice fading to the merest whisper. "I am yours."

Neridia couldn't take her fingertip off his palm, that strange, warm energy sparkling down every nerve of her body from just that tiny contact. She couldn't stop herself from staring up into those incredibly blue eyes-

Wait.

She was staring *up* into his eyes.

Neridia blinked. She shot a swift, disbelieving glance downward, expecting to find that he was standing on a rock...but he wasn't. His bare feet were at the same level as hers.

And he was *taller than her*.

She had only a split second to gape at the impossibility, before he crashed down to his knees in a spray of water.

"Forgive me," he said brokenly, pressing his forehead to her hand like some ancient knight swearing fealty. "I have failed you. Forgive me."

"Please stand up!" Neridia seized both his forearms, tugging. "I want to-I mean, I've never-just *stand up!*"

He allowed her to pull him back to his feet, unfolding again to his full height. Neridia's breath caught in her throat.

I'm dreaming. This has got to be a dream.

She barely came up to his *chin*. His deep chest was thick with muscle, the gleaming skin a shade or two darker than her own. Every line of his body screamed power, from his impossibly broad shoulders to the hard curves of his thighs. He was so outsized and yet so perfectly proportioned that he seemed more a work of art than a man; some sculptor's final masterpiece.

"You're tall," she said stupidly, and could have kicked herself. It was what other people always said to *her*. "Sorry! I meant, you're *taller*. Than me."

He started to sink back to his knees, and she hastily waved her hands to stop him. "No! I like that you're tall! Um, not that you care or anything, it's just-"

"I care," he interrupted her. His eyes were still very wide, as if he was as shell-shocked as her. "I care very much."

He brought up one of his hands, almost but not quite brushing her face. Very slowly, never actually making contact, he traced the curve of her cheek. Neridia trembled with the desire to lean into his touch, to close that last distance between them...but she didn't dare.

Despite his gentle words, the stranger's expression was pure agony. He had the look of a man abruptly confronted with everything he ever wanted...and could never have.

"Oh, my lady." Water ran down his face. *"Where were you?"*

Neridia could barely process the question, still lost in disbelieving wonder. "When?"

"Now. Then. Always." The man dropped his hand, gesturing out at Loch Ness. "All this time, you were here?"

She nodded. "I've always lived here. Why?"

Her simple assent seemed to hit him like a blow to the gut. He closed his eyes tightly, as if he couldn't bear the sight of her any longer.

His obvious pain made her own heart clench in response. "What is it? What's wrong?"

"I...I..." All his previous eloquence had apparently deserted him. "I searched for you, my lady. I swear to you, I searched."

He searched...for me?

Some long-silent part of Neridia's soul sang in pure joy, even as she tried to wrap her rational brain around what was happening.

Before she could ask him what he meant, the man took a deep breath. His chiseled features settled into a look of grim, stoic determination. Setting his shoulders as though lifting a heavy burden, he opened his eyes.

"What is your name?" he asked her.

"Neridia," she said. She braced herself for the inevitable comment. "Neridia Small."

He shook his head. "Not your air name. Your *real* name."

Caught off-balance by this unusual response to her painfully ironic surname, she could only blink at him.

"Come." The stranger turned, and started wading deeper into the loch. "Swim with me."

Neridia found she'd actually taken a step after him. The chill kiss of water against her knees brought her crashing back to sanity.

"Wait!" she called after his retreating back. "I can't-*wait!* I don't even know your name!"

He was chest-deep in the water already. He looked back over his shoulder at her, and her heart broke at the despair in his eyes.

"I will tell you," he said.

And then-

CHAPTER 3

For the first time in his entire life, John didn't want to shift back to his true form.

I must. She asked for my name. I must tell her.

But the instant she heard the swirling music of his name, she would know how badly he had failed her.

Sea dragon names were not like human names. A human name might carry some hidden meaning or association—like his own air-name, "John Doe", which he had been told was traditionally given to one whose true identity was unknown—but it could not capture the true complexities of a person. Humans were more than their names.

But sea dragons were not.

A sea dragon's name grew and changed over time, recording their deeds and proclaiming their honor for all to hear. John's own true name had started as the same simple five-note sequence that all male noble-born infants bore, but by now it had lengthened into a symphony that took a full three minutes to sing in its entirety.

And it started with the unmistakable, thundering chord that proclaimed the bearer was a Knight of the First Water. Sworn defender of the Pearl Throne.

Mateless.

The day that chord had been prefixed to his name had been the proudest of John's life. Now, he would have given anything to be able to undo it.

It is already undone, insisted his inner human. John could practically feel its fists clenching round his bones, trying to prevent him from shifting. *She is our mate! All other loyalties mean nothing now. Abandon knighthood, abandon oaths, choose her!*

John savagely flung the puny creature down to the deepest, lightless depths of his mind. Just to listen to such whispers was dishonorable. He was the Emperor's servant, sworn to his duty. Nothing could change that.

He held onto that thought as if it was a sword, steeling himself for what he had to do. His mate—*his mate!*—was still gazing at him from the shore, making no move to follow him into the water yet.

He longed to swim with her, just once. If only he could hear the heart-rending beauty of her own true name, before he forever shattered the growing bond between them with the sound of his own…

No. Every second I delay is another small lie. I have taken a vow of candor. I must tell her.

He shifted, and for the first time it felt like shouldering a burden rather than being set free. Closing his eyes so that he would not have to see her face, he sang his name.

Or rather, tried to. His throat closed up after that first terrible, traitorous chord—*Knight/Poet/First Water!*—and he could go no further. What point of telling her the rest of him, the victories he had won and the treasures he had claimed? None of it mattered.

All that mattered was that he had betrayed her. He had not searched hard enough, long enough. He had bound himself to another's service too soon, too hastily.

They could never mate.

He did not want to look at her. Did not want to see the shining joy snuffed out from her striking, noble face, bleak betrayal clouding those summer-sky eyes. Almost, he turned to flee, to disappear back into the sunless depths of the lake without a backward glance and save them both further pain.

But only an honorless coward fled from a battlefield. And now, more than ever, he had nothing left but honor.

Taking a deep breath, he forced himself to open his eyes.

It was far worse than he could ever have imagined. The raw horror in her expression cleaved him to the very heart. She backed away, trembling all over, her eyes wide and…

…Terrified?

John instinctively swung his head round, momentarily convinced that some dreadful monster of the deep must have unexpectedly arisen behind him. But there was nothing there. Nothing to provoke such fear.

Nothing except himself.

Surely not.

That was a thought even more ludicrous than a colossal squid suddenly breaching from the calm lake. Why should his mate *fear* him?

"I don't understand," he sang to her, harmonies of bewilderment and growing concern swirling around the simple melody.

She clapped her hands over her ears, recoiling as if from a torrent of meaningless noise. There was absolutely no sign of comprehension in her face.

Her full lips moved, whispering human words. A single, senseless phrase:

"Loch Ness Monster."

He stared at her incredulously. "Monster?" he repeated in disbelief, in his own language.

He was talking to her back. She was running, flat out, straight away from him, as if all the sharks of the sea were on her scent.

"Wait!" The air shook with the force of his roar. "What is wrong? Come back!"

She screamed in response, speeding up. He tried to follow, but his huge bulk was unwieldy out of water. Every shining, plated scale was like an iron weight; his clawed feet sank heavily into the mud.

Shift, idiot! his inner human howled at him.

For once, the feeble creature actually spoke sense. John shrank back into human form, scrambling up the sloping shore. In his haste, he momentarily forgot how to run on two legs, and promptly tripped over a rock. He fell, catching himself with an outflung hand.

His palm landed on something small and smooth. Something familiar.

"Wait!" he called out, picking up the pendant. His human voice was so weak in comparison to his true one. "Come back! You dropped your-"

He stopped, dead, staring at the pearl in his hand.

"Treasure," he finished in a whisper.

She dropped her treasure.

She dropped *her* treasure.

No dragon, under the sea or above it, *ever* abandoned treasure. No matter what the circumstances. It was as unthinkable as abandoning a limb, or a child. John had seen sea dragons *die* rather than lose a treasure.

Yet she had dropped this one. The one that she had, not long ago, been quite willing to fight five angry men to defend…

John's mind spun as if caught up in a whirlpool, facts fitting together to form the inescapable conclusion.

She hadn't shifted to fight off her attackers. She hadn't given any sign of understanding sea dragon speech. She'd fled in terror at the sight of him.

His mate wasn't a sea dragon. More than that, she wasn't even a shifter.

His mate was a *human*.

CHAPTER 4

Neridia was almost back to the pub before she realized her pearl pendant was gone.

Up until that point, she'd simply been running for her life, in the instinctive animal panic of a small creature fleeing from a much larger predator. The warm, friendly, *normal* glow from the pub windows called out to her like a beacon across a storm-tossed sea. Sobbing out loud in relief, she stumbled toward the door, reflexively clutching at her pearl pendant for comfort-

Only for her hand to encounter nothing but her own bare neck.

With a sinking feeling, Neridia remembered that she'd been holding the pearl in her hand when the...the *creature* had reared up out of the water.

And now she wasn't.

I dropped it. I dropped Dad's pearl.

The sheer awfulness of the realization brought her back to herself, clearing her blind terror. She leaned against the rough stone wall of the pub, gasping for breath, and tried to make sense of what had just happened.

That can't have been real. I can't really have seen...it.

But every detail was etched in her memory with crystal clarity.

Water streaming from the glittering, indigo scales as that massive, horned head reared up, up out of the lake. The luminous, deep blue eyes, each bigger than her own torso, rising into the air like twin alien moons.

Neridia shuddered all over. It had looked at her. It had roared, each exposed tooth longer than her entire arm. And then it had *started toward her*-!

And she'd dropped her most treasured possession, right at the monster's clawed feet.

She touched the bare hollow of her throat again. Her father had been a shy, gentle man, for all his size. He'd always kept his head down, avoiding confrontation, and he'd taught her to do the same. She was sure he would have told her to forget the pearl, go into the pub and find help.

Neridia drew in a deep, shaking breath. Then she pushed open the door of the pub.

She was relieved to see that the gang of drunk men wasn't present in the snug, warm bar. Neither was Dave, but Neridia discovered that she didn't care at all about that. Her feelings for him had been utterly washed away by both his rejection of her...and the memory of the stranger's deep blue eyes.

"Excuse me," she said to the bartender. "Um, I accidentally left my purse at my table, earlier?"

"Yeah, your boy-ah, that is, the guy you were with, he handed it in." The man produced the small black bag from behind the bar, sliding it over the polished counter. "You okay, love? You look like you've seen a ghost."

No, just a monster. Neridia smothered a hysterical giggle.

"I'm fine," she said, her voice shrill and tense even to her own ears. "Thank you."

Grabbing her purse, she fled before he could ask any more questions. Back out in the air, she delved into her bag. Her fingers closed over her cellphone.

If I'm going to get eaten by the Loch Ness Monster, I'm at least going to take a picture of it first.

∽

Neridia wasn't sure whether she was relieved or disappointed that the shore was empty by the time she returned. She edged down the sloping rocks nervously, clutching her cellphone—camera app armed and ready—in front of her as if it were a gun.

The waters of the loch were as flat and still as a black mirror. Nothing broke the surface. Nothing made odd ripples, or gave any indication that something prehistoric and impossible might be lurking below the calm water.

Maybe I imagined it after all?

Neridia had always thought of herself as a sensible, logical person. Even as a child, she'd preferred nature documentaries and science books to cartoons and fantasy stories. She'd never been prone to flights of fancy.

But she knew that sometimes even the most scientific mind could play tricks. And what was more plausible—that she'd suffered some sort of hallucination, or that she'd *actually* encountered the Loch Ness Monster?

I didn't drop my pendant. Those thugs mugged me, and I must have fallen and hit my head. I blacked out and dreamed the whole thing. The monster, the fight...and the stranger.

Stupidly, the thought made her want to cry. She sniffed, angrily palming away the tears. Of course he hadn't been real. A man springing out of nowhere to rescue her? A man who looked like a Greek god and spoke like a knight from a fairytale? A man *taller* than her?

Of course, it seemed like even her subconscious mind hated her, given that her dream man had turned into a creature out of a nightmare.

Neridia sighed, her head drooping...and found herself staring at a footprint.

It was so big, she almost mistook it for a natural depression in the mud. But her trained conservationist's eye—used to tracking deer through miles of wilderness—picked out the shape of an animal track.

The round oval of the heel, the faint marks of webbing between the toes, the deep gashes caused by long, curving claws digging in for grip...

Neridia's heart thudded painfully against her ribs.

I didn't imagine it. It really happened.

Fumbling for her phone, she snapped a dozen pictures of the footprint, desperate to capture it before the water swept it away. It wouldn't prove anything to anyone else, of course—such a mark would be far too easy to fake.

But the footprint proved it to *her*.

It's real.

It's all real.

He's *real*.

"Hello?" she called out, timidly.

Nothing answered her but the soft murmur of the water on the rocks.

"I'm sorry I ran away earlier. I, I'd like that is, I want...I just want to see you again. You didn't even tell me your name."

Silence.

Neridia licked her dry lips. Then she edged into the water, shivering at its cold kiss on her skin. She went as far out as she dared, until the lake rose to her waist. Currents pulled at her, trying to tug her off her feet.

"Hello?" She looked down into the dark water, and saw nothing except her own reflection looking back. "Is anyone there?"

∽

All seas are one sea.

The water carried her face, her words, on hidden currents across the ocean. By the time the ripples reached a palace deep under the sea, the news of her existence was the barest whisper.

But it was noticed.

CHAPTER 5

*J*ohn ignored the first knock on his hotel room door, and the second. He could not, however, ignore the third.

It wasn't exactly a knock. More a kick. The door slammed back against the wall with a crunch of splintering wood.

"Right," Griff said, lowering his booted foot. Chase and Hugh flanked him, their expressions as grimly determined as if they were about to charge into an inferno. "What's wrong, John?"

John didn't pause in his packing. "Nothing, oath-brother. All is well."

Griff's golden eyes narrowed. "John, it's the middle of the night, you're dripping wet and practically naked, and you're flinging your hoard into your backpack as though the room is on fire. All is very definitely *not* well."

John gripped his favorite golden chain, the worked links digging into his palms. He forced himself to meet his oath-brother's eyes. He knew it was futile to try to dissemble—the griffin shifter's piercing gaze could see through any lie.

"On my honor, I swear to you that it is not a matter with which you can help." He made himself speak levelly, forcing back the melody of grief that wanted to weave around the human words. "But I must go."

"What, right now?" Chase said. "Where?"

"Home," John said simply.

They stared at him.

"Well," Hugh said, after a moment. "I for one am not going to volunteer to drive you to the damn seaside at one o'clock in the bloody morning."

"I shall swim." He could tell the lake joined up with the ocean eventually, though the distant song of the salt water was whisper-faint.

"Through a canal?" Hugh countered. "Through the middle of Inverness? It's a *city*, John. Even invisible, you'll be like a whale trying to squeeze down a drainpipe."

"Then I shall walk!" His roar rocked all three of them back on their heels. John took a deep breath, trying to steady his voice. "I must go. I must go *now*!"

Chase's jaw dropped. "My God. You actually found some trace of your missing Emperor, didn't you? In Loch Ness?"

"No—it is not that." John shook his head in quick denial. "I found something else. Something much worse."

Griff's brow furrowed. "Is there some sort of danger here?"

"No! I assure you, it is nothing of that nature. You need not fear for your mate's safety, nor that of any dry-lander. But I must report at once to the Knight-Commander of my Order. Please. Let me go."

The three other shifters exchanged baffled glances. He could sense the silent flicker of telepathic communication as they conferred with each other.

All mystical shifters could commune psychically with each other, but he kept his own mind closed, his mental walls thick and high. If his comrades sensed his inner turmoil, they would never let him go until they knew what had caused it.

"John," Chase said. John had rarely heard the mercurial pegasus shifter speak so seriously. "If you must go, then of course we'll help you any way we can. But we're your friends, and we're worried about you. Please, just tell us what's going on."

He wound the thick chain around his hand, trying to draw comfort from the reassuring richness of gold against his skin. "I...I..."

They said nothing, giving him space to speak if he chose. The warmth of their silent concern and friendship encircled him like a tropical lagoon.

Giving up, he sat down heavily on the edge of the bed. "I met my mate."

All three of them gaped at him.

"You what?" Griff said.

"Congratulations!" yelled Chase.

"Oh no." Hugh jabbed an accusing finger at John, looking as though he was personally offended by this revelation. "I distinctly recall you saying you didn't have a mate. You *promised* you didn't have a mate."

"I *shouldn't* have a mate." John fisted his hands, the golden chain cutting into his knuckles. "This should be impossible!"

"She's human, isn't she?" Chase turned to Griff, a wide grin spreading across his face. "You owe me a beer."

"And I thought I'd be pleased to lose that bet." Griff's forehead was still lined with concern. "But now I'm not so sure. John, why isn't this a good thing?"

"Because she is human," John said wretchedly. He dropped his head into his hands, running his fingers through his braided hair. "And even more than that, I am a Knight-Poet of the First Water. My oaths still apply. I cannot serve the Pearl Throne and also serve my mate."

"Oh. I see." Griff sat down on the bed next to him, the light touch of his shoulder against John's a silent reassurance that the griffin shifter had his back, no matter what. "So that's why you need to talk to your Knight-Commander. To resign."

"Yes." John was grateful that his oath-brother was taking the news so stoically. "I can no longer serve in my current role. I must beg the head of my Order to release me from my duty."

Griff let out a long sigh. "I can only imagine how difficult this must be for you. I'm so sorry. When will you be back?"

John raised his head to stare at Griff. "Back?"

"What, you thought we'd kick you off the team?" Chase said. "Of course you can come back. Fire Commander Ash hardly cares whether you're a knight or not, after all."

"Is the problem that you think your mate will want to stay here in Scotland?" Hugh said, sounding rather hopeful. "If you've both got careers at opposite ends of Britain, perhaps you could consider a long distance relationship? Physical contact is greatly overrated in my opinion."

John had the sinking feeling that, not for the first time, his comrades had utterly misunderstood him. "No. When I said that I could no longer serve, I meant as Walker-Above-Wave. I can no longer be the Emissary to the Land. I will not be coming back."

Silence spread out from his words. He could not bear to meet his friends' shocked eyes.

He looked down at his gold-wrapped hand again. "I will miss you," he said quietly. "I will miss you all. Please convey my regrets to Fire Commander Ash."

"No." Griff stood abruptly, turning so that they were eye-to-eye. He folded his thick arms across his broad chest. "You can tell him yourself, when he gets here for the wedding. He is your acting commander and you owe him the courtesy of at least handing in your resignation in person."

Much as John did not want to admit it, his oath-brother was right. Fire Commander Ash was an honorable man, and a good leader. When John had been new onto land, the Phoenix had taken him under his wing, saying only that he too knew what it was like to be a stranger in a strange place. Though the reserved Fire Commander would never be a friend in the same way as the other members of Alpha Team, John owed him a debt of gratitude. He could not simply vanish without thanking the Phoenix for the honor of serving under him.

Slowly, he nodded. "You are right, oath-brother. I can delay my departure a few hours."

"You'll delay your departure longer than that." There was an edge of anger in Griff's usually calm, amiable voice. He glared across at

John like a weapons-master about to discipline a particularly disappointing new novice. "Or have you forgotten that you have duties to *me* as well?"

Guilt stabbed him like a sword. In his selfish anguish, he *had* forgotten. He was supposed to be serving as Griff's second at his mating ceremony. John was still somewhat unclear as to why a mating ceremony needed a second—or "best man" to use the human term—given that it seemed highly unlikely that any duels would be occurring, but it was still a position of great honor and responsibility.

"I did not think," he admitted, ashamed of himself. "I beg your forgiveness. I will stay until after your mating ceremony, of course. But I cannot linger longer."

"Why not?" Chase asked. "Why can't you slow down, take some time to think this over before you go diving into the depths of the sea?"

Hugh raised an eyebrow at Chase. "Did you just actually tell someone to slow down? *You?*"

"I know, it's a historic occasion. Seriously, John. Neither your Knight-Commander nor your mate are going anywhere." Chase paused, a brief look of concern flickering over his expressive features. "Ah, she *isn't* going anywhere, is she?"

A hollow laugh forced its way out of his chest. "The last time I saw her, sword-brother, she was fleeing from me in mortal terror."

Chase brightened. "*Finally*. Someone managed to make an even worse first impression on his mate than I did!"

"No, *your* mate only fled from you *after* she got to know you," Hugh said. "As an impartial judge, I'm awarding John the victory here."

Strangely, his comrades' refusal to treat the matter with the gravity it deserved helped to ease some of his anguish. John's taut shoulders eased down a little.

"That's better," Griff said, his eagle eyes clearly picking up his body language. He reached out to grip John's arm for a moment, his fierce expression softening. "See, we *can* help you, John. If you'll let us."

He let out his breath in a long sigh, finally unwinding the golden chain from around his hand. "Actually, there is a matter with which I would be most grateful for assistance. Yours in particular, sword-brother Chase."

Rising, he picked up his mate's lost pendant from where he'd carefully placed it on his pillow. Closing his fingers over the shimmering pearl, he hesitated. It felt so good in his hand, as smooth and precious as her cheek would have felt against his palm. Its perfect roundness reminded him of the wondrous curves of her body.

It was a tiny piece of her. He wanted to keep it. To treasure it, always, as he could not treasure her...

It is not ours, his inner human said stubbornly. *We must give it back.*

With a sigh, he allowed his inner human's strange sense of "fairness" to push aside his more natural desire to add to his hoard.

"Here." He handed the pearl to Chase. "Could you see that this is returned to its rightful owner?"

The pegasus shifter had a talent for finding people. John had seen him put it to good use in many a rescue situation, unerringly guiding the fire crew to trapped victims. He could locate anyone within about a five mile radius, as long as he had a clear mental picture—from either his own memory or someone else's—to use as a focus.

Chase let out a low, impressed whistle, holding up the pendant by the broken chain so that the pearl caught the light. "Pretty. So's the woman you're thinking of. Is that her? Your mate?"

"Yes." John had lowered his mental shields to allow the pegasus shifter to pick his mate's image from his mind. "Last I saw, she was on the far side of the loch. Can you locate her, and return this lost treasure to her?"

"She's not in my range at the moment, but I'll track her down for you." Chase tucked the pearl away in his pocket. "What do you want me to tell her?"

"Nothing," John said, allowing a touch of steel to enter his voice. "Just return it to her. Do not speak to her. On your honor, swear that you will not."

"But-" Chase began.

"Promise me."

Chase's mouth snapped shut with a click. "I promise," he said after a second, sounding subdued. "But I think you're making a mistake. You don't truly understand how hard it is to live without your mate."

"Like living without air." John met his eyes levelly. "In the crushing depths, where the weight of water cracks your bones and your very heart struggles to beat. I understand very well, sword-brother."

"No, you don't." Chase shook his head. "It doesn't get better. It will feel like that, every second of every day. Always. Until you're together again."

"A wise man once told me," Griff said softly, "that I would rip my soul into pieces if I tried to deny my mate."

He'd been the one who'd said that to Griff. At the time, he'd wholeheartedly believed in the advice. Now, he could only marvel that Griff hadn't punched him in the face.

"I appreciate your concern. Truly. But the matter is settled. I will stay for the mating ceremony. Afterwards, our ways must part." He drew himself up to his full height, the top of his head brushing the ceiling. "I am a sea dragon. I can live without air."

CHAPTER 6

After a sleepless night and a long morning spent reading through website after website of pseudoscience, garbage, and flat-out lies, Neridia was no closer to coming up with a plan.

People have been searching Loch Ness for almost a century, without finding anything whatsoever. How can I hope to do any better?

She stirred her tea moodily, glaring out her kitchen window at the placid loch. All her life, she'd lived beside these wide waters. She knew all the moods of Loch Ness; twinkling and cheerful, sullen and clouded, rain-lashed and angry.

Now, she couldn't shake the feeling that the loch was laughing at her. It was a particularly fine summer day, and the water seemed to sparkle extra-brightly in the morning sunshine. It was as if the loch was going out of its way to draw a dazzling veil over the secret hidden in its depths.

How am I going to find him?

She had no idea. She only knew that she *had* to.

It was more than just the desire to recover her father's pearl. It wasn't just scientific curiosity, either. Even more than she wanted to know *what* he was, she burned to know *who* he was. Where did he come from? How could he do what he did? Why had he chosen to reveal his secret to her?

Why had he looked at her like she was both the answer to his prayers, and his own personal hell on earth?

The doorbell rang, breaking her fruitless pondering. Shaking her head free of the questions swirling in her mind, Neridia went to answer it.

Her first thought was that her unexpected visitors had to be the world's best dressed Jehovah's Witnesses. The two men were immaculately turned out in dark charcoal morning jackets and waistcoats, with ivory cravats and elegant floral buttonholes.

They also wore stunned and slightly disbelieving expressions as their gazes tracked upward from where they'd expected to find her face.

She was used to the latter. The former, however, was new.

"Can I help you?" she asked, warily.

For all their fine clothes, both men projected an intimidating aura of strength and power. Their muscled shoulders strained their tailored jackets. They weren't precisely *frightening*, but something about them prickled deep animal instincts.

"Well," the taller, darker one of the pair murmured in a strong Irish accent. "We're definitely in the right place."

The other one—a stocky, square-jawed man with startling golden eyes—cleared his throat, as if he was having to regather his composure. "So it seems. Apologies for bothering you, lass. I'm Griff MacCormick of the East Sussex Fire and Rescue Service. This is my colleague, Chase Tiernach-West."

Neridia blinked at them.

Firefighters? I didn't call for any firefighters. Especially not from the other side of Britain!

"We're here on behalf of another friend of ours," Griff continued. He had a local Highland accent, and was wearing a formal kilt under his morning jacket with the unselfconscious ease of a native Scotsman. "Someone you met yesterday."

Neridia flinched, wondering if they meant someone in the gang who'd attacked her. She sidled behind the half-open door, ready to slam it closed again. "I-I don't know what you're talking about."

Griff smiled at her, and the warmth of the expression chased away Neridia's mistrust. "Oh, I think you do."

Grinning, the dark-haired man—Chase—held up one hand. A thin golden chain dangled from his fingers. At the end of it, her father's pearl spun, gleaming in the morning light.

"We'd like to talk to you about a sea dragon," Griff said. "May we come in?"

~

"I'm his *what?*" Neridia stared at Griff.

"His mate," the firefighter repeated. He sighed, raking his fingers through his thick blond mane of shoulder-length hair. "This is the part humans always have trouble with. But just take my word for it. Every shifter has one true mate, just one person in all the world who is their perfect match. And you're John's."

Neridia rubbed the bridge of her nose, fighting down a bubble of mad laughter. "Let me get this straight. You're trying to tell me that a literal *sea monster* is my perfect partner? A sea monster who's also some kind of, of medieval knight from a secret underwater kingdom?"

"Sea dragon, not monster," Griff said mildly. "And, as he's always keen to point out, he's a Knight-Poet. I've never been able to work out why that's so important, but apparently it is."

Neridia threw up her hands. "Oh, good. My perfect match is a *pedantic* sea dragon-knight-monster-whatever. That's so much better."

Chase, who so far hadn't said a word, let out a muffled snort of laughter. Griff shot him an exasperated look.

"I know it must seem bizarre, but I promise you, John is your mate," Griff said, turning back to her. "It may not sound like you have much in common-"

"It doesn't sound like we have anything in common!"

"Well, there's one thing," Chase murmured, his eyes flicking over her body from head to toe.

"You can't base a relationship on height," Neridia snapped. "What are we supposed to do, bond over a hatred of low ceilings? Love doesn't work like that! You need shared goals, shared experiences, shared values. That's what all the relationship advice says. I should know! I've made spreadsheets!"

Chase cocked an eyebrow at Griff. "Ask her how well that's been working out for her."

Neridia scowled at him. "I am sitting *right here*. Is there some reason you won't talk to me?"

"He promised John he wouldn't," Griff said, one corner of his mouth lifting in amusement. "Fortunately, John forgot to extract a similar vow from me, otherwise we'd be having this conversation in mime. Anyway. No matter what you may think, you *are* John's mate. So we want you to come back with us. We need you to talk some sense into him."

Even though her head still screamed that all this was pure madness, her heart gave a little skip at the prospect. She didn't believe in all this talk of love at first sight, but she couldn't deny that she wanted to see him again. She could still remember the fizzing excitement sparked by the merest brush of her skin on his...

Neridia squeezed her hand around her father's pearl—she needed to find a new chain for it before she'd be able to wear it again—for focus, trying to rein in her ridiculous emotions. More than ever, she wished that her parents were still with her. She could really have used her mother's keen perception or her father's quiet wisdom about now.

What would you think of all this, Mom? What would you tell me to do, Dad?

Her mom had been an energetic force of nature, always throwing herself gleefully into any new experience. She would have doubtless have told her to go, without a second thought. But her father had been a cautious, thoughtful man. He would have warned her to be cautious now. He wouldn't have wanted to see her get hurt.

She'd wanted to get her pearl back, and she had. She'd wanted to know who and what the mysterious stranger had been, and now she did. Could she really hope for anything more? Was it worth the risk of being rejected, right to her face?

I don't think I could bear it, if he looked at me coldly and turned away...

"From what you've said, it doesn't sound like your John wants to talk to me," she said. "How can I really be his mate, if he's so determined to stay away?"

Chase spread his long-fingered hands. "Tell her that her mate is very noble, very honorable, and occasionally very, very stupid."

"Chase is right," Griff said. "Like I said, John's a sea dragon knight. He follows a strict code of honor, oath-sworn to uphold certain Knightly Vows. And, unfortunately, one of those vows is chastity. He thinks it would be dishonorable for him to take a mate."

"And you think *I* can change his mind?" Neridia said incredulously.

"You have to." Griff grimaced. "Not that it'll be easy. John is the most stubborn person I've ever met. He'll stick to what he thinks is the right path, even if it leaves him just a hollowed-out husk. But we're his friends. We can't stand by and let him destroy himself."

"I lost my mate for a few years," Chase addressed empty air, as if just talking to himself. "Not being with her nearly drove me out of my mind. And *I* was doing everything in my power to actively get her back."

"*Your* mate?" Neridia stared at him. "Wait, are you a, a dragon shifter too?"

Chase's black eyes lit up. He started to push himself to his feet, but Griff grabbed his arm, shaking his head. Chase sat back again, looking a little disgruntled.

"Never provoke Chase to show off," Griff told Neridia wryly. "Especially not in a room this small. He's a pegasus shifter. I'm a griffin, by the way. Half lion, half eagle."

He said it so casually, as though it was no big thing. Neridia's head spun. "How many different types of shifter are there?"

Griff shrugged. "I don't think anyone really knows. Britain's a bit of a magnet for the more unusual types, though. These isles have a long history when it comes to mystical matters. Hence why John's here. He was sent to look for a sea dragon who was last seen on England's south coast."

It was like she'd been living in a dark cell all her life, thinking that was the whole world. And now someone had opened the door, and she saw how much she'd been missing…

"How-" she started, but Griff raised his hand, forestalling her.

"Much as I'd like to give you a full history of shifterkind, not to mention tell you more about your mate, I haven't got time." He stood, checking his watch. "I've got somewhere to be in-oh, shit. Twenty minutes."

"Well, *I* can fly that fast," Chase said with a smirk, also rising. "Pity I'm not the one getting married."

Neridia's jaw dropped. "Griff, you came to tell me all this on your *wedding day?*"

"I hope that gives you an idea how important it is," Griff said, mouth quirking even as he hastily struggled back into his morning jacket. "Don't worry, I cleared this trip with *my* mate, the bride-to-be. She's just as worried about John as we are. So, will you come?"

"With you? Right now?" Neridia looked down at her too-short men's trousers and unflattering t-shirt. "To a wedding? Like *this?*"

"I'm the groom, so I get to set the dress code." Griff held out a hand to her. "And anyway, it wouldn't matter if you were wearing a sack. John would still think you were the most beautiful woman there."

Neridia shook her head vehemently, backing away. "I…I can't. I need time. I need to think about this."

Griff opened his mouth, but Chase tapped him on the shoulder. "If you don't move your furry ass, my feathered friend, all of this is going to become academic. It's traditional for the best man to marry the bride if the groom doesn't show up, after all."

Griff blew out his breath, but didn't argue further. "Here" He handed Neridia a hotel business card. "This is where we're having the reception. John will be there this evening. That'll be your last chance to talk to him before he leaves forever. Please, promise me that you'll come."

Neridia bit her lip. "What if he's angry that you went behind his back like this?"

"Oh, I'm absolutely certain he's going to be utterly furious with me. But with you?" Griff smiled at her over his shoulder as he headed for the door. "Impossible. You're his-"

He paused abruptly, mid-sentence and mid-step. "Where did you get that?" he asked, his golden eyes narrowing.

Neridia followed the line of his gaze, and saw that his attention had apparently snagged on one of the paintings on the far wall. It was just a small watercolor study of Loch Ness at sunset, rendered in misty hues. It was nearly lost amidst the larger, bolder artworks surrounding it, yet Griff stared at it as if there was nothing else in the room.

"My dad was an artist. That's just one of his commercial pieces." Neridia gestured at the whimsical silhouette of the Loch Ness Monster her father had painted in the background. "He always complained that he was selling out to the tourist trade, but they sold like hotcakes. He must have painted hundreds like it. Why?"

"Huh." Griff's eyebrows drew together. "You said he 'was' an artist?"

"He passed away," Neridia said, as levelly as she could. Even after four years, it still hurt her throat to say the words. "But if you really like the piece, the local art gallery probably still has-"

"Is this *really* the time?" Chase interrupted. "Griff, your mate is a lovely and patient lady, but I suspect even she may become somewhat miffed if you're late for your wedding because you were too busy critiquing art. What's so important about an old painting?"

"Maybe nothing." Griff shook himself, turning away…though his gaze lingered thoughtfully on Neridia for a moment longer. "Or maybe you have more in common with John than you think."

CHAPTER 7

*J*ohn had descended into the deepest abyss of the ocean, and fought krakens there, blind in the utter blackness. He had patrolled under the miles-thick ice in the Arctic circle, where the cold was so strong it froze even a dragon's blood. He had faced down raging infernos, and walked on two legs into the fire's heart, where no sea dragon had ever dared to venture before.

He wished he was in any of those places now. The darkest, coldest waters or the fiercest fire would be preferable to this comfortable, beautifully-decorated human ballroom.

Serving as Griff's second for the human mating ceremony had turned out to be the hardest thing he had ever done. John had exerted every ounce of willpower he possessed in order to maintain an appropriately polite, pleased expression throughout the afternoon, but in the deepest, most secret depths of his soul he'd writhed and roared in bitter jealousy.

The sheer radiance in his oath-brother's eyes as he'd joined hands with his equally radiant mate, their obvious perfect happiness as they were united forever…John coveted it with an intensity beyond any mere gold-lust.

There can be no greater treasure. I want that for myself. I would give everything I possess, down to the last pearl, if I could feel that happiness for even one single, shining second.

But the one thing he would not trade away was his honor. No matter how his inner human howled in envy, no matter how much he longed to join with his own mate as Griff had joined with his, he could not.

And so John stood and sat and smiled throughout the interminable human mating ceremony, and longed with every fiber of his being for the day to finally end.

When I am home, all will be well. In the depths, where there is no air to remind me of her with every breath. The salt sea will cradle me and wash away the taint of the land. I will be myself again.

"Is the mating ceremony complete *now?*" he asked Hugh plaintively, as across the ballroom a grinning Griff twirled his mate through the start of what was apparently some traditional human dance.

"Oh, no," Hugh replied. He leaned back against the wall in their shadowed corner, watching the happy couple. "This is only the first dance, for the bride and groom. After this, you still have to dance with all the bridesmaids."

John stared down at him in dismay. "*All* of them?"

Griff had seven sisters, all of them eagle or lion shifters. The bride did not so much have a group of bridesmaids as an entire honor guard. If Hayley had formed them up into a phalanx, she could have comfortably routed a small army.

"All of them," Hugh confirmed. "Oh, and then we have the tossing of the bouquet. Then there's more dancing, and drinking, and later on we have to shower Griff and Hayley with confetti. That'll probably be around midnight."

If the strength of a mating bond was at all related to the length of the mating ceremony, then Griff and Hayley were going to be the most thoroughly joined pair in the entire history of shifter kind. "And you are certain that my presence is required for all of this?"

"Absolutely." Hugh took a sip of champagne. "The ceremony would be utterly ruined if the best man wasn't there for the whole thing. If you leave now, Griff and Hayley's mate bond will be shattered, and it will all be your fault."

John looked hard at him. He could not help but have a sneaking suspicion that the paramedic might not be being entirely truthful. He also couldn't help but notice that Hugh had not let him out of his sight for the entire day.

"Shield-brother, I am beginning to think that you have been assigned as my keeper," he said, eyes narrowing. "And that you are trying to delay my departure."

"My honor is deeply insulted by the mere suggestion." Hugh drew himself up to his full height, which put the top of his white-haired head somewhere around the level of John's sternum. "I demand satisfaction. I challenge you to a duel."

John blinked at him. As far as he could tell, the paramedic was entirely serious.

"As the challenger, I get to name the time and place," Hugh added. "I pick next Tuesday."

Despite himself, the corner of John's mouth twitched up. "A valiant effort, shield-brother. But I apologize for my inadvertent insult, and thus you must withdraw your challenge."

Hugh shrugged one shoulder, leaning back against the wall again. "It was worth a try."

"I am deeply touched by your efforts to force me to linger," John said gently. "But delaying the inevitable only compounds the pain of parting. I must go."

Other couples were joining Griff and Hayley on the dance floor now. Chase and his mate Connie whirled past, Connie laughing as the pegasus shifter spun her clean off her feet. Red dragon shifter Dai Drake stepped a more sedate measure with his mate Virginia, one of his strong arms around her waist, the other cradling their slumbering infant daughter. Even Fire Commander Ash had been compelled to take part, forcibly hauled by both hands onto the dance floor by swan shifter Rose, the owner of the Full Moon pub.

This is how I wish to remember them. All of my dearest friends, joining together in celebration.

Almost all of his dearest friends, that is. John glanced sidelong at Hugh, who was also watching the dancers. The paramedic's handsome face wore his usual faintly sardonic expression, but there was a hint of wistfulness in his ice-blue eyes.

"You too watch from the side." John rested one hand on Hugh's shoulder. "But if I could find a mate unexpectedly, perhaps you are also mistaken in your belief that you must be forever solitary. I hope that it is so."

"Believe me, that would turn out even worse for me than it's worked out for you." Hugh scowled at him, that momentary vulnerability hidden once more behind his spiky defenses. "If you're going to go, then just go. No need to start wishing me ill-fortune on your way out."

"I shall leave before I can make further blunders, then." John shifted his grip to clasp Hugh's forearm, in the gesture of one warrior to another. "It has been my honor and my privilege to call you my friend."

Hugh's fingers tightened on his arm. Though the paramedic's expression remained uncaring, the physical contact meant that John could sense the true sorrow behind his comrade's sarcastic manner.

It also meant that he could not help but be aware of Hugh's loud telepathic shout, even though it wasn't aimed at him.

I'm losing him! Chase, for God's sake tell me she's nearly here!

"Tell you that who is nearly here?" John said out loud.

Hugh jerked his hand away as if burned. "Didn't your mother ever tell you it's rude to eavesdrop?"

A terrible suspicion formed in his mind. "Yes," he said, coldly. "But not as rude as it is to cowardly attempt to undermine another's honor. *That* would be a truly unconscionable act. Especially from a comrade-in-arms."

The guilty look that flashed across Hugh's face told John all he needed to know. Anger lit in his blood at the betrayal.

How could he? How could they?

Hugh was opening his mouth, but John did not give him a chance to make whatever feeble excuses he planned. He turned his back on the paramedic—only to discover his path blocked by Chase.

"Now, calm down-" Chase started, holding up his hands.

"*Out of my way,*" John snarled at him, fingernail-scratch harmonics of outrage nearly drowning out the human words.

Chase was barely half his own mass. John held his full strength in check, but the pegasus shifter still slammed back into the wall with a thump, all the breath knocked out of him. Heedless of both the shock in Chase's eyes and Hugh's startled curse behind him, John started to stride on—and was one again forced to stop in mid-step.

"You going to hurl *me* into a wall, John?" Dai said, broad shoulders set and green eyes blazing.

The red dragon shifter would indeed have been a much more formidable opponent, but that was not what made John pause. Dai still cradled his sleeping infant, her tiny head nearly hidden in his large hand.

"This is a low tactic, kin-cousin," John growled, quietly so as not to disturb the child.

"I'm no knight. And I'm prepared to fight dirty if that's what it takes to stop you from making the worst mistake of your life."

"If it is a mistake, it is mine to make!" John's hands curled into fists, shaking. "How *dare* any of you presume to know what is best for me? No dry-lander could ever hope to fathom the ocean's heart. Now stand aside!"

"You are beginning to attract attention, gentlemen." John started at Fire Commander Ash's quiet but ice-cold voice. "Control yourselves."

Soft-footed as ever, the Phoenix had managed to appear right at his elbow without him noticing. Rose was at Ash's side, brow furrowing as she looked around at them all. The enigmatic swan shifter had the ability to see what was truly inside a person's heart. John wondered what she was seeing now.

"I will not have any of you casting a shadow over Griffin's happiness today," Ash continued, his dark, cool gaze sweeping over his crew. "What is the problem here?"

Dai jerked his chin at John. "He was trying to slip away."

John reflexively straightened to attention as Ash's eyes turned to him. "Commander. As I told you this morning, my other duties call, and I must answer. My task here is finished. I no longer have excuse to tarry."

"But your *mate*-" Chase began, but Ash lifted one hand slightly. The pegasus shifter instantly fell silent.

"I am aware of your attempts to entice John's mate here without his knowledge." Though the Fire Commander's level voice and set expression never changed, disapproval radiated from him like heat from a furnace. "John, do you wish to see her?"

John opened his mouth to say *no*, but the simple word lodged sideways in his throat. He *did* want to see her. With all his heart, he longed to. He could not dishonor himself with a lie.

"It is not a matter of my desires," he said at last, painfully. "It is a matter of necessity."

Ash nodded slightly, as if in understanding. "Daifydd. Stand aside. Let him pass."

"Stay right there, Dai, or you won't be setting foot in my pub again." Rose put her hands on her ample hips, scowling round at them all. "John, listen to your friends. I know what's in your heart. It isn't duty that's driving you into the sea. It's fear, plain and simple."

"Rose." Ash made a slight, abortive motion, as if he'd started to put a restraining hand on her shoulder but then checked himself. "It is John's decision. We must respect it."

"Oh, I could smack you sometimes." Rose rounded on Ash, glaring up at the Phoenix without the slightest hint of trepidation at so disrespectfully addressing the most powerful shifter in Europe. "You're just as bad as he is. All that stoic suffering. Well, what about John's mate? Doesn't *she* get a say in this decision? Why does John get to unilaterally decide what's best for them both?"

John had the rare experience of seeing the Phoenix look discomfited. The crack in Ash's calm lasted only an instant before sealing over again, his expression settling back into its usual impassiveness.

"Chase," the Fire Commander said, turning to the pegasus shifter. "Where is John's mate now?"

Chase hesitated, his black eyes sliding away from his commander's as if not quite able to meet his gaze. "Ah. Well. At this precise moment in time, she's...not actually in my range."

"What? She's still at least five miles away?" Hugh slapped the heel of his hand against his forehead with a groan. "I chase my own tail all day trying to keep this overgrown idiot from wandering off prematurely, and now you tell me she's not even *coming?*"

John should have been grateful that his mate understood the hopelessness of their situation just as well as he did. He should have been thankful for her own honorable nature and strength of will. He should have been relieved.

Instead, he felt as though he'd been disemboweled.

They went to find her and bring her to me...and she refused?

Ash lifted one eyebrow at Rose. "It would seem that John's mate is of the same mind as he is."

"No," Rose said firmly. "It would seem that Chase is drunk."

"*Excuse* me?" Chase looked mortally offended. "I've only had one bottle of champagne! It takes a lot more than that to put me under the table, as you should know."

"Well, all I know is that your pegasus is utterly addled. But my swan isn't. There's nothing wrong with my ability to sense mate bonds." Rose's full lips curved into a smile as she pointed triumphantly across the room. "John's mate is standing right there."

CHAPTER 8

Neridia's nerves failed her right at the entrance to the reception room. Clasping her father's pearl—safely strung round her neck once more—she tried to summon up the courage to push open the closed door and take that final, irrevocable step. She could hear fiddles and drums playing a bright, lively tune inside, and what sounded like hundreds of people dancing and laughing.

I can't. I can't do this. They're all going to stare at me.

"Hi!" said a bright voice behind her, from somewhere around the level of her thighs. "Are you Sir John's sister?"

Neridia nearly leaped out of her skin. Whirling round, she saw a small blond boy of about five or six beaming up at her. From his adorably miniature morning suit and waistcoat, Neridia guessed he had to be part of the bridal party.

"Wow," the boy added, leaning back and craning his neck. "You're *really* tall. Are you a sea dragon knight too?"

"Um, no." A little awkward in her one good formal dress, Neridia crouched down on her heels. "I'm not. A knight, or a sea dragon, I mean. I'm…Griff invited me."

The boy beamed at her. "That's my da. What kind of a shifter are you? You smell funny."

"Danny!" A muscular blond man had appeared around the corner, evidently just in time to catch the boy's words. "Don't be rude."

"I didn't say she smelled bad!" Danny protested. "Just different. I was only asking, Daddy."

Daddy? Neridia stared from one to the other. Danny's features were definitely a tiny version of the older man's. *But I thought he said Griff was...?*

"Apologize to the nice lady, Danny," the blond man was saying firmly. He had a slight Scandinavian accent to match his Nordic cheekbones and hair.

Danny rolled his eyes. "Sorry," he muttered.

"I apologize for my son," the man said to Neridia. "He's still learning proper shifter manners. Do you—*hold kæft den er stor!*"

Neridia had no idea what language he'd just lapsed into, but—given that she'd just risen to her full height—she would have placed money on the translation being, "Holy fuck you're huge." She flinched.

"I-I'm looking for John," she said, trying to sound dignified and not like she wanted to flee like a frightened rabbit. "John Doe?"

"Yes," the man said faintly, still staring up at her wide-eyed. "Yes, I imagine that you are. He's in there."

Neridia licked her dry lips, glancing at the indicated door. "Could you possibly let him know I'm here?"

The man's mouth twisted bitterly. "Ah. Sorry, but no. Apparently I dishonor him with my mere presence. If I tried to speak to him, he'd probably challenge me to a duel on the spot."

He really means it. What kind of medieval barbarian would assault someone just for speaking? *Oh, this was a bad idea. I shouldn't have come.*

"You don't need Daddy to find Sir John," Danny chirped up. "You really can't miss him."

Before Neridia could stop him, the little boy flung the door wide open. At least a dozen heads turned at the sudden motion—and did double-takes, gawping up at her. Neridia froze like a deer in car headlights.

"See?" Danny said happily. "There he is."

Neridia didn't need his pointing finger. John's gigantic form towered over everyone else in the room. He was in profile to her, slightly stooped, apparently arguing with the knot of people around him. His hunched, defensive posture made Neridia think of an animal at bay, searching for an escape route as hunters closed in.

Then he looked up, and saw her.

Time froze. The room, the crowd, everything seemed to fall away. In all the world, there was only him, and her.

He started to walk toward her, the crowd parting before him like water. Neridia moved forward too, matching his pace. It wasn't a conscious decision. She could no more *not* move toward him than the tides could resist the pull of the moon.

They halted at the same time, barely a foot apart. Before, he'd just been a silvered silhouette in the night. Now, she could finally take in every detail.

The last time she'd seen him, he'd been practically naked. Now, fully clothed, he was if anything even *more* jaw-dropping. His perfectly-tailored morning suit clung to the planes of his chest and accentuated the astonishing breadth of his shoulders. Although his massive arms would have made any bodybuilder cry into his steroids with envy, he actually had a swimmer's build, with long limbs and a wedge-shaped torso narrowing to slim hips. He was just all scaled *up*, to the point where his sheer physical size became overwhelming.

His eyes were the deep liquid indigo of the ocean depths, mysterious and unfathomable. With a start, Neridia realized that his *hair* was blue too, perfectly matching the shade of his eyes. There was no question of it being a dye job; even his eyebrows and eyelashes were the same alien hue.

He isn't human. He really isn't human.

His dreadlocks swept back in intricate braids along the sides of his head before falling freely down his back in a thick, textured mane. Small golden charms were strung onto the narrow strands, gleaming like sunken treasure. They chimed and clicked as he gracefully sank to one knee, taking her hand and pressing it to his forehead.

"My lady," he murmured, in that glorious cello-deep voice that sent thrills through her very bones. "You came."

"Is he *proposing*?" someone whispered off to the side in delighted, scandalized tones.

Neridia was abruptly aware of the circle of fascinated stares and murmurs surrounding them. Face flaming, she grabbed hold of John's suit lapel, awkwardly tugging him up. He appeared totally unselfconscious as he rose again, as if what he'd just done was as normal as shaking her hand.

"All right, people!" Heads turned as Griff's firm Scottish voice cut over the whispers of the crowd. The griffin shifter jumped up onto the band's podium, clapped his hands together briskly for attention. "Next dance is the Circassian circle! Ladies on the right, gentlemen on the left, if you please!"

Something about his no-nonsense tone demanded obedience. Neridia breathed a sigh of relief as their unwanted audience broke up, drifting away. Still holding John's lapel, she retreated, drawing the sea dragon shifter back with her to the edge of the dance floor.

"You are upset," he said, his eyebrows drawing together a little. He turned his head to glare out at the crowd, one hand clenching into a fist. "Has someone here caused offense?"

"I'm all right. It's just that they were all staring." She looked at him hopefully, searching his chiseled features for any sign of understanding. "Doesn't it bother you?"

From his quizzical look, he didn't. "It is natural that they stare. I am a sea dragon. Dry-landers cannot help but marvel at my presence." His matter-of-fact tone made the words a simple statement of truth rather than a boast.

Neridia wrapped her arms around herself, hunching her shoulders in the habitual, futile attempt to make herself look smaller. "Well, I hate it."

His oceanic eyes darkened. "I am sorry. Yet again, I am the cause of your distress. It was I that attracted the unwanted scrutiny." He sighed, looking away from her. "Even after nearly two years on land, I still cannot fit in."

She peeked up at him, drawn to that strong, noble profile with a hunger that scared her. It was more than just appreciation for his physical looks. Something about him, some vital essence, pulled her to him as if she was caught in a riptide.

This is ridiculous, she tried to tell herself. *I know practically nothing about this man, and everything I do know just highlights that we have nothing in common. For pity's sake, every word out of his mouth makes it clear that we're from completely different worlds!*

And yet, and yet...

"I will never fit in here." His voice was so soft she could barely hear him over the sound of the band striking up a sprightly tune. He was still looking away. "I must go."

"Must you?" She felt as if she balanced on the edge of a cliff, looking down into a gleaming, beckoning sea; a reckless inner voice whispering *jump, jump* even as common sense held her back.

He met her eyes again at last, and the naked longing in his took her breath away as surely as water closing over her head.

"I should," he whispered.

They stared at each other, yearning, yet separated by a chasm that seemed impossible to bridge.

Out of the corner of her eye, Neridia noticed an elegant, middle-aged woman with ebony-black skin staring in their direction as she whirled past. Abruptly, she broke away from the other dancers, striding with firm steps straight toward them.

"Rose," her abandoned partner called, a note of warning in his voice.

The woman took no notice of him. She had the wisest eyes Neridia had ever seen, calm and kind in her soft face. Neridia found herself unable to resist as the woman took hold of her left wrist in one hand, and John's in the other.

A shock went through Neridia as the woman closed John's calloused fingers over hers, and she felt his swift, sharp intake of breath. Without pausing, the woman moved the two of them into a ballroom hold, as briskly as if positioning a couple of mannequins.

"There," the woman said, stepping back and surveying her handiwork with satisfaction. "That's better."

Without another word, she went back to her previous partner, grabbing his hands. The two were quickly swept up again in the swift, energetic dance circle.

Her hand clasped in his, and his broad shoulder under her palm... it was like an electrical circuit had been completed. Neridia found that she couldn't let go again. She didn't *want* to let go again. Not ever again.

His long fingers tightened on her waist fractionally. She could feel the strength in his grip, and how carefully he controlled it, and how his hand trembled as he pulled her closer. She could feel the heat radiating from him, warming her to the core. She could feel the rapid beat of his heart, perfectly echoing her own.

"What are we doing?" he whispered, his breath soft against her ear.

"I think we're dancing." Neridia wasn't quite sure when they had started, but they were definitely swaying gently, in such perfect unison that it wasn't clear who was leading and who was following.

She felt more than heard the noise he made, a deep rumble of longing that vibrated in her own chest. "When a sea dragon meets his mate, they dance. Circling ever closer, twining together, in the heart of the sea."

They were spinning now, circling around a point between their two bodies. "Like this?"

"Like this."

Neridia closed her eyes, leaning her cheek against his shoulder. She felt weightless, his strong hands bearing her up as if she floated on the surface of the ocean, gently rocked by the waves.

"Neridia," he murmured, his musical voice turning her name into a melody of longing edged with discordant pain. "We must-"

"Shh." She tightened her fingers on his. "Let me pretend to be a sea dragon, just for one dance. Just while the music still plays."

All the breath sighed out of him, ruffling her hair. "Just one dance," he agreed, softly.

Round and round, so gently, so sweetly. It wasn't remotely in time to the music, but Neridia didn't care. Her feet moved to a different tune, the hidden currents of desire, the secret song of her heart.

"John," she said, after a timeless while.

"Mmm?"

"Are you humming?"

"Yes. Do you wish me to cease?"

"No, I like it."

Neridia was silent for a few more minutes, listening. Somehow he was able to hum chords, and notes that she could only feel in her bones rather than hear with her ears. It was as if someone had transcribed whale song into a duet for bassoon and cello; haunting, alien, beautiful.

"John?"

"Mmm?"

"The musicians stopped playing some time ago, didn't they?"

"I had hoped you would not notice," he confessed.

Opening her eyes, Neridia peered over John's shoulder. They were the only ones still dancing. Wedding guests chattered and mingled nearby, throwing occasional curious glances in their direction.

Neridia sighed deeply. "I guess we have to stop," she said reluctantly.

"Yes. We should."

Despite his agreement, John didn't loosen his grip. Neridia too found that she couldn't bring herself to let go.

It was possible that they would have still been dancing at daybreak, except that a large white and pink bundle abruptly came flying out of nowhere straight at the back of John's head.

"Look out!" Neridia yelped, shoving him aside.

Reflexively, she caught the bundle—and found herself holding a bouquet of roses, slightly the worse for wear.

"Wow, you certainly hurled that, Hayley!" A laughing auburn-haired woman in a beautiful leaf-green bridesmaid's dress pushed her way through the crowd, searching. Chase followed in her wake, a broad grin on his face. "Come on, who has it?"

Belatedly, Neridia realized she had just caught the bridal bouquet.

Hastily, Neridia shoved it at the nearest person, who turned out to be the blond man she'd met before. "Here!" she called, waving at the bridesmaid. "He's got it!"

The blond man spluttered in protest, but Neridia pushed him forward. The bridesmaid's gaze fell on him, and she let out a whoop of laughter.

"It's Reiner!" she announced, nearly unable to get the words out through her giggles. "Reiner caught it!"

"Yay!" Little Danny hopped up and down next to Reiner, beaming up at his father. "You're getting married next, Daddy!"

"I most certainly am *not*." Reiner turned, lifting one hand as if about to point Neridia out. "It was-"

John stepped forward, coming between him and Neridia. The sea dragon's broad shoulders bunched ominously.

"-me," Reiner finished. "Yes, I caught it. Apparently."

"Well, that's certainly…unexpected." Griff appeared through the crowd, his golden eyes dancing with amusement. He clapped Reiner on the shoulder. "Congratulations. Let's hope that this means you'll meet your mate soon."

"Like *that's* ever going to happen." Reiner held the bouquet between finger and thumb, flowers dangling, as if it was a bundle of dead rats. "This is just adding insult to injury."

"I wasn't aiming for Reiner," Griff's bride complained, coming up to take her new husband's hand. Her white lace dress clung to her voluptuous body, accentuating the unmistakable curves of mid-pregnancy. "I was trying to hit—um, never mind. Where's your mate gone, John? I'm dying to meet her."

Chase was looking worried, glancing around as if he'd lost something. "She's not here. John, don't tell me you let her slip away *again*."

They couldn't see her, shielded from view as she was behind John's tall form. It was a novelty to be able to *hide* behind someone. John's hand reached behind his back, opening toward her in silent inquiry.

He remembered that I hate to be stared at. If I want him to, he'll protect me, get me away from all this attention…

Nonetheless, Neridia took his hand, allowing John to draw her forward. Chase started violently as she stepped into view, as if she'd appeared out of thin air.

"How are you *doing* that?" the pegasus shifter demanded of her.

Neridia shrank back from his outburst. "I'm not doing anything."

"But-but-you aren't there." Chase pulled at his curly hair, staring at her somewhat wild-eyed. "I can see you, but you aren't there! Is nobody else bothered by this? Is it just me?"

The auburn-haired bridesmaid, who Neridia guessed had to be Chase's mate, firmly took the champagne glass from the pegasus shifter's other hand. "And that's enough alcohol for you, evidently."

"Hello again," Griff said to Neridia with a warm smile. "I'm glad you decided to come. This is Hayley, my wife." He lingered on *my wife*, clearly savoring the words. "Hayley, this is-"

"This is the treasure of my heart." John's deep voice was very quiet, but every word rang like some great, solemn church bell. "This is the moon to the sea of my soul. Pearl-bearer, hope-carrier, burdened but unbowed. This is my lady Neridia, who bridges worlds with a touch, whose courage I cannot capture in speech nor song."

"Um," Neridia said, into the echoing silence that followed. "Hi?"

John turned to address Griff and Chase, his words coming slower now, as if he was having to force each one out. "And if ever I have served you, if ever I have earned your friendship, I beg that you will grant me one last boon. If ever she is in need, come to her call. Protect her, as I cannot."

The breath froze in Neridia's lungs. She felt as if a great weight of water crushed her down, squeezing her chest.

He's leaving. This is goodbye. Forever.

"Well, yes, of course we—wait, what?" Chase cut off his apparently automatic agreement. "John, you can't be serious. You're *still* intent on leaving?"

Rather than answer Chase, John looked down at Neridia. "The dance is over." All music drained from his tone, leaving his voice as bleached and bare as washed-up bones. "And you are human again, and I still am not. I do not have the strength to bear this further. Please. Release me. Let me go home."

She wanted to cling to his hand. Every part of her soul cried out to keep hold of him, to never let go. But she could not deny the truth in his words. She could not ignore the agony in the depths of his indigo eyes.

Slowly, she opened her fingers, and let him go.

CHAPTER 9

"*Wait*," Griff said suddenly.

John's back was already turned. Face hidden, he squeezed his eyes tight shut for a moment, fighting for control. His fists clenched, blunt human fingernails digging into his palms. His true shape pressed tight against the underside of his skin.

No more delays. No more. I will break if I do not return to my true self soon. This form is too weak, too frail, to bear this pain. I need to lock away my heart behind the armor of my scales.

"The time for words has passed, oath-brother," he said without looking round. "Farewell."

"*Wait*," Griff repeated. He grabbed John's arm, forcing him to pause. "You still owe me a life-debt. I'm calling it in."

The sheer affront of it nearly blinded him with sudden rage. He jerked himself free of the griffin shifter's grip. "I have done you service after service-!"

"Yes, and I have tried time and time again to persuade you that we're even, and you have never accepted." Griff met his glare without flinching. "Not even that last time, with Danny and Hayley—you said it didn't count, because I'd turned out not to need your help after all. Were you lying, all this time? Is the debt paid?"

John made himself breath deeply, twice, in and out, before he could trust himself to speak. "I am a Knight-Poet of the First Water, vowed to candor. I never lie. The debt is not paid."

It was the deepest gesture of trust a sea dragon could make, to refuse to allow a life-debt to be repaid. It was laying your throat bare to your oath-brother's blade, confident that he would never use the weapon you had handed him. He'd thought Griff understood that.

I am a fool. Of course no dry-lander can ever truly comprehend our ways.

"Well, I'm calling the debt in now," Griff said firmly. "I have one last task for you, before you disappear for good. I need you to take Neridia home."

"Griff." Neridia had overheard. "Please, don't."

Out of the corner of his eye, John caught a glimpse of her stepping forward. He quickly looked away, staring across the room before the sight of her could weaken his resolve yet further.

"It's, it's all right." Her beautiful voice stumbled on the painful lie. "Let John go. Please, don't torment him any more."

"I'm sorry, and doubly so if this all turns out to be a mistake. I have a horrible suspicion that even if I'm right, this is just going to make everything worse…but John has to go to your house."

"My honor," John grated out through gritted teeth, "is not a leash round my neck for you to jerk at your whim. I warn you, *oath-brother*, that if you do this we will not part as friends."

"I know," Griff said quietly. "But this is too important. Neridia, you need to show John that painting."

~

The journey to Neridia's dwelling-place seemed endless. She lived on the far side of the loch, which was no distance at all for a sea dragon, but a considerable journey when one was forced to travel by land.

John did not like travelling in cars at the best of times; he had to contort like an eel to fit inside even the largest vehicle, and to have the world streaking past without any effort from his own muscles was deeply disconcerting. To be forced to cram himself into one of the hellish metal devices now, agonizingly aware of Neridia's bare arm mere inches away from his, was a fresh depth of torment.

Though he kept his eyes firmly fixed on the dark waters of the lake blurring past outside, he could not close his nose to her enticing scent. He breathed as little as possible, tried to find a position that didn't break his spine, and began to mentally recite the Creed of the Knights of the First Water.

By the time they finally stopped outside a small stone cottage, every bone in John's body screamed protest at the constant jolting, he'd reached the Forty-Ninth Rule of Honorable Duels…and he was more rigidly hard than he had ever been in his entire life.

"Um. Well," Neridia said, breaking the silence that had smothered them for the entire journey. She turned off the infernal vehicle. "Here we are."

John contemplated first whether he *could* unfold from his contorted position, and secondly whether he *wanted* to. But his shameful state showed no sign of subsidence. He could only hope that the ridiculously thick, all-enveloping human garments he wore would conceal his lack of self-control.

"I still don't understand why Griff insisted on this," Neridia said, as she led him into the house. "Did he say anything more to you?"

"No," John said, shortly.

John hadn't given his oath-brother—his *former* oath-brother—the opportunity to explain himself. Filled with anger at his comrades' betrayal, he'd stormed out of the ballroom, removing himself from their presence before he lost his temper entirely.

Privately, John was certain that Griff had just been seizing on any excuse to force him to spend more time in Neridia's presence. Doubtless the griffin shifter's eagle-sharp senses had allowed him to see just how close to breaking John truly was. He must have hoped that the enforced proximity would push him over the edge.

I will endure. I must endure. Only a few moments more.

His packed hoard, armor and sword were safely stored in the back of Neridia's vehicle. As soon as he had discharged this ridiculous duty, he could seize them, and disappear into the depths of the lake. He would be gone, and never again have to know the torment of breathing the same air as her, walking on the same land as her, so close and yet so terribly apart.

"Well, this is it." Neridia gestured uncertainly at a small painting hanging on the wall of the living room. "So? Does it mean anything to you?"

John glanced at the unimpressive thing. "It is a painting of the lake. With a sea dragon in it. There. Honor is satisfied. I shall not trouble you further."

For fuck's sake! his inner human yelled at him. *Idiot!* Look *at it!*

His inner human's vehemence caught him off guard. Without his own volition, John's gaze was dragged back to the tiny painted silhouette.

He still could not see anything special about it, certainly nothing to so agitate his inner human. It was just a sea dragon. Perfect in every detail, from the noble curve of the horned brow to the majestic sweep of the neck-ruff…

Wait.

John had seen many human depictions of sea dragons. They had all been laughably inaccurate. No human had properly seen a sea dragon for thousands of years, after all, not since Atlantis had sank beneath the waves. All humans had to base their fanciful pictures on were half-remembered legends and tall tales.

But this…*this* sea dragon was painted with utter accuracy, as if drawn from life.

And more than that, it was a very particular sea dragon.

"Who painted this?" John said softly, staring at the unmistakable profile.

"My father," Neridia said, sounding puzzled. "That's what Griff asked too. He-what are you doing?"

He'd seized her chin, gently but firmly tipping her face up to the light. Heedless of her muffled protests, he tilted her head first one way, then the other, staring at her features as if seeing them for the first time.

How was I so blind? How could I not see it before?

The elegant arch of her brow, the strong set of her jaw, the glory of her eyes…it was not merely the fact that she was his mate that made every line of her face shine with noble beauty.

"Why are you staring at me?" Neridia jerked free from his suddenly slack hand. "What's going on?"

"*Where is he?*"

Neridia took a half-step back, eyes widening in alarm. "I, I don't know what you're saying."

He'd spoken in his own language. He fumbled for human words, tongue half-numb with shock. "Where is he? Your, your father, where is he now?"

Neridia's hand crept up to close around her pearl pendant. "He died four years ago. He-*John!*"

He'd crashed to his knees, not gracefully, but as if felled by a sword-stroke.

"The Emperor is dead." Shaking in every muscle, he bowed his head in the full genuflection due to her. "Long live the Empress."

CHAPTER 10

Neridia stared down at John's bowed head. "What?"

"You are the one I have been seeking, Your Majesty," he said to her shoes. "You are the Heir to the Pearl Throne. Your father, may he rest in the ocean's heart, was the Pearl Emperor, King of Atlantis, Ruler of all the Shifters of the Sea, Commander of Wave and-"

Neridia had a suspicion the list of titles might go on for some time. "My *father*? That's ridiculous. My father was no sea dragon!"

"Look, Your Majesty." John unfastened one of the charms from his braided hair, holding it out to her without lifting his head. "Look at this, and then at the painting."

Neridia took the small golden disc, squinting at it. A minute sea dragon's head was engraved on one side in exquisite detail. Something about it struck her as terribly familiar.

It was exactly the same profile her father had painted in the picture. Exactly the same as the way he'd always drawn the "Loch Ness Monster."

"Coincidence," she said, trying to convince herself. "He was an artist, he had a good imagination. Or, or maybe he just saw a sea dragon some time."

John shook his head, gaze still fixed on the ground. "Your Majesty-"

"Don't call me that!"

He ignored her interruption. "I saw him in human form once, Your Majesty. I was no more than a mere child at the time, but I could never forget his imperial face. I should have recognized you at once. I *would* have done, had I not been blinded by...what else you are to me."

"This, this is..." Neridia clenched her fist around the charm, her hand shaking. "This is nonsense. You're wrong. My father couldn't even swim! He was terrified of water!"

That jerked his head up at last. "What?"

"He wouldn't even go outside if it was raining. My mom always said it was just a phobia, something he couldn't help, and that I mustn't upset him by asking questions about it."

"And the lake told me that no sea dragon had visited its depths," John murmured, his eyebrows drawing down. "I do not understand. How could he bear to never take his true form?"

"Because being human *was* his true form! He never went near the lake. He liked to look at it from a distance, but he was paranoid about getting too close."

John's blue eyes widened in sudden realization. "Because if his reflection crossed water, he could have been seen."

"What?"

"It is one of the sea dragon arts. Scrying, seeing what is reflected in the surface of distant bodies of water." John's brow was furrowed in thought. "It is not my chosen art form, so I do not comprehend more than the very basic principles of it. But I know that our most talented Seers have been searching for him ever since he vanished. If he did not wish to be found, he could not risk going near open water."

"Then why would he choose to live near a *lake*, for pity's sake?"

"Because he was still a sea dragon," John said softly. "And no sea dragon could bear to live without at least the sight of water. What it must have cost him, to gaze upon it every day, yet still keep his exile..."

"But why?" Neridia realized she was yelling, and tried to get herself back under control. "If, if what you're saying is true, and he really was...*why?*"

"Why did he leave the sea? Why did he abandon the Pearl Throne, his duties and responsibilities, without a word of warning, not even to the Order of the First Water, his sworn guardians? I have long pondered that mystery, without a glimmer of insight." John rubbed his hand across his face, mouth tightening into a grim, heartsick line. "But now...now, I think I am beginning to understand his mind."

"My mom," Neridia whispered, as the answer struck her too. "He loved her so, so much. When she passed away, a few months before he did, it was like part of him had died too. I think she must have been his mate."

John nodded, slowly. "And he could not both rule the sea and serve his mate. No human may enter sunken Atlantis, and the Emperor can only rarely leave our city."

"So he gave up his title, and the sea. He picked her." John stiffened, and Neridia belatedly realized how he must have taken her words as an accusation. "No, I didn't mean—I was just wondering how he could do that. I thought honor was everything to a sea dragon."

"It is." John's tight shoulders eased down a little. "But the Emperor was not a Knight, bound by vows of chastity as I am. What would be dishonorable for me would not have been for him. I have no doubt that your father kept his honor, even though he gave up his Throne."

Neridia found that she was holding her pearl, as she so often did for comfort. For most of her life, it had rested in the hollow of her father's throat, gleaming against his slate-dark skin. He'd given it to her a few days before he'd died, and until yesterday it had never left her throat in all the four years since. Yet now, its familiar smooth surface seemed suddenly new and foreign.

Did he bring this with him? Is it a sea dragon treasure, a royal *treasure? Did it have some special meaning?*

When she'd first put it on, he'd looked at her so strangely. As though underneath his shining pride had been a deep, fathomless sadness...

"What I do not yet understand," John said, frowning, "is why he never told you of your heritage. You are the Heir to the Pearl Throne. Even if *he* never intended to return, he should have been preparing you to take your rightful place. Why did he not?"

He sounded genuinely baffled. Neridia stared at him, unable to believe that he'd failed to see the blindingly obvious.

"John, *I'm* human." She held out her arms, displaying her ordinary, utterly un-dragonlike self. "Even if I am half-sea dragon, I'm no shifter. My father must have been able to tell that."

He looked at her as if she'd just announced she was a small purple rabbit. "Of course you are a sea dragon, Your Majesty."

"No, I'm not! I think I should know! And for pity's sake, stop calling me that!"

He shook his head stubbornly, charms chiming together in his long hair. "When we first met, when I first knew you to be my mate, I was absolutely convinced that you were of my kind. It was not until you fled that I began to doubt. Now, it is obvious that my first impression was indeed correct. I was merely fooled for a time by the misleading reflections on the surface, and did not see through to the true currents beneath."

Neridia pressed her fists to her forehead. It was all too much. "I didn't even know sea dragons *existed* until yesterday."

"You have been kept in a dark vault, like a hidden treasure." John rose to his feet at last, holding out his hand to her. His fingers trembled, ever so slightly. "But no longer. Come, Your Majesty. It is time to take your true form."

CHAPTER 11

What if she's right? John's inner human asked uneasily. It was pacing in his mind, back and forth like a caged beast. *What if she is just human?*

John ignored the creature's whispers as he led Neridia down to the waterside. It was a human trait to fret about the future, imagining the worst case so vividly that it crippled them from acting in the present. Sea dragons were unhampered by such weakness. A sea dragon saw what was so, and acted upon it, without hesitation or self-doubt.

Of course his mate was a sea dragon. What else could she be? Honor and strength shone from her like the very moon above.

No wonder I could not resist her. No wonder she draws me so strongly. My true self recognized her, even through weak human eyes.

He looked around, assessing the surroundings with professional scrutiny. Until Neridia—no, he must stop thinking of her in such familiar terms. Until *Her Imperial Majesty* could be provided with an appropriate retinue, he had sole responsibility for her safety.

"May I have your permission to ask a question, Your Majesty?"

Her Imperial Majesty glared at him. "Are you really going to keep calling me that?"

"Yes, Your Majesty." She had not given him permission. He kept his back very straight, gaze fixed somewhere over her left shoulder, and waited.

The wind blew. Insects sang in the plants edging the loch.

The Empress sighed, holding up her hands in surrender. "Now I know why Griff called you the most stubborn man he'd ever met. Okay, fine. What did you want to ask?"

"Is that dwelling-place derelict?" He pointed at the only other house in sight, a larger stone cottage set some distance away. The windows had been boarded over, and parts of the roof were skeletal.

"Yes." A shadow flickered across her royal face, as if she had been stabbed by an old pain. "That was my parents' old house. My childhood home. It burned down. That was how my dad, how he, he…the firefighters did all they could, but it was too late."

Shame washed over him at this failure of his profession, although four years ago he hadn't even left the sea, let alone become a firefighter himself. "All the sea grieves with you, Your Majesty. Did the investigation identify a cause for the tragedy?"

"They said the whole house had been soaked in gasoline, so thoroughly that they thought he must have done it himself." Her lips tightened. "My mom had passed away a few months back, and everyone knew how devoted he'd been to her. The police recorded it as a suicide."

He frowned. "Sometimes shifters do indeed lose the will to live after the death of their mates, but…your father had you. I cannot believe he would choose to end his own life, leaving the Heir to the Pearl Throne unguarded and unaware of her own heritage."

"I didn't think it was suicide either. There was this man, you see. He was at my dad's house, the day before the fire. I only saw him briefly, and my dad said he was just an old friend who'd unexpectedly dropped by…but he gave me the creeps for some reason." She hugged herself, shivering a little. "But since the police already thought they knew what had happened, they weren't much interested in trying to track down some random guy just because I had a bad feeling about him."

"You have all the knights of the sea at your personal command now, Your Majesty. We will find him, should you command us to do so, even if we must scour the entire earth."

She sniffed, hastily swiping the back of one hand across her eyes. "That doesn't sound very practical."

"Practicality is not one of our vows, Your Majesty."

That won him a small smile, though her lower lip still trembled a little. "I kind of got that impression, yes. Why were you asking about the house, anyway?"

"I wished to be certain that it was uninhabited, Your Majesty. Since this location seems secure, we may proceed." John began stripping out of his confining human clothes.

He was pulling off his shirt when he realized that she was simply staring at him, making no move to follow suit. "Do you require assistance, Your Majesty?"

"You want me to take off all my clothes and jump into the lake? Right now?"

"Yes, Your Majesty."

"Are you *insane*?"

"No, Your Majesty."

She rubbed her forehead. "You really weren't kidding about the lack of practicality thing. John, this is Scotland, not the Bahamas! Even in summer, I'll freeze solid in there. Not to mention the fact that I can't even swim!"

"You will neither sink nor freeze, Your Majesty. You are a sea dragon. You are made for colder waters than-"

"I'm not, I keep telling you, I'm *not!*" She sat down heavily on a rock, burying her face in her hands. "Why did you have to turn up? Why did I have to find out any of this? Why can't you just leave me alone, like you said you would?"

The Empress was weeping.

Without thinking, he reached out—and then snatched his hand back as his knightly training overruled instinct. One did not presume to *touch* the Imperial presence. He knelt instead, stone cold and sharp under his knees. "Your-"

"If the next word out of your mouth is *Majesty*, I shall *hit* you," she snarled through her tears.

Etiquette, his inner human said, *can go fuck itself.*

"Neridia." She looked up at the sound of her name, her face wet and vulnerable. He brushed her hair back from her damp cheek, his fingertips barely grazing her skin. "I am your mate. I know your soul, even the depths that you yourself do not. Trust me."

Her eyes brimmed with tears. "You're really certain about this?"

"As certain as I am about my own true self." He touched her chest above her heart, then his own. "I was born a sea dragon, and was taught human form as a small child. But you were born in human shape, like a dry-land shifter. And is not unheard of for a dry-land shifter to come late to their other form."

She took a deep breath, swiping her tears away with the back of her hand. "Really? You aren't just saying that?"

"Candor *is* one of my knightly vows. I cannot lie. I promise you, your situation is not unique. Ask Griff, when you next see him. He too only learned to shift as an adult."

She looked out at the lake. "My parents never let me swim," she murmured as if to herself. "I've never been in the water. Not properly."

Gently, he took her hands, lifting her to her feet. "Then allow me the great honor of bringing you home."

She wore a silky garment the color of sea foam. Still holding her gaze, he reached behind her to find the tiny tab of the zipper. She did not protest as he slowly drew it down. The delicate straps slid over the soft curves of her shoulders.

Courage, courtesy, compassion, chastity, charity, constancy, candor. John mentally clung to the mantra of the Seven Knightly Vows as if to a lifeline as Neridia's dress fell away. *Courage, courtesy, compassion, chas-*

Silk pooled around his mate's feet, leaving her clad only in the barest wisps of lace, and all thought drained away.

Her curves held both the abundance of the earth and the rolling waves of the sea. Her skin evoked the rich tones of fertile soil, warmer than his own ocean-tinged hue. Her navel was a tiny perfect whirlpool; her collarbones graceful as the wings of gulls.

He might have stared in dumbstruck worship until the end of time and tides, but she shivered, wrapping her arms around herself. "I'm cold."

Every drop of his soul cried out with the desire to embrace her and warm her against his own body. But if he did…

I would never be able to let go again.

He forced himself to step back, though it felt like fighting against the strongest ocean current. He cleared his throat. "The, the water shall warm you, Your Majesty."

He turned away, crouching down to put one hand just above the surface of the water. The lake rose up to meet his touch, waves rubbing against his palm like a dolphin's arched back. He could hear the water's anticipation, its shivering eagerness to greet the Empress.

Gently, gently, he cautioned the water, as best he could with a mere human voice. *Feel the warmth of my blood; all seas are one sea, and your currents flow through my veins. Give back your stored summers, remember the heat of distant sands. Embrace my lady gently, as I cannot.*

"Here, Your Majesty." He motioned her forward. "The way is prepared for you."

She cast him a dubious look, but kicked off her shoes. Her eyes widened as her bare toes dipped into the water. "It's warm!"

"The lake is your loyal subject, Your Majesty, as are all waters. It is anxious to please you."

The water murmured with pleasure, caressing the Imperial ankles. John tightened one fist, fighting for control as the lake whispered and sighed over the silkiness of her skin. Linked to its currents as he was, he could not help but feel everything that the water did. The elegance of her instep, the perfect shells of her toenails, the soft swells of her calves…

The Empress waded out further, and John bit back a moan as the water crept past her dimpled knees and up her thighs. The lake sang in ecstasy as it lapped higher, tasting her intoxicating salt-

"John?" Waist-deep, she looked back at him in concern. "Are you coming?"

"A, a moment," he gasped, hunched over.

Courage, courtesy, compassion, chastity, charity, constancy, candor! He mentally shouted his Knightly Vows, drowning out the water's sensual song. *Courage, courtesy, compassion, chastity, charity, constancy, candor!*

His crisis retreated a little, leaving him not quite so much on the brink of utterly shaming himself right there on the shore. Straightening, he strode into the water—raising rather more concealing spray than was strictly necessary.

"You'll ruin your suit," she said as he splashed over to join her.

"It is a necessary sacrifice, Your Majesty." He wished that he could ask the lake to drop the temperature to sub-arctic levels in a very localized area. "Come. We must go deeper. Your true form will require more space."

The Empress hesitated, biting her lip. "I can't swim."

"You can swim." He took her hand, drawing her forward. "You were born able to swim, Your Majesty."

She grabbed at his hand as her feet left the bottom, eyes suddenly panicked. "John-!"

"Let your body recognize what your mind has forgotten." He wove a calm melody around the human words, urging the water to cradle her as gently as a soft-scaled hatchling. "You spent the first nine months of your existence floating, rocked by the tides of your mother's heart. You knew water long before you ever knew air. You merely need to be reminded."

He was floating too now, balanced on his back, his long legs positioned protectively underneath her. The lake swirled around them both, supportive and welcoming. He felt her rigid muscles ease a little at the friendly, buoyant touch of the water.

Cautiously, she relaxed into the embrace of the lake. She kept hold of his hand, but her free arm drifted out, fingers opening like a delicate anemone unfurling.

"Oh," she whispered. "*Oh.*"

"See, Your Majesty," he whispered, heart near breaking with pride and longing. "You are home."

She rolled over onto her own back, effortlessly, with barely a swirl of her hand. Closing her eyes, she tipped her head back so her ears were under the water.

He gazed at her calm profile as she floated alongside him. There was a tremor in the deeps, a sense of a great power stirring. He could practically *see* the glisten of her scales, the royal sweep of her horns. The sense that a sea dragon swam alongside him was strong, so strong…

She opened her eyes again, looking at him rather ruefully. "I really have no idea what I'm supposed to be doing now."

"You are so close, Your Majesty. Can you also not sense it? Your true self, rising from the depths?"

She shook her head, droplets of water caught like a coronet of diamonds in her dark hair. "I just feel like me."

The lake murmured in frustration. *She holds back. Something stops her from uniting with the flow.*

The thin gleam of gold around the Empress's neck caught John's eye. He followed the line of the chain down to the shimmering pearl resting in the hollow of her throat.

Could it be…?

"Tell me about this, Your Majesty," He gently hooked a finger around the necklace to draw the pearl out of the water. "You said your father gave it to you?"

"Yes, just before he died. He'd always worn it before then. I don't know why he suddenly decided to give it to me—he just said that it was my turn to have it. He made me promise to wear it, always. He wasn't a superstitious person, but he seemed to think it would somehow protect me." She cast him a curious sidelong look. "Why are you asking about my pearl now?"

"We have no paper under the sea. Our Scribes work in pearl, starting from a simple kernel of meaning, and wrapping it in layers of shining nuance. The very best can capture our songs, creating pearls of great power."

The Empress put her hand to the pearl. "You think my pendant is magical?"

"I myself possess a pearl imbued with tales of our greatest knights, set into the hilt of my sword, to lend me their fortitude and endurance. If a pearl can be enchanted to strengthen, I suspect one can also be made to weaken."

She was silent for a long moment, treading water. Then she reached behind her neck to unfasten the chain. "Will you look after this for me?"

"With my life." He took it from her.

She watched anxiously as he fastened it around his neck. "Do you...feel any different?"

"I cannot say that I do. You, Your Majesty?"

She shook her head. "No. Are you still able to shift?"

Experimentally, he reached for his true form—and quickly stopped as he felt his skin prickle with the start of the shift. "Yes. Perhaps I was mistaken."

"Well, maybe you'd better keep it on for now. Just in case there's a delayed effect or something." She floated on her back once more, staring up at the night sky. "John, I don't think this is working."

"Patience, Your Majesty. It may simply take time."

She blew out her breath in a long sigh. "Is there any way to speed things up?"

His inner human grinned. *Oh yes. There most definitely is.*

It was, of course, absolutely right. And John was most definitely *not* going to share the information with Her Majesty.

We must, his inner human argued. *Candor is one of our vows. We cannot break a Knightly Vow, can we?*

The cursed creature could be as cunning as an octopus when it was trying to get its way. John set his jaw, trying to ignore its blandishments.

Of course, even the Knightly Vows must be broken if a higher duty calls, his human said, its eyes gleaming slyly in the darkness of his soul. *And our first duty is to the Pearl Throne. Not to the Order of the First Water, not to knightly oaths. Not even to our mate. Our first duty is to the* Empress. *And if her best interests conflict with other oaths...*

His heart suddenly thumped against his ribs.

No. That is human sophistry. I must not be tempted-

"John?" He'd taken too long to respond. The Empress's eyes widened as she stared at him. "There *is* something, isn't there? Something you don't want to tell me."

"I…" He could not tell a flat-out lie. "Yes, there is. But it would not be wise. Please, trust my judgment on this, Your Majesty."

Her mouth set in a stubborn line. "No. If you're still going to insist on calling me that, then you can damn well treat me like your Empress. I *order* you to tell me whatever it is."

His inner human pumped a fist in the air in exultation. *Yes!*

Yes, echoed the lake, currents urging them together.

He would still have refused, if he could. But his Empress had commanded, and he had to obey.

"We could…" He swallowed, mouth dry despite the water all around. "We could mate, Your Majesty."

CHAPTER 12

She had water in her ears. Neridia shook her head, trying to clear them. "I'm sorry, could you say that again?"

"We could mate," he repeated, even more reluctantly.

She *had* heard him right the first time. In her shock, she forgot to tread water, and promptly swallowed a wave. All her subconscious swimming skill deserted her. She slipped under the surface, flailing.

"Neridia!" John's strong hands closed around her waist, bearing her up. "I mean-that is-Your Majesty."

Neridia clung to his broad shoulders, gasping. She instinctively wrapped her legs around his waist...and her breath caught for a different reason than her brief dunking.

Only her underwear separated their bare torsos. She could feel every ridge of his muscles, hard against her own softness. Even in the bizarrely tropical waters of Loch Ness, his naked skin burned, igniting fire through her blood.

Her hands slid over the water-slick swells of his shoulders. "When you say mate..."

"Join. Unite our souls." He was as solid as a rock in the water, supporting her without any apparent effort, but she could feel the pounding of his heart. "If we were mated, we would be able to touch mind-to-mind, sharing everything. You would *know* what it is to be a sea dragon, as surely as I do."

Her stomach sank, and her hands stilled. "So this mating would just be a meeting of minds?"

He met her gaze. "No," he said softly.

Her heart leapt again, but she forced herself to stay still. "What about your vows? I thought you were sworn to chastity."

"Before all else, I am sworn to the Pearl Throne. My highest duty is to serve the Empress. To serve you."

"Even if it means sacrificing your honor?"

"It would not be a sacrifice," he whispered. "To be your mate would be the greatest honor of my life."

Their faces were very close now. His eyes were very dark with desire, his breath coming short and fast. Her own heart was beating so hard, her blood sang in her ears.

"Neridia." He brought up a hand, preventing their mouths from closing that last fateful distance. His calloused fingertips traced the curves of her lips. "If, if we do this…it is forever. Do you understand?"

"Yes. *Yes.*" Her body yearned for him so fiercely she was physically shaking, her thighs trembling against his hard flanks. "But—are you really sure *you* want this?"

He made a low, inarticulate noise in answer, half-moan, half-growl. His hand clenched around the back of her head, pulling her against his mouth.

Neridia melted into the fierce kiss, lost in the glorious feel of his lips against hers. His demanding tongue pressed into her, deep and hot, sparking an answering throb of need between her legs.

One hand still tangled in her hair, his other slid down over her hips, underwater. Neridia sucked in her breath as he slipped under her panties, exploring the soft curve of her butt. He tightened his grasp, fingers deliciously rough against her skin, pulling her more firmly against his hips. His unmistakable erection pressed into her stomach even through the thick, sodden fabric of his dress pants.

"Um." Neridia broke the kiss, gasping for air. "Shouldn't we get out of the lake?"

He pulled back a little, his brow furrowing. "Why?"

"Well, we can't, you know…" Neridia caught her breath as his hips flexed, rubbing his hard length against her body. "Not in the water!"

"We are sea dragons." He ducked his head to kiss the junction of her neck and shoulder, sending delicious shivers through her. "This is how sea dragons mate."

"I've only just learned to swim!" She squirmed against him, tormented by the exquisite, nipping kisses he was trailing across her skin. "This is a bit advanced, you know!"

"Trust me, my lady." Despite his words, he unwound her arms from his neck. "And trust yourself."

Lithe as an eel, he twisted out of her grip. Before she knew what was happening, he dove, disappearing under the black water.

"John?" Every nerve aflame with thwarted desire, Neridia flailed gracelessly, trying to see where he'd gone. "John!"

She gasped as his arms encircled her from behind, pulling her against his hard body. His *naked* hard body. The feel of his thick length pressed against her inflamed every inch of her skin. She couldn't help rubbing back against him, the slick, swollen head of his cock sliding along the crack of her ass. He let out a deep groan, arms tightening, his muscles as hard as his shaft.

Neridia threw back her head as his hands came up to cup her breasts through the wet lace of her bra. Nearly blind with pleasure, she writhed against him, her ass thrusting against his cock as he rolled and teased her nipples.

"John!" she cried out, as the pulsing pleasure between her legs grew to an unbearable wave. "*John!*"

He held her through her climax, supporting her with his muscled body as she came. He made a deep, satisfied hum of pleasure as she collapsed back against him. She had no idea how he was keeping them both afloat; *she* certainly wasn't capable of swimming at the moment.

His hand drifted down the curves of her stomach, slipping under her panties again. She jerked as his fingers gently parted her folds, his calloused fingertip brushing her swollen clit.

"Too soon?" he rumbled in her ear, his circling finger pausing.

"No. *God*, no." Even though she was still trembling with the aftershocks of orgasm, she wanted more. She *needed* him, all of him, inside her-

She bit back a curse, grabbing his wrist. "Wait. I'm pretty certain neither of us has a condom to hand right now."

He went still, though she felt his chest heave as if it took a great effort to force himself to stop. "I do not know what that is."

"Birth control?" She twisted her head round, looking up at his uncomprehending expression. "You know, to prevent pregnancy?"

He blinked at her. "Humans need to do something to *prevent* pregnancy?"

"Uh...don't sea dragons?"

He shook his head. "We must do the opposite. If we wish to have young, we must mate at specific times of the year, after certain rituals."

"Um, well. I'm half-human. I don't know whether that's true for me."

"Perhaps, but it is certainly true for *me*." His finger started to circle again. "I am not currently fertile."

If she was sensible, she knew, she shouldn't take his word for it. On the other hand, if she was sensible, she wouldn't be having sex in a lake with a sea dragon.

Tipping her head back, Neridia abandoned all thought of being sensible.

His touch rocked her with swelling waves of pleasure, echoing the way the lake's waves rocked their bodies. Cradled in his arms, in the lake, she felt wonderfully small and weightless. For once, she didn't have to worry about being too big, taking up too much space.

"Neridia." His voice was rather rougher than usual. Though his fingers kept their slow, teasing rhythm, his cock pressed hungrily against her back. "I, I cannot-forgive me, I wanted to do you justice. But I do not have the fortitude to endure much longer."

In response, Neridia reached round, sliding her hand between their bodies. He groaned as she closed her fingers around his thick shaft, hips jerking involuntarily.

"I don't *want* to wait longer." She stroked him, her breath coming as fast as his at the feel of his hard, slick length against her palm. "I want you, now."

He growled, deep in his throat. His hands grasped her hips, pulling her higher up his body so that his cock pressed against her entrance.

Neridia shut her eyes, all the world narrowing down to the sensation of him pushing into her. He went slowly, though his whole body shook with the effort, giving her time to stretch around his huge girth.

As he slid into her, inch by inch, her awareness expanded. She could not only feel the exquisite slide of him entering her, but also his astonished delight at the feel of *her* warmth embracing him, her slick depths welcoming him in. His pleasure and hers mingled in her mind, echoing and doubling, until she couldn't tell where she stopped and he began.

They both cried out as he buried himself fully in her. Neridia clenched around him, and felt him lose all control at last. He plunged into her, powerful and rhythmic as the sea, sweeping her away on a tidal wave of sensation.

"Neridia!" He sang her name as they both came, in a thundering chord of triumph and wonder.

She *knew* that the music was words, and what those words were. She could hear them in her head, as clearly as if he'd spoken in English.

My mate!

～

They drifted for a time, entwined in each other's embrace on the surface of the lake. Neridia leaned her head on his chest, listening to the slow, quiet sound of his heartbeat, and the deeper, equally quiet sound of his mind.

She couldn't exactly read his thoughts, but she could sense something of their nature, like the way rippling water revealed the currents below. She knew that he was tired, and relaxed, and profoundly, deeply awestruck.

This last thought was so unexpected that she lifted her head to look at him. "*You're* awed by *me?*" she said in disbelief.

His fingertips traced light, spiraling patterns down her spine. "How could I not be, Your Majesty?"

Annoyed, she splashed him. "Don't start that again. Anyway, if you're the Empress's mate, doesn't that make you the Emperor?"

His hand stilled. She could sense that this honestly hadn't occurred to him. "It would make me…the Royal Consort, if I am remembering the protocol correctly."

"Well then," she said in triumph. "You're royalty yourself now, so there's no need for formality, your Royal Consort…ness."

His shoulders shook with his deep chuckle. "I bow to your impeccable logic, Your—my mate."

"That's better."

Still feeling that all this had to just be a dream, she ran her hand over the smooth planes of his chest—only for her skin to snag against his. Rubbing her fingertips together, she realized that they were waterlogged by the long immersion in the lake.

She let out a deep sigh, holding up her hand to show him her wrinkled skin. "I guess we have to get out. If we stay in here much longer, I'm going to turn into a raisin."

He kissed her fingers, tongue flicking lightly over the tips in a way that made her toes curl. "No. You will turn into a sea dragon."

Apprehension cut through her glowing contentment like a bucket of ice water dumped on her head. "John, I don't think anything's changed. Well, I mean, it *has*, but…I still just feel like myself."

"You feel like yourself because you *are* still yourself," he said serenely. "You are what you have always been. A sea dragon."

He flicked himself vertical with an effortless twist, balancing upright in the water. She was forced to slide off his chest, rather less gracefully doggy-paddling at his side.

He smiled at her, his usually solemn face alight with joyful anticipation. "Watch me, my mate. Learn how to take your true form."

He disappeared under the surface with barely a ripple, smooth as a seal. She couldn't see him through the dark water, but she still knew exactly where he was. She could sense him swimming down with strong, swift strokes, moving with the unconscious grace of a fish.

Then he did…something.

She caught her breath. *He's shifting.*

It was as quick and easy as pouring water from one container into another. One moment he was as human as her. The next-

She tumbled head over heels, thrown backward by the shock wave of displaced water. All the breath was knocked out of her lungs, bubbling away. Unable to tell which way was up, she panicked, hands clawing as she sank.

Neridia!

A vast, scaled back rose up beneath her, pushing her to the surface once more. Neridia scrabbled for purchase on the slick, hard scales as she spluttered.

I am sorry. Something huge curved above her, blotting out the moon. *I was too eager, and did not give myself enough space to shift. Forgive me.*

Pushing her hair out of her eyes, heart hammering, Neridia looked up.

It's John. It's just John.

There was no *just* about it.

He was vast. His long, fluid body filled the water around her, encircling her in graceful coils. His head was bigger than her car. His eyes were the same deep blue as in his human form, but now each one was at least three feet across. They glowed faintly in the darkness, like some phosphorescent deep-sea creature that lived beyond the reach of the sun.

Two long, elegant horns swept back from his temples, each dividing into six short, jutting points like a deer's antlers. The overall shape of his head reminded her more of a Chinese dragon than a Western one; intelligent and noble rather than brutally reptilian.

A sort of ruff or mane fringed his head, running a little way down the back of his serpentine neck. Gold glittered amidst the flowing blue tendrils. She wondered if they were the same charms woven into his hair when he was in human form, somehow transformed to match his new size.

Yes. My honor-tokens are made to have two forms, the same as myself. It is the art of our Smiths to create twinned items that shift as we do.

If his human voice was reminiscent of a bassoon and a cello playing in harmony, in *this* form he sounded like a whole orchestra. As before, she could somehow tell what he was saying, the words taking shape in her head as his melodious dragon-speech shook the water.

Tentatively, she put her hand up. He curved his neck in response, lowering his head until the huge, blunt tip of his wedge-shaped muzzle touched her palm. She spread her fingers out. Her entire hand didn't even cover a single *scale*.

He was so big, so *unapologetically* big. He occupied space with a casual, unconscious assurance, as if it was his *right* to take up as much room as he needed. She couldn't even imagine doing the same herself.

Try, he urged her.

In her mind, she could clearly picture what he'd done, how easily he'd shrugged off human form and exploded into his true glory. She could see in *his* mind what she would look like as a dragon, as huge and powerful as he was.

She took a deep breath, filling her lungs to their fullest extent, and let go of his side. Relaxing her limbs, she allowed the water to close over her head.

And tried.

CHAPTER 13

𝓑y the time John had managed to soothe Neridia into a fitful slumber, the moon was past zenith. It shone through her bedroom window, the silver light washing over her tear-streaked cheeks. Even in sleep, her body curled in a tense, unhappy ball, like a hermit crab huddling into a stolen shell.

She tried so hard. Oh, my mate, my heart, my Empress. You tried so hard.

She doubtless would still have been in the lake, her salt tears mingling with the agitated water, had John not bodily carried her out of it. He'd wrapped her in towels and his own arms, kissing away her sobbing frustration. He'd sung to her as he would have sung to an overwrought hatchling, soft notes of reassurance and certainty: *All will be well. No defeat is final. Sleep, rest, and be fresh for battle tomorrow.*

Now, at last, she slept. With infinite care, John untangled his fingers from hers. She murmured fretfully, hand searching across the bedcovers, and he held his breath—but she lapsed back into exhausted slumber. Barefoot, he eased out of the room, closing the door silently behind him.

We can't leave her now, his inner human fretted. *This is a terrible idea. Go back.*

John shook his head slightly, dispelling the intrusive thoughts.

Even though he too wanted nothing more than to remain at his mate's side, guarding her dreams, he had his duty. He had already delayed too long.

His possessions were still safely stored in the rear compartment of Neridia's vehicle. He opened the smaller rucksack for a moment, just to reassure himself that his hoard was secure. He had a sudden vision of adorning Neridia's glorious body with the gleaming pearls and gold, and had to fight down a surge of lust. He made himself zip the bag up before he succumbed to the temptation to go back inside.

Instead, he opened his large duffel bag. Carefully, piece by piece, he unwrapped his armor.

In the golden age when Atlantis stood proud above the waves and the entire ocean reverberated with sea dragon songs, a knight like himself would have had an entire retinue of pages and squires to assist him. He would have stood in solemn contemplation, arms outstretched, while each shining piece was fastened to his body with pomp and ritual. One of the knights of old would not even have been capable of preparing for battle alone.

Those days were long gone. John donned his armor as he always had, without assistance.

First the soft, supple kraken-leather leggings, fitting over the muscles of his legs like a second skin. He wrapped his forearms in lengths of the same material, tying the ceremonial knots one-handed with the ease of long practice.

Over the under-armor, the armor proper. Greaves to protect his lower legs, and cuisse over his thighs, fastened round the backs of his legs with strong, rough sharkskin. Long, cunningly articulated boots, each so finely wrought that they flexed as easily as his living feet.

He slid his vambraces over his forearms, whispering a praise-poem to their many past wearers as he buckled the straps. The hard, translucent material gleamed like mother-of-pearl, but it was stronger than any human metal. Both its name and the secret of its manufacture had been lost long ago.

His pauldrons were made of the same substance, encasing his shoulders like the spined carapace of a deep-sea crab. He pulled the straps tight across his chest, flexing to make sure they were properly settled into place.

The helmet completed his armor. He left the visor—fashioned to resemble a sea dragon's snarling visage—raised for now, leaving his face bare. His torso and back too were left uncovered, of course. Griff had once taken him to a museum to see armor worn by human knights, and John had laughed harder than he ever had before in his life. A sea dragon knight had no need to hide inside a thick shell like a turtle; he was trained to catch his opponent's blows on his shoulders and forearms, with the agility allowed by his lightly-covered form.

And no sea dragon knight had need of armor on his *back*. The only thing that belonged there was his sword.

John picked up the weapon, running his thumb reverently over the fist-sized pearl set on the end of the pommel. It shone faintly at his touch, recognizing him as its rightful wielder. The strength of ancient knights whispered in his blood, a battle-hymn of honor and glory that shielded his soul as surely as his armor protected his skin.

He drew the sword with the barest whisper of steel. With the excitement of Griff's mating ceremony—not to mention subsequent events—he had been shockingly lax in his discipline. He had not performed even the most minimal exercises for an entire day.

The blade leaped through the air like a dolphin as he executed the first few strokes of a practice form, switching fluidly from a single to a double grip and back again. He winced at his own poor performance.

I cannot allow my edge to become dulled. I must maintain my discipline, now more than ever.

But given that performing the entire practice sequence would take two hours, it would have to wait. Grimacing, he flipped the sword over his shoulder, sheathing it in the scabbard across his back.

And finally, he was ready.

He walked along the shoreline, heading away from the house. Though it gnawed at his soul to move so far from his mate's side, he had no choice. He needed space and solitude for this task.

Fortunately, he did not have to go too far before he found what he sought. A hollow in the rocks had caught a fragment of the lake, forming a still, clear pool. John knelt next to it, closing his eyes and clearing his mind.

As he had told Neridia, he only knew the very basic fundamentals of scrying. Poetry was his art form, moving water and wave with words. But he knew the simplest skill of the Seer's art, that of reaching out to talk to another through a reflecting pool. He was poor at it, especially when forced to use fresh water rather than salt. In these circumstances, he would only be able to contact the two individuals to whom he was the most closely linked.

One of those was his sister. He reached out through the water to find the other one.

His questing mind encountered...nothing. No sense of the mystic currents that linked this small puddle to the great sea surrounding Atlantis.

That is odd.

Frowning, John opened his eyes. He was a poor Seer, but not usually *that* poor. He should have at least been able to see the psychic flow with his inner eye.

Perhaps there was too much human-wrought iron nearby, interfering with the energies of the water. Scrying was a more delicate art form than poetry, easily disrupted by human influence. Neridia's house was isolated, but there would still be pipes and wires connecting it to the wider human world.

Moving further away, John tried again, but with no more success. He kept going, becoming increasingly perplexed, until he'd gone so far from Neridia's house that it was out of sight entirely. The soft sounds of nature enfolded him, without a hint of human presence.

And yet scrying still eluded him. His poetry was completely unaffected—he experimentally sang a few words to the water, and saw the waves stir in response—but his inner eye was blind. It was as if he was surrounded by psychic fog.

He rubbed the back of his neck in thought—and stopped abruptly as his hand touched the thin gold chain. He had forgotten that Neridia's pearl still rested in the hollow of his throat.

I wonder...?

He unfastened the chain. The instant the pearl left his neck, the mental fog bank lifted. His inner eye cleared, showing him the delicate currents spreading out from the water.

So that *is what it does.*

He remembered how Chase hadn't been able to sense Neridia's presence earlier, when *she* was wearing the pearl. Evidently it interfered with all forms of locating magic, not just scrying.

The Emperor must have worn it to protect himself from being located by our Seers. And then, later, he passed it on to his daughter... just before he was murdered. Did he know that an enemy was stalking them? Did he choose to protect his daughter rather than himself?

There was no time to ponder the unraveling history further. Now that his inner eye was open, he could see the psychic currents swirling around him, urging him toward the lake.

Someone—a Seer of much greater ability than his own poor talents—was trying to contact *him.*

Hastily, John knelt next to the lake, peering down into the calm water. He barely caught a glimpse of his own face before the reflection blurred, reforming into a different man.

The other's helm was far more ornate than his own, crowned with gleaming golden horns and inlaid with pearl. Rainbow-edged reflections glimmered around his hulking shoulders, cast by the thousands of diamonds set into his ceremonial armor in a pattern resembling scales. Two swords were strapped across his back in a cross pattern.

John saluted, fist to heart. "Sir."

"Knight-Poet. At last." The Knight-Commander of the First Water let out a long, relieved breath, his knotted shoulders easing down a little. "I have been trying to reach you for an entire day. I was beginning to wonder if you still possessed all your limbs."

John felt a twinge of shame for having caused his superior concern. "I can only apologize for so shockingly shirking my duty to you, sir. I should have reported sooner. Recent events-"

"Have apparently taken you to the opposite end of the country from where I stationed you," the Knight-Commander interrupted him, his tone sharpening. "You are the Walker-Above-Wave, the enactor of my will on the land, and yet I find you gallivanting off on your own affairs. Is this how you uphold the honor of the Pearl Empire?"

John felt like a hapless novice again in the face of his superior's obvious displeasure. It had not crossed his mind that he should inform the Knight-Commander of his visit to Scotland; he had, after all, travelled around many other parts of the British Isles without any objection from his superior. Clearly, however, he had been in grave error.

And if my lord is this disappointed in me just because I failed to properly report my movements...how is he going to react when I reveal what else *I have done?*

John swallowed the nervous melodies of trepidation rising in his throat. "I can only repeat my apology, sir."

"You may apologize by performing your duties better in future," the Knight-Commander said, his tone making it clear the discussion was over. "You are to return to Atlantis immediately. I have need of you here."

"Sir." It was so wrong to refuse a direct order that John very nearly said *Yes, at once,* out of sheer reflex. "Sir, I cannot."

"Are you being physically imprisoned?"

"No, sir. I...I am honor-bound by a higher duty, sir."

"Walker-Above-Wave, Emissary to the Land from the Pearl Throne, Knight-Poet of the First Water, Sworn Seeker of the Emperor-in-Absence, and Firefighter for the East Sussex Fire and Rescue Service." Every syllable of his name was enunciated with razor-sharp clarity. It took all of John's discipline not to flinch. "I am the Knight-Commander of the Order of the First Water, Right Hand of the Pearl Throne, the Voice of the Empire-in-Absence, Foremost of the Council of Sea Shifters, and First-Ranked Seer of the Ocean's Eye. What *possible* higher duty could cause you to defy my order?"

John forced himself to meet his Commander's blazing gaze head-on. "My duty to the Pearl Throne, sir. To the Empress."

The Knight-Commander went utterly still.

When his superior still did not speak, John took a deep breath.

"Sir, I have completed the quest you laid upon me. With the deepest sorrow, I must report that the Emperor rests in the sea's heart. But he has not left us bereft. The Emperor had a mate, a human mate. He forsook the Throne in order to be with her on the land, and raise their daughter in secret. Now she is returned to us at last, our new Empress-in-Waiting."

"You have met her," the Knight-Commander said, so softly John barely caught his words. "And you consider her to be the true heir to the Pearl Throne."

"There can be no doubt. She is as much a sea dragon as you or I, sir. I can personally swear to that fact."

The Knight-Commander's gauntleted hand came up to rub at his chin. "You have seen her shift?"

John hesitated. "No, sir. She…this is all very new to her, and she has not been properly educated. It will take her time to learn both our ways and our form. But I swear on my honor, she is a dragon in soul. I know it beyond a shadow of a doubt."

"How?"

John braced himself. "Because she is my mate, sir."

"Your *what?*"

"The Empress is my mate." If he hadn't already been on his knees, he would have fallen to them. "Sir, Knight-Commander, forgive me. I had no way of knowing that she was on land when I was searching the sea. I took my vows in good faith. I did not intend this."

The Knight-Commander was silent for a long moment. Then he sighed. "You are not the first, Knight-Poet. They are not spoken of in our official histories, but…mistakes have occasionally occurred. This does not invalidate your oaths. You are still a member of the Order of the First Water."

John let out a breath he hadn't been aware he was holding. "Sir."

The Knight-Commander raised a warning finger. "But. You are sworn to the Pearl Throne. You cannot have a mate. It is easier to do so if one does not exist, but your unfortunate circumstance does not grant-"

The Knight-Commander stopped abruptly, mid-sentence. John had bowed his head, deeply, unable to look at his superior at all.

"You said you knew she was a dragon in soul," the Knight-Commander said slowly.

John stared at the ripples washing over the pebbles.

The Knight-Commander hissed a lashing, bitter melody of dismay. "You have already mated her?"

It took every ounce of courage he possessed to raise his face. "Sir. She ordered—that is, she requested that I do everything in my power to assist her in her attempt to shift. I could not refuse my Empress."

"There is no Empress!" The Knight-Commander's roar shook the surface of the water, momentarily blurring his image. "A half-human whelp can never sit on the Pearl Throne!"

"She is a true dragon, and the Empress, and you will speak of her with respect!"

An echoing silence followed his words.

"Sir," John added, belatedly.

"It is clear," the Knight-Commander said, sounding as though he was speaking through gritted teeth, "that you have walked on two legs for too long, Knight-Poet. You are acting like a human."

Coming from anyone else, it would have been a killing insult, one demanding a duel to the death. But this was the Knight-Commander, to whom John had sworn all his oaths in the Emperor's absence. He was the Voice of the Emperor-in-Absence. It was his right to rebuke his knights when they erred.

As, apparently, John had.

His shamed silence seemed to mollify the Knight-Commander somewhat. "I am your commander, and you have sworn your loyalty to me. Whatever else you may have done in a…moment of passion, I know that you will not break *that* oath. Return to Atlantis. We must discuss this matter in person, mind to mind."

The habit of obedience was so strong, he was physically shaking with the effort of staying still. "I cannot leave the Empress unguarded, sir."

"Given that she has successfully survived her entire life to date without you standing over her, I believe she can last another few days."

"Sir, it would be most fitting to dispatch an honor-guard to-" John began.

"I do not have anyone to spare at the moment," the Knight-Commander interrupted curtly. "I already have half the Order scouring the seas for the Master Shark. I cannot weaken Atlantis's defenses any further."

John's brow furrowed. "The Lord of Sharks is missing, sir?"

"He stood up in the middle of a delicate diplomatic meeting last night and strode out without a word, scattering the assembled dignitaries as though he'd just scented blood in the water. The entire Council is in an uproar, and demanding that I locate him immediately so that the negotiations can resume. That is why I was originally trying to contact you."

"Me, sir?" John said, startled. "Why?"

The Knight-Commander was the most skilled Seer in the sea. To him, every drop of rain was an eye, every puddle was an ear. John's own art-form of poetry was of much less use when it came to finding a missing person. He was at a loss as to why the Knight-Commander would need *his* help.

"Your place is not to ask why, Knight-Poet. Just to obey. If I want you back in Atlantis, then you will come."

The Knight-Commander was a formidable strategist, both on the battlefield and in the arena of politics. He must have some use in mind for John's particular talents. But John himself could not even begin to grasp what it might be. He still didn't see what the Master Shark's disappearance could possibly have to do with him…

Wait.

Last night?

As if he'd scented blood in the water, the Knight-Commander had said. John knew that was no idle metaphor. Shark shifters *could* follow the scent of their prey's blood, under the water and over it. Unlike ordinary sharks, however, they could do so even when that blood had not yet been spilled.

And they were particularly drawn to power. The scent of a particularly strong, unusual shifter could catch the attention of sharks for miles around. More than once in the course of his duties, John had had reason to curse shark shifters' abilities. As a sea dragon knight, his own blood-scent could be picked up by even the weakest sharks from fifty miles away.

And I am just the least and lowest of the Knights of the First Water. How far away could they sense a sea dragon of true power?

John's heartbeat pounded in his ears. "Sir? Do you happen to know the limit of the Master Shark's range, when it comes to tracking prey?"

The Knight-Commander looked at him curiously. "As far as I am aware, he has none. He *is* the Master of his kind, after all. Why?"

John opened his fist, looking down at the pearl in his hand. Neridia's pearl, the Emperor's pearl that blocked all forms of locating magic, which had never left her neck...

Until last night.

CHAPTER 14

"John?" Neridia rolled over, roused from her fitful dreams by a breeze over her bare shoulder. Rubbing bleary, sleep-sodden eyes, she sat up. "What is it?"

The hulking figure at the open window straightened, turning.

It wasn't John.

Neridia screamed, rolling frantically as the stranger lunged for her. His fingers missed her by bare inches as she fell off the far side of the bed. Still screaming, Neridia grabbed the nearest thing to hand—a 1969 hardback copy of *Fishes of the British Isles and Northwest Europe*—hurling it at straight at her attacker's face.

All seven hundred pages caught him right between the eyes. He staggered back, momentarily stunned.

Neridia had never before considered her mother's collection of vintage natural history books in terms of their use as offensive weapons, but now she was grateful for her somewhat eccentric reading tastes. She snatched up more hefty tomes from the bookcase next to her bed, pelting him with them as she scrambled backwards.

He ducked his head, taking the brunt of the barrage on his armored shoulders as he came at her again. He moved in utter silence, not making even the slightest grunt of pain as the weighty books smacked into him.

There was something nightmarish about his utterly expressionless face and flat, emotionless eyes. Something nightmarish...and also something familiar.

She knew that angular, heavy-browed face with its wide, brutal jaw. She'd only seen him once before, for a brief moment, but those rough-hewn features were unmistakable.

She'd met that grey, chilling stare once before...looking out from her father's window, the day before the fire.

The day before he'd died.

Her attacker hesitated for a moment, looking back over his shoulder as if he'd heard something. Neridia didn't pause to see what had caught his attention. Throwing the last book at him, she dashed out the door. He didn't follow, but she was hardly going to stop to find out why.

Intent only on escaping, she didn't notice the wet, slippery puddle at the top of the stairs until it was too late. She cried out as her bare foot slid out from under her, nearly sending her tumbling. She only managed to save herself from breaking her neck by grabbing hold of the bannister. As it was, she landed badly on her ankle, twisting it.

"John, *John!*" she sobbed in pain and terror. Where *was* he?

NERIDIA! His mental roar filled her head.

She sobbed out loud again, this time in relief. She could feel every muscle in his legs burning as he sprinted flat-out to reach her. In only a few moments, he would be at her side.

Something wet trickled over her hand. The puddle she'd slipped in was spreading, fed by a trickling stream running impossibly *up* the stairs. A harsh, chemical reek filled the air.

Gasoline?

There was a soft scraping sound, and a light flared in the darkness at the bottom of the stairs. A face leered up at her, lit from below by the flickering match. It wasn't the intruder from her bedroom, but a different man—leaner, wirier, but with the same brutal cast to his features.

"Die, monkey scum," he hissed, and flicked the match into the gasoline.

~

JOHN!

John's pounding heart lurched at Neridia's mental scream of pure terror. He exploded into his true form, tearing away the roof of the house even as fire exploded through the lower level.

I have you! He snatched her up just in time, lifting her out in one forepaw a second before the flames could reach her.

Fire licked around his other foreleg, braced in the smashed, burning rubble of the staircase. He recoiled as heat gnawed at the thin, unprotected webbing between his long toes. Awkward as ever on land, he shuffled backward, trying to extricate himself from the ruins of the house.

"Look out!" Neridia yelled.

He roared in pain as burning liquid hit his flank. The stuff clung, roasting his flesh even through his armored scales. A moment later, a second burst of agony lit up his shoulder.

He was under attack. But where was it *coming* from?

Blindly, he lashed out with his tail, and was rewarded with an abruptly cut-off scream as he smashed someone into the side of the burning building. But it was clear he faced more than one opponent—yet another jet of fire shot through the darkness, missing his muzzle by mere inches.

The blazing inferno turned the night into a confusion of stark orange light and dancing shadows. His vision was adapted for the dimness of the ocean; this stabbing blaze seared his sensitive eyes as painfully as the smoldering oil still clinging to his hide.

He coiled protectively around Neridia, shielding her from the fiery blasts with his own body as he desperately searched for a way out. He had the advantage of strength, but his very size crippled him on land. He made an excessively easy target to hit.

Neridia pounded her fist against the side of his claw. He couldn't even feel the tiny impact, but her urgency poured down their mate bond. "Shift! Before they burn you alive!"

One moment! he replied telepathically, clenching his teeth in pain as another gout of fire lashed his flank.

Despite the smoke swirling in the air, he breathed deeply, filling his mighty lungs to full capacity. Then, at the top of his voice, he sang.

It was not his finest work. The circumstances were hardly conducive to the reflective, calm state of mind required for truly great poetry. But what it lacked in finesse, it made up for in passion, and in desperation. And, of course, in volume.

And, in volume, the rain answered.

It fell like a hammer blow, shocking and brutal. Every cloud in the sky gladly came at his call, pouring out their hearts in the name of the Empress. The blazing house spat and fought against the downpour. Flame ran in rivers as still-burning oil was washed away.

Water slicked his scaled hide, soothing the pain of his burns. But more importantly than that, it ran over *everything*. Nothing could hide from it.

Here! sang the rain as it found his attackers, each individual raindrop a tiny, triumphant note as it struck their flesh. *Here! Here! Here!*

Now he knew where they were. There were ten of them, though two were already crumpled and dead. The eight remaining were spread out around him. They'd evidently been closing in, but the unexpected assault of the rain had shattered their formation.

John took advantage of their momentary distraction to shift back to human form. He caught Neridia in one hand, drawing his sword with the other. "Can you run?" he shouted over the din of the downpour.

"I twisted my ankle." She clung to his side, struggling to stay upright on her injured foot. "What's happening? Who *are* they?"

He very much wanted to know the answer to that question himself. With the rain's assistance, John located the nearest one—a man crouching behind Neridia's vehicle, separated from the main group.

John squeezed Neridia's hand, silently sending her a mental image of his plan down their mate bond. She nodded in understanding. She moved behind him, holding onto the straps of his scabbard for support. Together, as quickly and silently as they could, they circled the vehicle, relying on the torrential rain to hide their movements.

As he crept up behind the lurking man, John saw that he had one hand outstretched. Liquid fuel gathered in a floating ball over the man's palm, running out of the open cap of the car's tank.

A hiss of disbelief escaped John's throat. Only one group had the power to manipulate oil in that way…and they were meant to be dead.

The Brotherhood of Extinction!

They were an outlawed cult of plesiosaur shifters, who mourned their long-extinct kin and were filled with hatred for the humans that had inherited the world. They had an affinity for fossil fuels, thanks to their own prehistoric nature, and could manipulate oil the same way he himself could manipulate water. They were assassins and arsonists, happy to whore their skills out to the highest bidder…especially if it gave them the chance to spread destruction and chaos on land.

The Sea Council had finally authorized the Order of the First Water to exterminate them several years ago, on the advice of the Knight-Commander. John had gladly assisted in wiping the ocean clean of the honorless pond scum.

Evidently the Order of the First Water had missed some.

The plesiosaur shifter whipped round, eyes widening as he caught sight of them. He ignited the oil and flung it, but John dodged, spinning Neridia safely out of the way. Before the assassin could launch another fireball, John was on him. His blade passed through the plesiosaur shifter's neck with barely a hint of resistance.

Neridia cried out as the body dropped, blood mingling with the mud. But there was no time to comfort her—they'd attracted attention. Six jets of fire lit up the rain, homing in on their position. John pulled Neridia down, covering her with his own body as the fireballs hit the car. Heat washed over his back as the vehicle ignited.

The remaining seven assassins were closing in fast, moving through the rain as smoothly as sharks. Tugging Neridia up again,

John desperately tried to keep his armored form between her and the circling assassins, every sense alert for the next attack.

The odds were very bad. The Brotherhood of Extinction were vicious beasts who fought without honor, stopping to any low trick to ensure victory. Even without Neridia to protect, he would have been hard-pressed to take down this many of them single-handed. Hampered by the need to shield her, he was badly outmatched.

My brothers, assist me! he called out reflexively in his mind. But his fellow firefighters were too far away to reach telepathically. And even if they had been closer...they thought he had returned to the sea. They would not be listening for his call.

He could not seek refuge in the lake; with Neridia still unable to shift, they would be even more at a disadvantage there. He would be constrained to stay on the surface while the assassins would be free to harry him in their agile plesiosaur forms.

I must rush them, he decided grimly. *Force them all to focus their fire on me, and endure long enough to slay them all.*

Neridia's fingers dug into his arm as she sensed his intention down the mate bond. "John, no!"

He pushed her forcefully away, toward the ditch that ran alongside the road. "Hide! Find what cover you can!"

He spun on his heel, sword poised and ready. At his command, the rain lifted around him. The fierce light from the blazing car backlit his form, highlighting every edge of his pale armor. He was as exposed as a pearl in an opened oyster.

"Primitive throwbacks!" He hurled the taunt into the night, contempt and derision clear in every note. "I shall send you to join your pathetic kin in the oblivion of extinction!"

As he had hoped, his insults maddened the Brotherhood. Hissing in outrage, they closed in on him, flinging blazing balls of crude oil.

He dodged and spun, fighting for his life, for *her* life. His sword cut down one, two, three—but the last deliberately clawed his way up the blade even as he died, fouling John's backstroke. In the two seconds it took him to free his weapon, the remaining four had regrouped.

The assassins raised their hands, uttering an ugly, guttural chant. A great wave of crude oil swirled up before them, drawn from the tanks strapped to their backs. John sprinted toward them—but too late.

One of the plesiosaur shifters tossed a lit match. John flung up an arm in futile reflex, shielding his face as the towering wall of fire roared over him.

The hungry flames flowed around him like water parting around a rock. The inferno swirled barely inches from his skin, yet he could not even feel its heat.

My apologies for the abrupt intrusion, said a familiar cool, calm voice in his head.

Blinking, John looked up. A large, bird-like shape hovered over him, wings spread protectively, every feather burning brighter than the firestorm raging all around.

I do not wish to imply that you need aid, Fire Commander Ash continued, as politely as if this was a mere social call. *But if you permit it, we would very much appreciate the honor of sharing this battle with you.*

Dumbfounded, John could only incline his head in wordless assent.

The Phoenix turned incandescent eyes on the Brotherhood of Extinction. Shock was clear in the assassins' pale faces. One broke and fled, but the remaining three stepped up their chant, pushing with their hands as they tried to force the fire to obey them.

The Fire Commander's eyes flared white-hot. The fire doubled back, embracing the plesiosaur shifters in their own blaze. They didn't even have time to scream before they were nothing more than drifting ashes.

John hesitated, torn between chasing down the last fleeing assassin and running to Neridia's side. His dilemma was resolved by two more winged forms swooping down out of the sky.

We'll take care of your mate, Griff sent to him. The golden griffin spread protective wings in front of Neridia. Hugh slid off his back, hastening to support her. *You get the last one!*

This way! Chase was already pursuing the fleeing assassin, his black hooves flashing over the stony ground. *He's heading for the water. Cut him off, Dai!*

"Do not kill him!" John shouted, as Dai—in red dragon form—came hurtling out of the sky like a thunderbolt. "I want him alive! I want to know who sent them!"

Dai rumbled acknowledgment. Opening his huge jaws, he breathed out a blast of fire, trying to cut off the assassin's escape route—but with a final, desperate burst of speed, the plesiosaur shifter dodged around the leaping flames. John cursed as the assassin plunged into the lake, form blurring into a long-necked, finned shape.

John splashed into the water himself, intent on pursuing the assassin in his own true form—but the lake swirled urgently around his legs, current grasping his ankles like hands trying to hold him back.

What are you waiting for? Chase demanded, cantering up to him. The pegasus spread his wings, preparing to launch himself after the fleeing plesiosaur. *Hurry, he's getting away!*

"Wait!" John caught a handful of the pegasus's long black mane, stopping him from taking off. "The water is warning us away. Something is lurking in wait."

The plesiosaur shifter was already nearing the middle of the lake, swimming for its life. Suddenly it thrashed, its paddle-like fins flailing at the water as if attempting to climb out of it.

Dai landed behind them with a thump, spines bristling and teeth bared. *What the-?* he began.

With a last despairing shriek, the plesiosaur vanished backward under the water, still struggling. Blood swirled on the surface of the lake.

The dark, triangular shape of a shark's fin emerged, rising up.

And up.

And up.

I have an idea. Chase's usually swift, boisterous mental tone was subdued as the monstrous fin sank silently back into the depths once more. *Let's not go into the water.*

CHAPTER 15

"But how did you know to come?" Neridia asked Hugh as he examined her ankle.

"You can thank Dai for that." The white-haired paramedic jerked a thumb over his shoulder at the enormous red dragon who was working with John to put out the remaining fires. "Or more precisely, his grumpy, over-tired baby. He was walking around the hotel, trying to soothe the brat back to sleep, when he saw every cloud get sucked across the sky in this direction. He knew it had to be John's doing."

Good thing he woke us all up straight away. Neridia started as Griff's rolling Scottish voice spoke inside her mind. He was still in griffin form, holding one broad wing over both their heads to shelter them from the continuing drizzle. *We got here just in time. Whoever these thugs were, they were enough to give even John trouble.*

"I think John recognized them," Neridia said. "I guess they must come from the same place he does."

She flinched as both Hugh and the griffin stared at her. "What?"

"You can hear him?" Hugh said, sounding startled.

"Um, yes. In my head, the same way I can hear John. Why, is that wrong?"

"Not wrong," Hugh said, his ice-blue eyes narrowing thoughtfully.

"But usually we can only communicate telepathically with other mythic shifters."

The griffin cocked his head, feathers raising with evident interest. *So I was right. Your father was the lost sea dragon Emperor, wasn't he?*

Neridia looked down at her knees. "That's what John thinks. But whatever my dad might have been, I'm just human."

Hugh and Griff exchanged glances. "Hmm," the paramedic said, not sounding entirely convinced. "Well, medically speaking, I can pass no judgment on what species you are, but I do know that you've badly sprained this ankle. Hold still."

He laid his hand on her ankle, skin to skin. Neridia caught her breath as a tingling warmth spread out from his touch.

"How are you doing that?" she asked in amazement as the dull ache faded away to nothing.

"With great annoyance and discomfort," Hugh replied, through gritted teeth. His expression was set in a pained grimace, as though healing her was hurting him in some way. "Why do all my patients have to screw like bunnies before they get injured?"

Embarrassment flooded up her face. "How did you-?"

Hugh doesn't like to talk about himself, Griff said telepathically. The griffin's hooked beak fell open in an unmistakable smile. *But it seems congratulations are in order. You and John are mated?*

Neridia squirmed, her blush deepening. "Um. Yes."

"So much for chastity," Hugh muttered, without looking up from her ankle.

The griffin buffeted the paramedic with his free wing. *Don't mind him. He's just cranky. We're all delighted for you and John.*

His warm mental tone conveyed his sincerity. Neridia looked away, her throat tightening. He was so obviously pleased for his friend, she couldn't possibly tell him that *she* wasn't sure she shared in his delight.

In the lake, it had felt so natural, so *right*. But in the cold light of her burning home, the full impact of her hasty decision was finally hitting her.

I'm joined to him forever, she thought as she watched John's towering silhouette, backlit by sullen flames. *No matter what. And he's from a different world...*

A world full of monsters.

He hadn't flinched or hesitated in the face of the fire-wielding assassins. He'd cut them down with a practiced, ruthless efficiency, as if it was all in a day's work. As if this sort of thing was *normal* in his world.

And he wants me to join him in that world. Forever.

Neridia hugged her knees, cold and numb. All she wanted at the moment was for everything to be back to normal. To be safe and secure in her own home, surrounded by her own familiar things.

But that was something she could never have again.

John was calling great streams of water out of the lake, directing them onto her house to douse the fire. The red dragon—Dai, Hugh had called him—stomped out smoldering patches with his huge taloned feet, apparently impervious to the flames. Chase, in pegasus form, flew in wide, sweeping circles above the fire, keeping watch for any further signs of attack. The final man, who John had briefly introduced as Fire Commander Ash, didn't appear to be doing anything other than standing and watching, his hands behind his back.

Despite the firefighters' efforts, it was clear that there was no saving her home. The cottage was a roofless, blackened shell. One wall had completely collapsed, torn away by John's raking talons in his haste to save her.

My home, my things...all my father's paintings. Everything I had. Gone.

John's head jerked round, like a dog hearing its master's call. Leaving the other firefighters to finish putting out the remnants of the blaze, he strode over to her.

"Oh my mate, my heart, do not despair." He sank down to one knee at her side, pushing up the dragon-faced visor of his helm. Underneath, his face was streaked with soot and sweat. "You still have a home, though you have never been there. Your palace awaits you under the sea, with a thousand treasures to replace every one that you have lost."

Thanks to the strange bond between them, Neridia could tell that he honestly thought this would comfort her. She was suddenly, abruptly furious.

"I don't *want* a palace or treasures!" She jerked her shoulder away from his outstretched hand. "Maybe you dragons only care about gold and gems, but I don't. My dad's paintings, my mother's books and all my things from my childhood, those were *my* treasures. They can't be replaced!"

His armored shoulders hunched, as if her words were blows. "I am sorry, I did not mean…forgive me, my mate. I swear on my honor, I will take care of you."

"Yes, because that's been working out really well so far," she spat. Distantly, she knew that she was being monstrously unfair, but the burning anger in her belly was better than that black despair. "If it wasn't for you, I wouldn't *need* anyone to take care of me! If I'd never met you, I'd still have a home!"

Her unfair accusation hammered him to both knees, head bowing. The wash of his shame down the mate bond brought her back to her senses. She might not really have meant what she'd said, but *he* believed it, every word.

"Oh, John, no." She twisted round as best she could with Hugh still holding her ankle, reaching out to her mate. "No, I'm sorry, I didn't mean any of that. I'm just upset and taking it out on you. None of this is your fault."

"But it is." He didn't raise his head. His arm was cold and hard as stone under her hand, every muscle knotted tight. "They found you because of me."

What are you talking about, John? Griff asked telepathically.

"I unknowingly stripped away the veil that has kept the Empress safely hidden from her foes." John dug under one of his vambraces with two fingers, extracting her pearl pendant. "Her father the Emperor, in his infinite wisdom, bestowed this powerful treasure on her. It prevents the wearer from being located by magical means."

Neridia, already reaching to reclaim her pendant from his palm, looked at him in surprise. "Is that what it does?"

He nodded as she refastened it around her neck. "I deciphered its true nature mere moments before the attack. You *must* wear it, Your Majesty. It is clear that your enemies have been lying in wait, searching ceaselessly for you. Do not remove it again for even a moment."

"As the medic who has to patch people up in the wake of this sort of thing, I wholeheartedly endorse this plan." Hugh sat back on his heels, shaking out his hands as if he had pins-and-needles. "Please try to avoid this happening again in future. John, let me see those burns."

"My trivial wounds are not worth-"

"Dying over," Hugh completed tartly. "Much as I'm sure you'd love to be in hideous physical pain as punishment for your so-called failure, you'll find it hard to redeem your honor if your sword arm drops off with gangrene. Now hold still."

Do you have any idea who these enemies could be? Griff asked, as John grudgingly submitted to Hugh's ministrations.

"Those we faced tonight are honorless worms who call themselves the Brotherhood of Extinction." John indicated the nearest corpse—which Neridia had been trying hard to avoid looking at—with a jerk of his head. "But I fear they are not our true foes. They are mere assassins-for-hire, selling their foul services to any who can pay their fee. I have reason to believe that they are working for the Master Shark."

A chill ran down Neridia's spine. "That big fin in the lake…that was a shark shifter?"

"Yes. The Master Shark, the lord of the shark shifters. He is their representative on the Sea Council. Many years ago, he was their sovereign King, but the Emperor—your father—conquered him and his people. The sharks were the last of the shifters of the sea to submit to the authority of the Pearl Throne, and they have never been willing subjects."

Griff clicked his beak. *That definitely sounds like someone who would be happy to keep the Pearl Throne unoccupied.*

John nodded grimly. "The Emperor graciously granted the fallen Master Shark a place of honor on the Sea Council, despite the near-unanimous objections from the other shifter representatives…but there is no satisfying a shark's hunger. Ever since the Emperor's disappearance, the Master Shark has always sought to wrest more power away from the rightful talons of the sea dragons."

"Well, to be fair," Hugh said, shifting around to lay his hands on another blistered patch on John's side. "You *are* something of an irritating bunch of arrogant bastards. I can't imagine a shark who used to be a king in his own right would be very happy about the prospect of having to bow down to sea dragon royalty again."

"This Master Shark…" Neridia said slowly. "Would he happen to be a tall, pale-skinned man, with cold grey eyes and a heavy forehead and jaw?"

John's head jerked up in surprise. "You have seen him?"

"I woke up to find him climbing in through my bedroom window. I ran away, straight into a trap." Neridia swallowed, her mouth dry. "John, there's more. That's not the first time I've seen him. Remember I said I saw a creepy guy at my dad's house, right before he died?"

"Before *his* house burned down. It cannot be a coincidence. The Master Shark must have been behind both attacks." John's fingers clenched in the mud. "The Emperor—he *assassinated*—"

Human words seemed to fail him. He broke down into a snarling, hissing song in his own language, the tendons on the side of his neck standing out with the force of his rage.

"Um." Hugh edged away from his patient. "I'm not sure whether to ask for a translation of that."

The mate bond was giving Neridia a very precise image of exactly what John intended to do with the Master Shark when he got his hands on him. A small, savage part of her echoed his anger, crying out for revenge for her dad's murder…but mostly, she just felt scared.

The Master Shark killed my dad. My father was a sea dragon, and the Emperor, with incredible powers at his command…and the Master Shark was still able to kill him.

And now he's after me.

John cut off his tirade mid-note. "I swear on my honor, I will not fail you again," he said fiercely, his chest heaving for breath. "I *will* protect you."

We'll all protect you, Griff added, his feathers bristling. *No mere shark is going to get past Alpha Team.*

"I thank you." John looked sidelong at the griffin, uncharacteristically hesitant. "...Oath-brother."

Griff's fierce golden eyes softened. He lowered his head, the great hooked beak nudging John's shoulder in a silent gesture of affection and forgiveness.

Hugh pointedly cleared his throat. "As the person who has to wipe up the blood when it all goes horribly wrong, can I ask if there's actually a *plan* to stop the Big Bad Shark?"

"Yes," John said, and Neridia took heart from the calm confidence in his voice. "We must get Her Imperial Majesty to safety. To the one place where she will be safe from all attack."

"Where's that?" Neridia asked.

"Home, Your Majesty. We must go to Atlantis."

CHAPTER 16

"Absolutely not," the Knight-Commander said flatly, his image ripping on the surface of the lake.

John struggled to maintain the scrying connection. It was hard to focus his mind's eye on the mystic currents in the glare of daylight, and doubly hard to do so this close to human habitation. He had not dared to go too far from the hotel where Neridia was breakfasting. Even now, his heart cried out to be back by her side.

"Sir, there is no choice," he said to the Knight-Commander's reflection in the water. "The Empress is as safe as she can be on land at the moment, with the firefighters of Alpha Team guarding her back, but this is only an interim solution. My colleagues have other duties of their own. Much as they wish to help, they cannot protect her night and day forevermore. The only place she will be safe is in Atlantis."

"No human has ever entered Atlantis!"

"But she is not human," John said, a hint of growl creeping into his voice despite his best efforts to observe proper etiquette. "She is a sea dragon, and the Empress-in-Waiting. With respect, sir, not even you have the authority to forbid her from entering her own domain."

"Until she formally ascends the Pearl Throne, I have every authority," the Knight-Commander retorted, a warning snarl singing in his own tones. "You forget yourself, Knight-Poet. I am the head of the Sea Council, and the Voice of the Emperor-in-Absence. At the moment, your mate is nothing. Unless she can shift, she cannot lay claim to any sea dragon title, let alone that of Empress-in-Waiting."

John held onto courtesy by his fingernails, though his blood burned at this slight to Neridia's honor. "She will shift, sir."

"Given that she did not last night, when both her own life and the life of her mate were in grave peril, I very much doubt that she ever will." The Knight-Commander gave him a penetrating look, his voice lowering. "Wishful thinking is a human trait, Knight-Poet. It does not become you. I begin to wonder whether you have been away from the sea for too long."

The accusation struck through his anger like a sword finding a crack in flawed armor. John dropped his gaze, unable to meet his commander's green-gold eyes. He *had* succumbed to the whispers of his inner human last night, allowing it to persuade him to bond with his mate. At the time, it had seemed so natural...but had it been his human's judgment rather than his own?

The Knight-Commander let out a long sigh, shaking his head. "Your duties have kept you away from Atlantis for too long, Knight-Poet. But regardless of my concerns for your honor, I fear I have no choice but to order you to remain on land. You said that the pearl she wears conceals her from my scrying?"

"Yes, sir. From all forms of locating magics, including a shark's ability to track her Imperial blood-scent. It is how she remained undetected for so long. I assure you, she will not remove it again now that she understands its importance."

"In that case, I command you to remain at her side. I do not wish to lose track of her again. You, at least, I can still scry. But you will not bring her to Atlantis without my express permission. Is that perfectly clear?"

"I hear and obey, sir." John took a deep breath, steeling himself for further battle. "But sir, I must repeat that I cannot guarantee Her Maje-"

The Knight-Commander's eyes narrowed.

"Ah, that is, Neridia's safety while she remains on land." It felt horribly wrong to say her name so baldly, without honorifics, but there was no sense in antagonizing the Knight-Commander further. "She will only be secure in Atlantis. I beg you to reconsider your position."

"Even if she was the crowned Empress, her safety would come secondary to the safety of the entire Pearl Empire!" The Knight-Commander slammed a fist down, sending ripples across the water. "Damn it, Knight-Poet! Would you seek to undo everything I have worked for these last twenty-five years? Can you not see what a disaster it would be, should the rest of the Sea Council catch scent of her existence?"

John stared at him, taken aback. "You have not already told them, sir?"

"Of course I have not. The instant the other lords discover there may be a half-human heir to the Pearl Throne running around, it will tear the Council apart. Some would seek to destroy her, like the Master Shark. Worse still, others would seek to crown her immediately."

"But surely that is what *we* seek, sir," John said, utterly bewildered. "To put her in her rightful place on the Pearl Throne."

The Knight-Commander's chest rose and fell in a long sigh. Raising a hand, he pulled off his glittering helm. John froze. He had hardly ever seen his commander's face before. It was a privileged usually reserved for his most trusted knights.

"You have a hatchling's romantic view of royalty." The Knight-Commander rubbed his lined forehead. He looked tired, as though he hadn't slept for days. "An untutored, naive Empress on the Throne? A *human* Empress, ignorant of our ways, with all the power of the ocean at her command? Who could guess what catastrophic whim might take her fancy? She might demand that we allow more of her kind into Atlantis. She might overturn laws simply because her weak human mind cannot comprehend the demands of our honor. She could destroy the Pearl Empire itself! For sea's sake, *think*, Knight-Poet."

John did so. "I think," he said, after a moment of reflection, "that you gravely underestimate her, sir."

"And *I* think that you are blinded by your mate bond." Dropping his hand, the Knight-Commander fixed John with a piercing stare. "Which is another matter of which we must speak. I have not forgotten that you broke your vow of chastity."

John bowed his head. "I, I believe that I did so for honorable purposes, in the service of the Pearl Throne, but...I stand ready to receive whatever discipline you see fit, sir."

The Knight-Commander let out a somewhat exasperated breath. "The usual fate of knights who break their oaths is execution, which is hardly practical at this point in time. As your circumstances were indeed...unusual, I will exercise my right as the Knight-Commander of the Order to waive the full consequences. *Once.*"

John's heart had been lifting at this unexpected show of mercy, but at the last word it lurched sideways in his chest. "S-sir," he stammered. "You cannot mean— sir, we are fully-bonded mates. To demand that we stay apart-"

"Is the only hope of salvaging your honor. And so the only hope I have of saving one of my most promising young knights from utterly destroying himself." The Knight-Commander put his helmet back on again, his tone turning formal. "I will say this only once, Knight-Poet. There is no place on land or sea where I cannot find you. If I ever have reason to believe that you have dishonored the Order, I will personally hunt you down and execute you myself. Do not break your vows again."

CHAPTER 17

The journey south was a nightmare. Neridia had rarely had the chance to travel beyond Scotland before, and normally she would have been glued to the train window, fascinated by glimpses into unfamiliar places and other people's lives. But now, the slow change of scenery from the beautiful wilderness of the Highlands to the industrial towns of the north of England just made her feel homesick. Every minute, every mile, took her further and further away from everything she'd ever known.

I might never come home again.

Her old life was a smoking ruin behind her. Fire Commander Ash had said that he would handle reporting "the incident," as he had put it, to the police, and that she did not need to be involved in the matter. Neridia had no idea *how* he was intending to explain away a burnt-out cottage surrounded by dead bodies, but something about his quiet air of authority made it impossible to doubt that he would.

I wish he could have handled my boss for me too.

Neridia had a sick feeling that she wouldn't have a job anymore, after her boss got her rather vague voicemail about a "family emergency." As her boss frequently liked to remind his staff, there was a long line of people hungry for any job opening in conservation.

She didn't have a home. She likely didn't have a job. All she had was the slim contents of her bank account, the pearl around her neck, and the few clothes they'd managed to salvage from the fire.

And John.

He was the only thing that enabled her to face the terrifying journey into the unknown, to keep putting one foot in front of the other. Her entire life might lie in ashes, but whenever she looked at him, a small, secret voice in her soul whispered: *Yes*. She clung to that strange sense of certainty, trying to have faith that everything would be all right as long as they were together.

She would have liked to cling to *him*, or at least to hold his hand, but he was in constant motion—patrolling the train carriage, or finding some need to confer with his fellow firefighters, or just fidgeting with the blanket-wrapped hilt of his disguised sword. The mate bond was like a taut rope between them, betraying his deep tension. He was on high alert, every sense straining for any hint of further attack.

Though she knew his duty compelled him to keep a constant vigil, she couldn't help wishing that he would just sit *down*. That he would put his arm around her, hold her close and whisper to her that everything would be okay.

Deep down, all she wanted was for him to reassure her that it wouldn't matter if she never shifted, if she could never go to Atlantis, if she never became the Empress. That whatever happened, they'd figure it out together.

But he was a knight. He was under a vow to speak the truth.

So Neridia bit her tongue, and clasped her hands together tightly in her lap, and didn't ask him to tell her comforting lies.

London, and hordes of people; hundreds of stares and gasps and not-so-whispered comments as they forged their way through the crowds. Neridia didn't see a single woman who was even close to her own height, and of course John towered above everyone. More than one group of tourists openly took pictures of them, gawping as if they were animals in a zoo.

John took it all in his stride, not even seeming to notice the camera flashes and pointing fingers. Neridia tried to hide in his shadow, but apparently even a seven-foot-tall, blue-haired slab of pure beefcake wasn't sufficient distraction to allow her to pass unnoticed.

By the time they finally made it onto the train to Brighton, she felt physically bruised by the weight of so many eyes. It was a relief to curl up in another private first-class cabin, closing her own eyes in miserable exhaustion.

It felt like only a moment before John was gently shaking her shoulder. "Only a little further now, my mate. Take up your courage for just a while longer."

Heartsick and sore in every muscle from the long, jolting journey, Neridia stumbled after him in a daze. She barely registered the short taxi ride from the station. She stared blankly out the window, not really seeing the lights of the buildings flicking past. It was evening now, and it felt like they had been traveling forever.

"Here, my lady." John opened the taxi door for her, holding out his hand. "We are here."

Stepping out of the taxi, Neridia's spirits lifted a little. There was a sharp, clean tang in the air that cleared her muzzy head. It was nothing like the sweet scent of the Highlands, but there was still something strangely familiar about it. She closed her eyes for a moment, breathing deeply.

Somehow...it smells like home.

Opening her eyes, she found that John was watching her, his own blue gaze deep and clear. "It is the scent of the sea, my lady," he said softly. "We are very close to it here. Have you truly never visited it before?"

She shook her head. "I've never been to the seaside. My father avoided water so thoroughly, it never occurred to me to go myself, not even after my parents passed away."

John had been leading her towards a small Victorian townhouse, but now he hesitated with one foot on the front step. "I had thought to rest here on land for tonight, but if you are impatient to see your true home...?"

"Oh God, no." Neridia quailed at the thought of adding *more* stress to this exhausting day. She didn't share John's unshakeable certainty that the ocean would unlock her dragon form at last. "I'm in no rush. I'd rather see your house. Is this it?"

"Yes." John unlocked the front door, ducking his head as he entered. "My territory is humble, my lady. But it is yours."

John wasn't kidding about the humble part. The house was spotlessly clean, and also terribly empty. There wasn't a single painting or picture on the walls, though holes marked where some had once hung. Dents in the worn carpet suggested that there might have once been a sofa and armchairs in the front room, but now it contained only a single hard, straight-backed chair and a crate full of battered books.

It was about as far as it was possible to get from her own colorful, art-filled home. If she didn't *know* that John lived here, she would have sworn that someone had just moved out.

"It's, um..." Neridia struggled to conceal her dismay. "It's very... well, there's a lot of space."

"It used to be my oath-brother Griff's dwelling. He generously shared his territory with me when I first came to the land, needing a place to stay. He has since moved in with his mate, of course." John gestured around at the empty room apologetically. "I am afraid that most of the furniture went with him. I did not feel the need to replace it. Human dwellings feel very claustrophobic to one used to the open ocean."

Neridia peered into the box of books. It was a wild assortment, everything from bodice-ripper romances to history textbooks. It looked like John had just swept an indiscriminate armload up from the shelves of a charity shop and bought the lot.

"I thought you said sea dragons didn't have books," she said.

"We do not have paper under the sea, but we do learn to read and write your human tongue." John unwrapped his sword from its concealing blankets as he spoke. "I must confess, I have acquired a fondness for books during my time on land. Human minds are endlessly inventive, if frequently rather mysterious. I learn a great deal from your literature."

Neridia noticed that John was currently reading *Fifty Shades of Grey*. She decided not to ask what he was learning from *that* particular book. Nonetheless, she was strangely comforted by the eclectic collection. It was a tiny touch of normality in his otherwise alien lifestyle.

John hung his sword up on two hooks placed where an ordinary person might have a television. "You are hungry, my mate. I shall prepare food."

"Food sounds good." Neridia followed him into the kitchen. "What can I do?"

"You can rest," he said firmly, shooing her back out again. "Allow me to take care of this task. Go, settle into the territory. It has been a long day, and I can sense your exhaustion."

Neridia would rather have helped him cook, but she had a hunch he didn't want her company at the moment. Her sense of him down the mate bond was strangely elusive, as if he was trying to keep his distance from her mentally as well as physically.

It's been a long day for him too, she told herself, squelching down her own feelings of rejection. *He probably just needs some space to decompress.*

Leaving John to it, she wandered upstairs. The upper floor of the house was just as barren as the rooms below. The master bedroom was completely empty, even the wardrobe. Neridia guessed that must have been Griff's room. From the looks of things, John hadn't used it at all since his former housemate had moved out.

Somewhat to Neridia's relief, the second bedroom did actually contain a bed. She'd been starting to fear that John slept on the floor, if he slept on land at all. At least here he wasn't a complete ascetic. The bed dominated the small room, clearly custom-made for his immense height.

Plenty of room for two.

Despite her tiredness and homesickness, the thought sent a thrill through her. She ran her fingers over the soft coverlet, scarcely able to imagine that tonight she'd be curled up underneath it. With him.

I hope sea dragons don't only *mate in water.*

A shriek split the air, sending her heart leaping into her throat. She cast around wildly for a weapon, but there wasn't anything sharper than a pillow in sight.

Empty-handed, she ran for the stairs. "John! What-?"

The hellish noise cut off abruptly. John looked up at her sheepishly from the hallway, lowering his hand from the smoke detector in the ceiling.

"I am sorry to alarm you." Acrid fumes curled around his head, drifting from the kitchen doorway. "The matter is under control now."

"That's not what it smells like." Wrinkling her nose, Neridia ducked round him into the kitchen. Whatever John had been trying to cook was completely unidentifiable, just a black mess welded to the bottom of a pan. "What happened?"

John gazed mournfully down at the cremated remains. "Me. We do not have fire under the sea, or cooking. My oath-brother has done his best to teach me the basics, but I must confess that I still struggle with the techniques."

"Sea dragons don't *cook?*" Neridia said incredulously. "What do you eat?"

"Fish, mainly." John dropped the ruined pan into the sink. "Or squid. Shark or kraken, as a delicacy. We hunt and eat in dragon form. For us, the pleasure of the meal comes in the catching of it more than the consuming."

Just when I think he can't get any stranger…

"I shall try again." Squaring his shoulders as if he was facing off against assassins, John opened the fridge. "This time it will go better, I assure you."

"This time, I'm helping," Neridia said firmly. "What have you got?"

John rummaged in the fridge, as if hopeful that something new might have miraculously appeared in it within the past ten minutes. "I have…chicken eggs, miscellaneous plant parts, butter, and some surprisingly solid cow milk. Do these things together make a meal?"

"It makes omelets." Neridia disposed of the carton of milk, which was practically about to walk away on its own. "Without the milk."

It felt good to take charge, to at last have something that *she* could do. The familiar motions of chopping vegetables and whisking eggs soothed her frayed nerves. John followed every movement with the fascinated concentration of someone trying to work out a magic trick.

When they finally sat down to the end result, his delighted surprise at the first forkful sparkled down the mate bond. It heightened her own appreciation of the flavors, as if she too was tasting it for the first time.

"How do you *do* this?" he said, staring at the simple omelets as though she'd transmuted lead into gold.

Trying to explain the concept of seasoning turned into a broader discussion of herbs, which somehow led into him quizzing her in detail about the best meals she'd ever eaten, and what had made them special. For the first time since her house had burned down, Neridia found that she was actually enjoying herself.

"You have a great passion for this art," he said as they finished the meal. "And you are a true master of it."

The warm glow of his respect filled her even more than the food. "Hardly. I'm just an amateur. But I've always liked to cook."

One more thing I'll have to give up, if I learn to shift.

The thought ruined the pleasure of the moment, tensing her shoulders again. John's eyebrows drew together a little as he picked up on her change of mood. For a second, she thought he started to reach out a hand to her—but then he abruptly stood, gathering up the plates.

"You should try to sleep, my lady." He kept his back to her as he started to wash the dishes. "You will need your strength for the coming day. Do not fear. I shall guard the territory while you rest."

Her sense of him had gone remote again, as if he'd withdrawn into some deep cave in his mind. His spine was very straight, every muscle standing out in his back.

Neridia gathered up her courage. Going over to him, she tentatively slid her hands around his waist. He went very still.

"I, um." Neridia was sure she was blushing. "I know you take your duties as my bodyguard seriously, but I was kind of hoping you might take some of your other duties equally seriously tonight...Royal Consort."

She felt him draw in a deep, shaking breath. This close to him, their skin separated only by the thin fabric of his shirt, he couldn't hide his emotions from her. She could sense the sharp leap of his desire…and the agonizing effort it was taking him to restrain it.

"John?" Confused, she stepped back. "Why are you holding back from me? Did, did I do something wrong?"

"No!" The word leaped from his lips in a vehement chord, like a trumpet blast. "Never think that, my mate. It is not you. It is me."

He'd been withdrawn ever since he'd talked to the leader of his Order, Neridia realized. "Is it to do with what you Knight-Commander said? About not letting me into Atlantis if I can't shift?"

His hands tightened on the edge of the sink, knuckles white. "Not that. I have no doubt that you will take your place on the Pearl Throne. But…but that is not all that he said."

Neridia had a sick feeling that something was wrong, terribly wrong. "Tell me, John. Whatever it is, I can feel that it's eating you up inside. I'm your mate. Please, just tell me."

He turned to face her at last. "He corrected my erroneous interpretation of our code of honor."

It took Neridia a second to work out what he meant. "You mean he's angry about you breaking your vow of chastity? But you did that to help me! Didn't you tell him that you only did it in order to try to teach me to shift?"

"There can be no excuses for oath-breaking. I understand that now, thanks to the guidance of my Knight-Commander." Though the mate bond cried out with pain and grief, his face was absolutely expressionless. "My honor has been strained near to breaking point. If I am not to shatter it completely, I must strictly adhere to my vows."

Neridia stared at him, too shocked to speak.

He bowed his head, his indigo hair shadowing his face. "I am sorry." His voice was the barest whisper. "More sorry than I have words to say. You are my mate, and yet I have done you a worse injury than any shark. This is all my fault."

"No it isn't!" Neridia grabbed his chin, forcing him to look at her. "You acted with honor, John. You didn't have any doubt of that before, not until this Knight-Commander of yours got into your head and twisted up your thoughts."

He stiffened, moving away from her hand. "The Knight-Commander is the strongest and wisest among us, and his honor is unquestionable. He is the very heart and soul of my Order. He *is* the Order of the First Water. He does not *twist up my thoughts*, as you put it. He provides discipline to keep me on the path of honor, when my own poor judgment would lead me astray."

"This isn't discipline, this is punishment!"

"This is mercy." John's jaw tightened for a moment. "The mandated punishment for oath-breakers is death."

"*What?* Why didn't you tell me this before?"

"Because as you said, before I did not consider myself to be breaking my oaths. I thought I was following the demands of my higher duty to the Pearl Throne. But I was in error. We are very fortunate that he has graciously allowed me the one indulgence. He will not overlook a second transgression."

Neridia felt like she'd been gut-punched. "So we can't—not *ever?*"

John hesitated. "It is probably a sign of my damaged honor that this has even occurred to me, but there is some hope."

"How?" She knew enough of him by now to be certain that he didn't mean he might consider resigning as a knight. "You think the Knight-Commander might relent?"

"Not precisely." John raked both hands through his hair, making the gold charms clink together. "I must explain some history to you. The vow of chastity was only added to the Creed of the Knights of the First Water about five hundred years ago, back in the reign of the thirty-eighth Pearl Emperor. One of the Emperor's knights was coerced by threats against his mate into turning a blind eye to an assassination plot."

"Oh. So that's the reason for the vow? It was introduced to make sure no knights could ever be blackmailed that way again?"

John nodded. "The Emperor survived the assassination attempt, and afterwards persuaded the Knight-Commander of the time to instigate the vow of chastity. The Knight-Commander dismissed the knights who already had mates, and subsequently only accepted new novices who were proven mateless. It was somewhat controversial at the time."

"I bet." Neridia caught her breath as the reason he was telling her this became clear. "Wait. You said the vow of chastity was the *Emperor's* idea?"

The corner of his mouth twisted slightly. "Perhaps what an Emperor persuaded a Knight-Commander to do, an Empress might persuade a Knight-Commander to undo."

Neridia's heart plummeted right down to her socks. "Oh."

John's expression softened as he sensed her dismay. "I know that it sounds like a difficult feat. The Knight-Commander is cautious, thinking only of the safety of the Pearl Empire, and will not easily be persuaded to change our traditions. But the Knight-Commander will be sworn to your service once you ascend the Pearl Throne, and Compassion is one of our most important Knightly Vows. He will not wish to see his Empress miserable. I believe he will relent in the end."

"But...all that can only happen if I take the Pearl Throne. If I'm Empress."

"You will be Empress." He took her hands, squeezing them in his own. "You will shift, my mate. I will take you to the sea, and you will find your true form, and together we shall go to Atlantis. I promise you, you *will* be Empress."

Neridia didn't answer. She looked down at their joined hands, unable to meet his eyes. With his utter certainty blazing down the mate bond, there was no way she could say out loud the terrible question in her heart.

But what if I don't want *to be Empress?*

CHAPTER 18

It was a day made for rejoicing. John had spent some hours during the night communing with the clouds, and as a result the morning dawned bright and clear. The brilliant summer sunlight made the old, pale buildings of Brighton gleam like fresh-polished shells. Seagulls wheeled across the azure sky in exuberant flight, their raucous voices filled with joy.

The sky, the wind, even the small minds of the birds; all things connected to the sea knew at some level that this was a historic day. For today, for the first time, the Empress-in-Waiting was coming home.

Even ordinary humans seemed to have picked up on the mood. It might just have been the unusually fine weather, but a sense of giddy delight permeated the entire city. Children jumped and skipped with just a little more energy than usual, shrieking as happily as the seagulls overhead. Lovers walked just a little closer to each other, laughing in the sun. Everyone was smiling.

Everyone, that is, except the Empress-in-Waiting herself.

As they made their way toward the seafront, John couldn't shake the feeling that he was escorting a prisoner to her execution.

Neridia had been withdrawn and quiet ever since the previous evening. She hadn't touched her breakfast, despite the fact that even *his* culinary skills couldn't render dry cereal inedible. Their mate bond was pale and subdued, her thoughts drawn back like a snail into a shell.

Alone in the happy crowd thronging Brighton's main street, she walked with head bowed and shoulders hunched, as if the bright sunshine were a howling gale. Though the broad road ran downhill, she was going slower and slower. John kept having to check his own stride to avoid outpacing her.

This isn't right, John's inner human fretted. *This isn't right at all. This should be one of the happiest days of her life. We have to do something.*

For once John was in full agreement with his inner human, but he was at a loss as to *what* to do. Though his poetry could move sea and rain, he had no idea what words might lift Neridia's mood. So far, he could not exactly claim a string of victories when it came to talking to his mate.

His inner human rolled its eyes in exasperation. *So don't talk.*

John clenched his jaw. It would be so natural, so *right*, to reach out to her, to stroke away the tension in her shoulders and kiss smooth the lines of worry furrowing her brow...but his vow of chastity kept his arms at his sides. His honor bound him like a net of gossamer threads—easy to break, but irreparable once broken.

He wished that he had thought to offer Neridia some of the surviving treasures from his hoard before they'd left his house. The pearls had been scorched by the fire, but he'd been able to rescue his gold and silver at least. He had nothing that would truly befit her status as Empress-in-Waiting, of course, but perhaps she might have taken some small comfort in being at least somewhat adorned.

He eyed a jeweler's window as they passed, wondering whether any of the diamonds on display might lift Neridia's spirits. But although he had only the haziest grasp on the peculiar human concept of money—Griff had always managed his finances for him—he suspected that only the cheapest pieces were within his means. He could hardly insult his mate by offering her such paltry gems.

Then his gaze snagged on the neighboring shop.

But perhaps there is something I could offer her...

"John?" Neridia queried, as he took her elbow. "What are you doing?"

"I," he said, steering her firmly inside the small shop, "am buying you an ice cream."

"What?" Neridia stared at him as they took their place at the end of the line of waiting customers. "Why?"

"Because you have not eaten anything today, and this will provide you with much-needed energy. Because you spoke so passionately about flavor combinations last night that I think you would enjoy this experience. Because the sun is shining, and I am told it is traditional to celebrate a beautiful day with the ritual consumption of a…" John had to pause to read the menu chalked above the counter, in order to remind him of the human word. "Ah yes, a 'cone.' And finally, because *I* experience an intense desire to eat sweet things when *my* inner human is agitated."

Neridia's lips had been slowly curving upward throughout this speech, but at his final words she blinked. "Your inner human? What do you mean?"

John noticed that the group of human boys ahead of them had half-turned, casting the two of them rather odd looks. He glared, and the youths quickly discovered a pressing need to examine the menu instead.

Nonetheless, he lowered his voice. "Many shifters experience a, an internal duality, shall we say. Shifters who are born as humans tend to have a separate animal-self contained within their soul. My sword-brother Dai, for example, would speak of his inner dragon. I am the reverse. I *am* a dragon, therefore my other-self is human."

"Like having a split personality?" Neridia sounded dubious.

"No, nothing so malign. It is just that the instincts of our other form always occupy a corner of our minds. They speak to us, in our own thoughts. That is how I am able to understand human perspective."

Sometimes, his inner human commented dryly.

Neridia fell silent for a moment, as the line shuffled forward. "So... would I have an inner dragon? Like Dai?"

This possibility had not occurred to him. "Perhaps. You are human-born, after all."

"Sometimes I feel—I hear—like a little voice, urging me to do things I normally wouldn't dare." Neridia bit her lip. "Does that sound crazy?"

"It sounds like you are a shifter," he said, smiling down at her. "What are these things that your inner voice encourages you to do?"

She peeked sidelong at him, her cheeks darkening a little. "Never you mind. What sort of things does your, um, inner human tell *you* to do? Apart from eat chocolate?"

John was saved from having to answer *that* one by the group in front of them dispersing, leaving them at the head of the line. The girl behind the counter did a double-take as she looked up at the two of them, but her professionally cheerful smile never wavered.

"What can I get for you today, folks?" she asked, brandishing her scoop invitingly at the spread of various flavors.

Neridia only needed to examine the tubs for a heartbeat before pointing at one. "Honey and ginger for me, please. What are you having, John?"

His inner human brightened hopefully, but John shook his head. "Your pleasure is enough for me. Although my inner—ah, that is, although I occasionally experience a craving for such foodstuffs, I do not indulge in them."

Neridia's forehead wrinkled. "Wait. Are you trying to tell me that you've *never* eaten ice cream? Do your vows forbid you or something?"

"No. It is simply a good test of discipline to deny myself such-"

Neridia turned back to the server. "He'll have triple chocolate. With fudge sauce. And marshmallows."

Which was how John found himself holding a brittle cone filled with mud-colored frozen cow excretions, topped with a tar-like ooze and sprinkled with what appeared to be tiny fragments of peculiarly solid white foam.

"You were right." Neridia's eyes closed in bliss as she licked her own, much less alarmingly brown confection. "This *was* a good idea."

John was no longer so sure of that. The slowly liquefying concoction was quite the most unappetizing thing he had ever had the misfortune to behold. It did not smell like fish *at all*.

Neridia giggled, obviously sensing his dismay. "Just try it, okay? For me?"

For the sake of putting a smile on his mate's face, he could endure any hardship. Steeling his nerve, John took a tentative taste.

I told *you so,* his inner human said with infinite smugness, into the stunned silence of his mind.

Neridia burst out laughing. "Your *face.* Now do you see what you've been missing out on?"

"Griff and Chase—kept trying to convince me—" John said indistinctly. He swallowed, clearing his mouth. "My brothers-in-arms on Alpha Team have attempted to persuade me to eat such things, many times, telling me that I could not imagine the delights that I was denying myself. I always thought they were merely teasing me. I believe I owe them a substantial apology."

"I'll say." Neridia's delight radiated down the mate bond like sunbeams through clear water. "Oh, I am going to have to take you to *so* many restaurants. I bet you've never eaten—um, John, you might want to slow down there."

He couldn't answer, having gone back to inhaling the incredible concoction like a starving shark. A second later, he found out the reason for the warning. A numbing pain rushed up from his mouth, as if his skull had been filled with ice.

Neridia winced, though she was still grinning. "And there's another first for you. Your first ice cream headache. I'm sorry, I should have warned you."

"It fights back?" John eyed the remaining inch of cone with increased respect. "Truly this food is fit for a warrior."

She was still laughing, wonderfully, as they rounded the last corner…and at last, came in sight of the sea.

The simple merriment in Neridia's face transmuted into something into something deeper, richer. Her own ice cream fell forgotten to the ground as she walked forward, her eyes fixed on the line where sea met the sky. John had to drag her back before she stepped straight out into traffic.

He could feel the way every part of her body yearned forward, pulled by the call of the ocean. The salt-song resounded in his own soul too, but he at least had enough presence of mind to guide her safely across the road and down to the beach.

Gulls swirled in a tight spiral high over Neridia's head, crying out in recognition, but she paid them no heed. Nor, for once, did she flinch from the wide-eyed stares of the humans they passed. All of her attention was focused entirely on the glittering water.

The waves rose higher as she approached, throwing up ecstatic plumes of white spray like handfuls of confetti. The tide dragged sea-smoothed pebbles back and forth across the beach in vast, rattling applause.

When the sea first kissed her feet in fealty, the whole ocean roared in such jubilation that John was nearly knocked flat. He could scarcely believe that even humans could fail to be deafened by the triumphant song, yet no one else on the beach reacted in the slightest.

Look! John felt like shouting, or singing. *Look! A wonder is unfurling, a moment to hoard forever in your minds, a memory to be polished and treasured all the rest of your days! Can you not see? Look!*

Yet the humans continued to walk, or sit, or lie in the sun, with only the occasional curious glance at the unusually tall woman standing so still in the ocean.

It might have been minutes, or hours, or years, before Neridia turned back to him. Her face was luminous, soft with wonder. There was a new depth in her blue eyes now. Forevermore, he knew, they would reflect the sea.

"Thank you," she said, so softly her voice was nearly lost in the murmur of the waves. "Even if—whatever else happens, thank you. For this."

"It is my honor and my privilege." He went to one knee in the surf, bowing his head. "My Empress."

Something flashed in her sea-struck eyes, too quickly for him to follow. She looked out at the horizon again, but her expression was guarded, no longer lost in awe.

"I still don't think I can shift." She hugged herself, her shoulders tensing. "The sea is, well, more than I could have possibly imagined, but…I'm still just me."

His inner human swore. *If she can't do it even now…oh, we are so screwed.*

"John, what if I can't ever do it?" Neridia said, unwittingly echoing his human. "If I can't shift, if I can't go to Atlantis, what will we do?"

"You will shift," he said firmly, forcing down the disappointment swelling in his own heart. He cast around for some glimmer of hope to offer her. "Perhaps…perhaps you are just too self-conscious at the moment. There are many humans present, after all."

Neridia blinked, looking around the crowded beach as if only just noticing the people all around them. "Um. Maybe it's just as well I didn't shift."

"We mythic shifters cannot be seen by mundane eyes unless we will it. But I know that you do not enjoy attracting attention. Perhaps your subconscious fears that humans will see your true majesty." John rose to his feet again. "We should return later, after dark, when the beach is empty."

Neridia looked happier, strangely, as though this was a stay of execution rather than an aggravating delay. "Okay. So what do you want to do until then?"

He spread his hands. "I have no preference. What would *you* like to do?"

"Well, actually there is something." Neridia splashed out of the sea, the waves chasing her up the beach as though entreating her to stay. "I didn't tell you this before, but my mom came from around here. She used to live in Brighton before she met my dad."

He lifted his eyebrows, another minor mystery becoming clear. "That would explain why this was the last place the Emperor was seen before he went missing."

"Yes, they only moved to Scotland after they married. My mom always said that she'd had enough of the ocean, but now I think they must have been trying to get as far away as possible in case anyone came searching for my dad." Neridia let out an amused huff of breath. "And Loch Ness *is* the last place anyone would genuinely expect to find a real sea dragon. Anyway, if you don't have other plans, I'd really like to go see where my mom used to work."

"Of course, if you wish." Personally, John would much rather have stayed by the ocean, but if traipsing round some human building would make his mate happy…

Neridia looked rather slyly at him, as though she'd sensed his lack of enthusiasm. "Oh, I think you'll find it interesting too."

CHAPTER 19

Neridia had a moment of doubt as they approached the aquarium, worrying that perhaps John might not approve of keeping fish in captivity. But her fears turned out to be groundless. John's stern face broke into a rare, breathtaking grin the instant he saw the sign over the entrance to the Sea Life Centre.

"Your mother worked *here?*" he said, laughter rolling under his words. "She was a scholar of the sea?"

"A marine biologist, yes," she said, relieved by his reaction. "She spent most of her career working on research ships." She paused as something occurred to her for the first time. "You know, my dad always said that they first met at sea. I always thought he just meant that he'd been crew on one of the research vessels, but now I wonder…"

John's eyes gleamed with amusement. "I suspect she found herself studying more than she had expected. I would very much like to know how their first meeting went."

Neridia shook her head wryly. "I bet *she* didn't run screaming from her mate in terror. Anyway, in between research tours she worked here as a marine conservationist. After she and my dad moved to Scotland, she changed focus to studying freshwater species."

John looked sidelong at her as they lined up for tickets, his expression turning thoughtful. "Was that why you too became a defender of the wild?"

Neridia rather liked his term for her job. "Yes. Even when I was tiny, she used to take me out on hikes around Loch Ness, teaching me the names of all the species. She was so proud when I went into the same line of work. Right up until she died, we worked together in local Highland conservation initiatives."

John abruptly looked grim. "Forgive me for dredging up old pains, but my duty means I must ask...was her passing suspicious in any way?"

"No, it wasn't like my dad. She passed away a few months before he did. She had a congenital heart condition. There was always the possibility that it could fail her, and, well, eventually it did." Neridia was silent for a moment, her throat tightening. "She always said that she had to make sure she packed in as much as possible into every day, because she never knew if it might be her last."

"A noble philosophy," John rumbled. "It sounds like your mother was a woman of great honor."

"Well, she would have to be, right?" Neridia forced a lighter tone. "I mean, she *was* the Emperor's mate."

He inclined his head, smiling a little. "There is that. I am pleased that they were well-matched indeed. And that they were able to find happiness together."

"Oh, you never saw two people so in love." Neridia sighed wistfully. "I wanted to be just like her, in every way. I even wanted to be a marine biologist too, originally."

"I imagine that the Emperor was somewhat alarmed when you first proposed *that*. I take it he managed to dissuade you?"

"Yes, my parents talked me out of it. Now, of course, I know why. But even though I ended up studying Highland ecology, I still love sea creatures."

"I am very glad to hear it," John said with utter solemnity.

She was starting to recognize the sly, subtle sense of humor hidden deep under his stern armor. The unexpected flash of it now lifted her spirits for real. She wished he would relax enough to joke more often.

Brighton Sea Life Centre was built underground, hidden beneath the streets and buildings. As they stepped inside, Neridia's initial impression was that it looked more like a cathedral than an aquarium. Subdued, shifting green and blue lights cast an eerie glow over the vaulted ceiling. Tanks and displays were tucked into dim alcoves like shrines. Wide-eyed kids drifted around, staring in hushed amazement at the jewel-like alien worlds revealed behind the glass portals.

"Oh, wow," she breathed, delighted by the unexpectedness of the architecture. "I had no idea it would be like this. No wonder my mom loved working here."

With the artfully designed exhibits occupying people's attention, for once neither she nor John were attracting too many stares. She glanced at him, and noticed that he was scanning the room, alert as ever for any threat to her safety. After a second, his shoulders relaxed.

"Come," he said, touching her elbow. "Let me show you my favorite display here."

"You've been here before, then?" she asked as they started across the hall.

"Several times, with Griff and his son Danny. It delights me to be able to share something of my home with them, even if it can only be a poor imitation of the sea's true wonders."

"I was worried you might be offended," Neridia confessed. "It really doesn't bother you, humans keeping sea creatures in captivity?"

"The great voices, the whales and dolphins, and the greater hunters…yes, it would distress me to see those caged. But here there are only small lives, small songs." John tilted his head a little, as if listening. "The water hums with their contentment. They do not care that they cannot roam freely, when they have food, companionship, mates. And they do a great and honorable duty by being here, where humans may see them. How can your young learn to treasure the sea, if they know nothing of the treasures within it?"

Neridia smiled up at him. "You've just summed up why education is part of conservation. And I'm glad you can tell the fish are happy.

Part of my mother's work was designing exhibits like these so that the creatures would be comfortable enough to display their natural behavior."

"Mommy, Mommy, look at the fish!" A little girl who couldn't have been older than five pointed into a tank, her face shining with excitement. "Look, they've all come to say hello!"

Neridia glanced at the tank herself—and did a double-take.

About fifty black-and-white striped fish were pressed to the glass as closely as the kids on the other side. They were all in perfect alignment with each other, in ranks like a marching band.

And every single one was looking at her.

Neridia stepped sideways, instinctively moving closer to John. In perfect unison, every fish turned to keep pointing straight at her.

"Why are they doing that, Daddy?" A little boy waved his hand in front of the fish, without getting a response. Next to him, a couple of teenagers had whipped out their phones to capture the odd behavior. "What are they looking at?"

Neridia quickly sidled out of the fishes' view—only to jump as a stingray in the neighboring tank plastered itself to the glass wall with a sound like a wet kiss. Within seconds, it had been joined by a dozen more, all shuffling and jostling to be the one closest to her.

"John!" she hissed, cheeks flaming with embarrassment. "Make them stop!"

"I am not certain that I can." Despite John's straight face, his shoulders shook with suppressed laughter. "They are simple creatures. They recognize you as their Empress-in-Waiting, and so they love you. They cannot help but seek to be close to you."

"Well, they can't!" Neridia tried to hide behind John, out of view of any of the tanks. "Tell them that if they don't stop it, we're leaving right now!"

"I speak to the sea, not to those that dwell within it." Nonetheless, John put his hand to the nearest tank. "But I shall convey your command to the water."

He hummed a low, resonant phrase under his breath, so deep that Neridia felt the vibrations of it in her bones. A moment later, a sudden current knocked all of the fish in the tank sideways, shattering the shoal. The fish swirled for a moment, trying to fight the water and regroup, but whenever one got lined up again on Neridia, the water tumbled it back.

"There," John said, as the fish grudgingly retreated into nooks and crannies amongst the rocks, looking for all the world as if they were sulking. "The water will force them to contain their enthusiasm. Shall we go on?"

To Neridia's relief, they were able to continue through the aquarium without attracting too much undue marine attention. Although creatures still hurried up to the glass as she came in sight, every time they were quickly forced to retreat again by sudden strange currents.

It's a pity the water can't do the same to the people...

Still, after the shock of the fishes' unexpected adoration of her, the more mundane stares of the other visitors in the aquarium didn't seem so bad. She was able to ignore the inevitable gawpers, her own attention happily distracted by the wonderful exhibits on display.

The jewel of the aquarium was an enormous tank with a glass tunnel running through it, so that visitors could walk along as if on the bottom of the sea. Of course, it hadn't been built with people of sea dragon height in mind, but Neridia quickly forgot the discomfort of her stooped back and tilted head, gazing up in awestruck delight.

Sea turtles flew over her head like birds, their grace belying their bulk. Some fish bumbled contentedly amongst the seaweed and rocks, nosing for morsels of food, while others shot through the water in shimmering schools, light flashing from their jeweled scales. Neridia noticed that each shoal tended to circle over her own head in a momentary living crown, but at least they were being relatively subtle about it.

John's favorite place in the aquarium turned out to be a small alcove set halfway along the tunnel, with a bench where visitors could relax and watch the fish. They found an unoccupied spot and sat down, their height allowing them a clear view despite the excited groups of children between them and the glass walls.

Neridia was so entranced by the fish, it took her a while before she realized that John's own attention was directed elsewhere. Alone in the crowd, he wasn't gazing upward at the sea creatures sweeping past. Instead, he was watching the children watching the marine life. Though his expression was as controlled as ever, there was a certain softness about his eyes that she'd never seen before, a sort of wistfulness.

"You'd like kids?" she said in surprise.

"I am a Knight of the First Water. It was never an option for me." He didn't look at her, his face in profile. "But yes, I would have liked to have had young of my own."

His hand rested alongside hers on the bench. Greatly daring, Neridia shifted her own hand, covering his. He didn't move away.

"I always wanted to have kids too," she said softly. "So maybe you do have the option after all."

She felt his breath catch. His longing echoed down the mate bond, sweet and sharp at the same time.

"One of the greatest responsibilities of the Emperor or Empress is ensuring the continuation of the bloodline." He glanced sidelong at her, hope rising in the indigo depths of his eyes. "I believe you have hit upon a compelling argument for persuading the Knight-Commander to release me from my vow of chastity, my heart."

She stared into the tank, watching fish dart amongst the rocks. "I still don't see why you think I'm going to be able to persuade any sea dragon of anything. I might be the daughter of the Emperor, but it's not like I have any power of my own."

"Ascending the Pearl Throne is not some mere ritual, nor is Empress an empty title." He turned his hand over, lacing his fingers through hers. "No one under the waves or above them will be able to deny your power, once you have taken your rightful place. The strength of all the sea runs in your blood. You have only to claim your inheritance."

This is it. I have to tell him. I can't let him go on thinking that everything's going to be fine once I'm Empress. Not when I don't even want *to be* Empress.

She felt sick to her stomach with nerves. Nonetheless, she took a deep breath, bracing herself. "John, I...that is, we have to talk."

He surged to his feet, every muscle in his shoulders and arms abruptly tense. For a horrible moment, she thought he'd anticipated what she'd been about to confess, and was going to storm away from her there and then—but all his attention was focused on something in the tank.

"Get up." His hand closed over her wrist, hard and urgent. "We must leave. Now."

"Why?" she asked, as he pulled her to her feet. "What is it?"

The tendons stood out on the side of John's neck. "Look at the sharks."

Blinking, Neridia looked up, into the tank. Previously, the few sharks within it had kept to the perimeter, endlessly circling the boundaries of their world as if looking for a way out. Now, however, they'd converged. Half a dozen of them formed a sleek, predatory triangle, for all the world like fighter jets flying in formation. Perfectly aligned, they pointed directly at them.

"What are they doing?" she asked, staring up.

"Revealing our position to their master," John said grimly, forcing a path through the still-oblivious visitors filling the tunnel. "He is here. The Master Shark is here."

CHAPTER 20

John cursed himself for nine kinds of fool as he tried to politely shove past the oblivious humans thronging the narrow tunnel. He had allowed himself to be seduced by the innocent pleasures of the day, by the taste of ice cream and his mate's smile. Now, unforgivably, he had permitted an enemy to come within striking distance of the Empress-in-Waiting.

Stupid, stupid, stupid! he raged at himself. He had never imagined that even the Master Shark would dare to attack Her Majesty so openly, in the sight of so many mundane witnesses. But he had underestimated the simple, direct brutality of a shark's mind.

Neridia clutched his arm, shrinking against his side. "John!"

He'd already spotted what she'd seen. Walking at an unhurried pace, cold gray eyes fixed unerringly on them, the Master Shark was coming.

There was no mistaking him, although John had only ever seen him from a distance before. His broad, muscular form stood at least a head taller than any of the surrounding humans, putting him only a few inches short of John's own height. Even dressed in a plain shirt and jeans rather than his usual utilitarian, iron-gray armor, he still exuded a sense of power.

Humans parted before him, their deepest monkey instincts making them recoil from the monster hidden under his white skin. He cut through them as easily as if swimming through still water. Sharks circled above their master's head, a crown of teeth.

Their own path was still blocked by a tour guide and a dozen children. He did not dare tell Neridia to run, not when the Master Shark could have dozens of his kind stationed at the exits. All he could do was thrust her behind him, shielding her from the approaching peril with his own body.

The Master Shark stopped, just feet away. Despite the crowd all around, a small circle of isolation surrounded them. Humans hurried past with quick, nervous glances at the looming predator in their midst, giving him a wide berth without really understanding why.

"Peace, Knight-Poet of the First Water." The shark lord's voice was as flat and dead as his eyes. "I am not here to fight. I only wish to speak with the Emperor's daughter."

"Your mere presence is an outrage to Her Imperial Majesty, traitor," John snarled. He had never wished more to have his sword in his hand. "You will not insult her ears with your worthless words. Stand aside."

The Master Shark stared through him, speaking to Neridia directly even though he couldn't see her. "Despite what you have been told, I am not your enemy. In fact, your father was my greatest friend."

"How *dare* you address-" John began, his fists clenching—but Neridia pushed his arm back down.

"Don't, John." She stepped round to his side. He could feel her shaking with fear, but her gaze was steady on the Master Shark. "I want to hear what he has to say."

My mate, no, John sent to her telepathically, unable to bring himself to break protocol by arguing with the Empress-in-Waiting out loud in front of others. *Whatever net he is weaving, do not swim into it. Remember who he is. Remember what he did.*

From the small shake of her head, he knew that she'd heard his mental plea. Nonetheless, she didn't back down. "You claim you were friends with my father?" she asked the Master Shark.

"More than that." The shark lord fixed her with his penetrating stare. "Do you know what it means to be someone's oath-brother?"

Neridia glanced up at John, and he knew that she was thinking of him and Griff. "I know it's a close bond. And that oath-brothers will do anything for each other."

The shark nodded curtly. "I was sworn to him, and he to me. I-"

"He is lying!" John burst out, unable to contain himself at this slur to the Emperor's honor. "The Emperor would never have sworn an oath-bond with any shark, let alone *this* shark. Our people have been mortal enemies since tides began! The Emperor *conquered* the sharks!"

"No," the Master Shark said, flatly. "But I will not waste air telling you the truth of the matter, for you would refuse to hear it. Suffice it to say, we were oath-brothers. I never called in his oath…but he called in mine. Just before his death."

"Before you murdered him." John could barely form human words, his voice warping with the melodies of vengeance.

Emotion flared in the Master Shark's grey eyes at last. It was just the briefest flash of rage, but the sheer power behind it hit John like a punch to the gut.

The Master Shark blinked, once, and the moment was gone as if it had never been. "I did not." He looked back at Neridia. "I say again, he was my oath-brother. I could never have harmed him. I would have died in his defense. My greatest shame is that I left him unguarded. I did not know, then, the danger that he was in."

"I saw you there." Neridia's voice was thin, but brave. "At his house, the day before he, he—the day before the fire. Are you claiming you had nothing to do with it?"

"On my honor, I swear I did not."

"The honor of a shark," John growled.

The Master Shark's impassive expression hardened. "I do not expect *you* to believe me, sea dragon."

"I don't believe you either," Neridia said, to John's relief. "You came after me with those assassins. You ordered them to set fire to my house, just like they set fire to my father's."

"No. I came to warn you. But even though I hastened to you as quickly as I could, I was still too slow. I arrived in the middle of the attack. I tried to get you to safety, but you fled before I could explain my intentions." The Master Shark shot John the briefest glance. "I could tell that you had already been prejudiced against my kind."

"I'm not buying it." Neridia shook her head, but there was more uncertainty in her expression than John liked. "If you didn't attack me, who did?"

The Master Shark's lips drew back a fraction, revealing the gleam of sharp, jagged teeth. "If I knew that, they would be dead. But I do know that you must not go to Atlantis. A hidden enemy awaits you there."

"So that is your ploy." John's own lip curled. "You are terrified of the Empress-in-Waiting claiming her true power, for you know it will be the end of your own. And since direct assault has failed, you resort to lying words to try to keep her from her throne. I would not have thought a shark would be so cowardly."

The Master Shark ignored him completely, focusing only on Neridia. "I captured one of the assassins that attacked you, but he did not know the name of the one who had hired him. All that he knew was that the order had come from Atlantis. If you go there, you will be putting yourself in mortal danger."

Neridia flinched—but then shook her head again, her mouth setting stubbornly. "John's right. You've got far too many reasons to be lying. Why should I trust you?"

"You shouldn't." An ironic, white flash of teeth. "Who would trust a shark? But perhaps you will trust your father. Consider his actions. All your life, he hid you from the Sea Council. He even gave you his pearl of concealment."

Neridia's hand flew to her pendant. "You know about my pearl?"

"I made it for him, as I made my own." The Master Shark parted the collar of his shirt, revealing an identical pendant resting against his muscular chest. "When we were young, we would sometimes use them to escape from our respective duties and adventure unobserved together. Later, of course, he used his to disappear permanently. I was the only person in the sea to know the truth. Before he left the ocean,

I told him that if ever he had need of me, he had only to remove the pendant. For decades, I stayed alert for his blood-scent calling out to me."

The Master Shark looked away, gazing into the depths of the tank as though seeing something quite different. "And four years ago, it did. I came immediately, as I told him I would. Your mother had died, and he could no longer deny the call of the sea. He wanted to finally return home."

"So that was why he gave me his pearl," Neridia whispered, her voice catching. "He was planning to go back to the Pearl Empire."

The Master Shark nodded slightly, still staring into the water. "I would have accompanied him back immediately, but he needed a few more days to finish wrapping up his human life. He asked me to tell no one of his imminent return. And he asked me...he asked me to protect you. I think, even then, he knew that he had enemies who would kill to stop him from returning to his Throne. He made me swear on our oath-bond that if anything happened to him, I would make sure no one in the sea ever discovered your existence."

"You spin tales like a seal," John snarled. "Neri-Your Majesty, do not listen to him. He is only trying to feed your doubts. He would cripple you with words, since he cannot do so with his teeth. Come away. We have heard enough of his lies."

The Master Shark turned on his heel, grey eyes hard as iron. "My last words to my oath-brother were that I would keep his daughter safe. I *will* keep my oath, sea dragon. I will eliminate any threat to her...regardless of whether such threats arise out of malice, or blind ignorance."

John didn't back down, matching the shark lord stare for stare. "As will I, traitor."

"John, stop. This isn't the time or the place." Neridia glanced nervously around at the humans still milling unconcernedly about them, checking that they weren't attracting undue attention. "Master Shark, why are you telling me all this?"

"To make you see the lengths to which your father went to keep you from the Throne." The shark lord gestured at her pendant. "He gave his very life to ensure that you would not be found. His dearest wish was that you would live your life free, on land, happily unaware of your own heritage. Why do you think he never told you of your birthright?"

Neridia's hand closed around her pearl pendant again, as if seeking comfort from the touch of the precious gem. "He, he thought I was only human. That I wouldn't be able to shift."

"He *knew* that you were only human," the shark lord corrected, his cold voice pitiless. "He did not want you to seek the Throne. He knew you did not have the strength to claim it. Think. Think on everything he did for you, and tell me that I am wrong."

Neridia's fist was shaking on her pearl pendant. She bowed her head, and said nothing.

"You are wrong," John's own fists were shaking too, though with rage. It took all his control not to smash the shark's teeth straight down his lying throat. "Neridia, my heart, my mate, do not listen-"

"Mate?" the Master Shark said sharply. "You are mates?"

"Yes." Regardless of the breach of protocol, John placed a possessive, protective hand on Neridia's shoulder. "I am the Empress-in-Waiting's mate. And so I know, *know*, that you are lying. She is a true dragon."

The Master Shark ran a hand through his close-cropped grey hair, his mouth tightening. "This is a complication I could have done without."

Join the club, John's inner human muttered.

The shark lord sighed, dropping his hand. "I had hoped to persuade you to escape your knightly keeper," he said to Neridia. "To disappear permanently into the human world. But I suspect you will not be willing to abandon your mate."

Neridia covered John's hand on her shoulder with her own, squeezing it. "You've got that right."

"Your cowardly plans come to nothing yet again, traitor," John said to the shark. "You cannot separate us. Even your power is as nothing compared to our bond."

"And so history repeats." The Master Shark's mouth twisted ironically. "And it seems I repeat my role."

"What do you mean by that?" Neridia asked warily.

"As I helped your father, so do I help you." The Master Shark pulled his pearl pendant out from beneath his shirt. "If you wish it, I will give you this."

Neridia stared down at the gleaming pearl, slowly turning on its chain. "I thought you said that was another pearl of concealment. I've already got one."

The Master Shark tilted his head at John. "But he does not."

Neridia gasped. "We could *both* disappear."

John was speechless with outrage. Only the thought of attracting the attention of the humans still surrounding them stopped him from snatching the pearl from the shark lord and crushing it under his heel, there and then.

How dare he? How dare *he?*

"I will give you a day to decide." The Master Shark turned, starting to walk away. "Ignore my warning, go to Atlantis, swim straight down the gullets of your enemies…or hide. Live out your lives on land. Be happy together."

"Like my father wanted," Neridia whispered, barely audible.

"Yes." The shark lord paused, glancing back over his shoulder. "He gave his life to keep you safe. Don't let his sacrifice be in vain."

CHAPTER 21

"I cannot understand why you are still contemplating his so-called offer!" John looked like he would very much like to punch something, preferably the Master Shark. "It is clearly a trap. He would say or do anything to keep you from the Throne!"

"But what if he's telling the truth?" Neridia shot back, her own fists clenching with frustration. "I don't understand why *you* won't even consider the possibility that he might *not* be lying!"

They'd taken refuge in a small pub called The Full Moon, at John's insistence. He'd explained that it was a shifter-only establishment, and it was clear he considered it to be the most secure location in Brighton. Neridia hadn't been impressed by the old, dingy building from the outside, but the interior had turned out to be surprisingly snug, with old oak beams and comfortable chairs.

The Full Moon was owned by Rose, the beautiful, middle-aged black woman Neridia had briefly encountered at Griff's wedding. When they'd walked into the bar, Rose had taken one look at them both, immediately shooed out the few mid-afternoon customers, and turned the sign on the door round to CLOSED. Then she'd called the other firefighters of Alpha Team.

At the time, Neridia had been grateful for the additional protection. Now, however, she could have done without the audience.

Dai and Chase were fidgeting uncomfortably, exchanging uneasy glances. Hugh had the expression of a man who'd rather be neck-deep in bodily fluids than where he was now. Rose was looking back and forth between John and Neridia like someone who'd placed a very large bet on the outcome of a tennis match, and didn't like the way it was going. Only Ash still appeared as cool and unperturbed as ever.

Neridia took a deep breath, trying to rein in her emotions. "Look," she said to John, more calmly. "I know you don't like it, but the Master Shark's story does hang together. When I glimpsed him at my dad's house, four years ago? My dad *did* say that he was an old friend who'd unexpectedly dropped by. He seemed genuinely delighted to see him again. I think they really were oath-brothers."

John opened his mouth, his expression thunderous, but Neridia didn't give him a chance to voice his objection. "And if the Master Shark is telling the truth about *that*," she forged on, "maybe he's telling the truth about everything else too."

John slammed his fist down onto the polished oak bar, making pint glasses jump and clatter. "And maybe he is not! You cannot seriously be contemplating throwing away your birthright, throwing away everything that you *are*, on the word of a shark!"

"You don't know them like we do, Neridia," Chase said. He looked grimmer than Neridia had ever seen him, his usually smiling mouth set in a hard line. "We've run into shark shifters before. One of them tried to kill my mate. Another nearly ripped Griff's family in half. You can't trust them. They're lying, evil bastards, every last one."

"Like all red dragons are greedy pyromaniacs?" Dai said, one auburn eyebrow rising. "My people's reputation is no better than that of the sharks, Chase. I'm with Neridia. We need to get Griff back down here from Scotland. His eagle eyes will be able to tell us if *this* shark is lying."

"No," John said, with utter finality. "I will not disturb my oath-brother."

"I don't know why you're so concerned about interrupting his honeymoon," Hugh said. He was keeping as much distance as he could between himself and John, though Neridia was certain that was more to do with the paramedic's strange sensitivity to mated pairs than the sea dragon's simmering wrath. "I mean, you *did* already call him out to a fire on his actual wedding night. It's a bit late to worry about disturbing him."

"Hugh's right," Dai said. The red dragon shifter folded his powerful arms across his chest, meeting John's angry glare without flinching at all. "I mean, that Griff won't mind taking a day out of his honeymoon to help. He'd *want* to be involved. He's not going to be happy about you not calling him."

John shook his head stubbornly. "As shield-brother Hugh kindly reminds me, I have already infringed on my oath-brother's sacred time with his new mate. I will not trouble him further with such a small matter."

"You call this a small matter?" Neridia couldn't believe her ears. "Our lives are at stake here, John! We need to know whether the Master Shark is telling the truth!"

"It does not matter whether or not he is telling the truth!" John shouted, painful harmonics scratching around his words like discordant violins. "Even if he is, it changes nothing!"

"How can you say that? It changes *everything!*"

Rose stepped firmly between the two of them, holding out her hands like a referee at a boxing match. "All right, time out. Both of you, take a deep breath and calm down. Remember, you're mates. You can work this out, but not by yelling at each other."

Neridia blushed, realizing the scene that they'd been causing. From the echo of embarrassment reflecting down the mate bond, John was equally mortified, though his own expression didn't show it. His face settled into a polite, neutral mask.

"My sincere apologies, Your Majesty." His voice was rigidly controlled again. "I spoke out of turn, forgetting my station. Please forgive me."

Neridia clenched her jaw, having to forcibly swallow the urge to scream at him again. "No titles. Like Rose says, we're mates. Just talk to me as your mate. I don't understand why you don't even want to find out the truth."

John closed his eyes, bowing his head. For a long moment, he was silent, as if composing a difficult poem.

"Neridia," he said at last, his deep blue eyes meeting hers. "Let us say that the Master Shark is correct. That he is not our true enemy, and an even more powerful hidden foe awaits us in Atlantis. What happens then?"

"Well…" Neridia hesitated, trying to work out where he was going with this. "Well, then obviously we can't go to Atlantis."

He shook his head slightly, gold charms glinting in his indigo hair. "A sea dragon does not flee a battle. We face the foe gladly, delighting in the joy of a challenge well-met."

"That's you, not me. *I* don't have a code of honor I have to follow."

"You may not have a formal code, but you have your own honor." He held her gaze steadily. "Would you truly be content to allow fear to defeat you, before you even know your enemy?"

He didn't mean it as a rebuke, she knew, but it stung nonetheless. "John, I'm not like you. I can't fight. I don't have magic powers. I can't even speak your language! How do you expect me to be able to defeat anyone, let alone some mysterious foe who's powerful enough to literally get away with murder?"

"I do not know," he said softly. "But I do know that you will not face this enemy alone."

His strength and certainty shone down the mate bond. His powerful warrior's soul infused her own, his courage almost washing away her own doubts. His utter confidence in her was so absolute, she nearly believed in it herself.

Yes, whispered that strange inner voice, fierce and joyous. *Together, we will fight. Together, we will win what is rightfully ours. No force in the sea or above it can stop us from claiming our Throne.*

Neridia flinched, spooked by the uncanny sensation of something else speaking with her own thoughts. She still wasn't sure whether she believed that it really *was* her inner sea dragon talking, as John had claimed.

It's probably just my imagination. Or maybe it's really John's *thoughts, and I'm picking up on them down the mate bond. That sounds more likely.*

Common sense came crashing back, drowning out the alien whisper. What was she thinking? She was just a human, and a too-big, ungainly, timid one at that. She hardly needed a shadowy enemy to prevent her from taking the Throne. Every sea dragon in the entire ocean would doubtless laugh themselves sick if she even tried to claim that she was their Empress.

"No," she said, hating the way that her voice came out weak and tremulous. "I can't do it, John. I just can't."

"You can, and you must. You are the Empress-in-Waiting. You must go to Atlantis. You must claim your Throne."

"I *can't!*" She pressed her fists to her forehead, feeling like her own thoughts were being squashed against the inside of her skull by the force of his willpower pressing down the mate bond. "I don't *want* the Throne! I don't want to be Empress! I don't even want to be a sea dragon!"

John rocked back on his heels as if she'd slapped him. His mouth opened and closed soundlessly, like a fish drowning in air.

"Please, for the love of God, someone set fire to something," Hugh begged the ceiling.

Dai and Chase were also looking desperately uncomfortable. Rose seemed on the verge of intervening again, but Ash caught her wrist, shaking his head slightly.

"I believe that this is a conversation that they need to have," the Fire Commander said to Rose. His calm gaze swept over his fidgeting crew. "But not, perhaps, with an audience."

The other three firefighters looked pathetically grateful for their Commander's suggestion. They all bolted for the door as if the room was on fire. Ash firmly escorted Rose out too, despite the bartender's attempted protests.

The instant the door closed behind them all, Neridia wheeled on John. Her pent-up worries and fears finally broke through her self-control, words rushing out of her like water spilling from a shattered dam.

"First you thought the lake would unlock my sea dragon form," she said, her voice shaking with the force of her emotions. "Then you were certain mating would, and then after that it was going to be the sight of the sea…when are you going to run out of excuses? When are you going to have to admit that yes, I really am just human?"

The mate bond was still reverberating with the thunderclap of his shock. "You—do not wish to be a sea dragon? You would deny your heritage?"

Her heart broke at the pain in his eyes, but she couldn't lie any longer. "John, I can't live in your world. From everything you've told me, I don't *want* to. It's too dangerous. I'm not brave enough, not strong enough."

"You are, if you would but believe-"

"I'm *not*. Please, John. Stop pushing me to be something I'm not. I can't take it any more. I can't keep having my hopes dashed again and again like this. We have to assume that I will never shift. We have to make plans based on reality, not dreams."

He shook his head in confusion, as though she was speaking gibberish. "But if you do not shift…you will not even have the option of coming to Atlantis. The Knight-Commander forbade it."

"I know. That means that there's only thing I can do. Run, like the Master Shark suggested. Try to forget all of this. Live out my life on land." She touched her pearl. "Like my father wanted me to."

"But you have seen the sea." He stared at her, for once looking utterly lost and helpless. "It is in your eyes, your soul, your very blood. And yet you would turn your back on it? Truly?"

No! cried that strange inner voice, in a chord of heartrending agony. Neridia pushed it away.

"Yes," she said firmly. "The sea is beautiful, but it's not my home. I belong on land."

He bowed his head, his vast shoulders slumping as if under a crushing weight.

"Perhaps you are human indeed, then." Defeat stripped all the music from his voice. "No sea dragon could bear to leave the ocean forever."

She sucked in her breath as his meaning hit her. "You won't come with me."

He didn't look at her. "You know I cannot."

Foolishly, she'd still been holding out hope that he would. That things would be different now that they were fully mated. That he wouldn't be able to bear the thought of living without her, any more than she could bear the thought of living without him…

"Why not?" she demanded, grabbing onto anger to save herself from falling into a pit of despair. "My father did! *He* chose to be with his mate!"

"Do not *dare* accuse me of loving you less than your father loved your mother!" He jerked his head up, his blue eyes blazing with a grief and rage equal to that in her own heart. "It is you who are choosing to leave me, not I you!"

"Oh no, don't you put this all on me." She was *not* going to cry. "I can't shift, I can't go to Atlantis, I don't have any choice! But you do. You could choose me, like my father chose my mother. He left the sea to be with her. Why can't you?"

"Because I am bound by vows, as he was not!" John shouted back, his voice rising to match her own. "If you are not the Empress, you cannot come before my duty to the Pearl Throne! I cannot choose you without utterly shattering my honor!"

"Then you love your honor more than you love me!"

The instant the words left her lips, Neridia regretted saying them —but it was too late. And she couldn't call them back. She couldn't even say she didn't really mean them.

Because she did.

She expected him to shout back, or flinch, or do…something. Instead, his side of the mate bond just went blank. If he hadn't been standing right in front of her, she wouldn't even have been able to tell that he was in the same room. His face was utterly expressionless.

Then, without a backward glance, he left.

∼

He came back after midnight, right when Neridia had lost all hope that he would ever return at all.

She'd cried an ocean's worth of tears in his absence, sobbing into Rose's soft shoulder. The motherly woman hadn't tried to console her, or tell her that it would be all right. She'd just held her, and let her cry, her own wise eyes infinitely sad.

When Neridia had cried herself dry, Fire Commander Ash—who had silently observed the entire outpouring of her grief—had finally stirred. Despite his apparently unmoved expression, she'd had a sudden, odd certainty that he understood even better than Rose what she was going through.

"Neridia," he'd said, very quietly. "If you wish it, if this is too painful for you to bear…I can destroy your mate bond."

She'd stared at him, dumbfounded. "You can do that?"

"I am the Phoenix. There is nothing I cannot burn." He'd hesitated, his eyes flickering for the briefest moment. "You must be absolutely certain, though. It is irreversible. And you would lose not only the bond itself, but also all memories of your mate. But perhaps that is better than grieving over what you cannot have."

She'd promised that she'd think about it, though her strange inner voice had cried, *No, no, no!* And she *had* thought about it, even as Rose had roundly scolded Ash for daring to suggest such a terrible thing. She'd kept thinking about it as Rose had shown her to the pub's small guest bedroom, telling her to call if she needed anything, anything at all.

But there was only one thing she needed. Her mate.

And if I can't have him…maybe it is *best to forget.*

Now, slowly, she became aware of the faintest glimmer down the mate bond. The tiny sense of his presence was a mere firefly spark in the bleak darkness of her soul, but even that was enough to make her hold her breath, scarcely daring to hope.

He came soft-footed into the room, closing the door gently behind him. He was just a looming shape in the darkness. She couldn't see his face, couldn't get any hint of his thoughts through the mate bond.

But he was there.

"John?" She sat bolt upright on the bed, swinging her legs over the side. "What-?"

His finger brushed her lips, stopping her half-formed words. She trembled, even that tiny contact setting her blood on fire.

He traced the shape of her lips, her cheek. His hand cupped the side of her face. She could feel the callouses on his palm, thickened by years of wielding a sword. The rough skin was a harsh reminder of what he was—a sea dragon knight, bound by unbreakable vows.

And yet, he there he was.

He came back. He came back to me. He came back.

"John," she breathed.

He bent down in answer, his mouth covering hers. She didn't dare say anything more, for fear that he would change his mind. She just closed her eyes, opening her lips to him.

In the darkness, she could pretend that he was just a man. She could pretend that she was just a woman.

She could pretend that things could be simple between them.

He framed her face with his hands, fingers tangling in her hair. His tongue slid deep into her, as if he wanted to lay claim every inch of her body, the entirety of her soul.

His hands moved down, skimming her neck, her shoulders, her sides. Finding the hem of the old t-shirt she was wearing, he broke the kiss just long enough to lift the garment over her head. She shivered at the rush of cool air over her bare skin. He pulled her closer, recapturing her mouth, his body hot against hers.

Down the mate bond, she sensed his desperate hunger. She was already wet, but his powerful desire for her heightened her own need. She fumbled for the buttons of his shirt. The fabric was slightly damp, clinging to the swells of his shoulders as she tugged it off.

She ran her hands over the smooth, hard planes of his chest, his nipples tightening under her palms. She still only knew him by touch, and as a half-seen form in the night. She craved to finally look at him properly, but she didn't dare reach for the bedside light. She didn't want him to see *her*.

He was trading away his honor for her. The sight of her all-too-human form might make him realize what a bad bargain it was.

Instead, she pulled away from his kiss, ducking her head. He made an inarticulate noise of protest, but the growl turned into a low gasp as she ran her tongue along his collarbone. She could taste the salt of the sea on his skin, and a deeper, wilder scent that was all his own.

She explored him with her mouth, slowly, savoring every hard line of his muscles. His fingers ran lightly over her own back, exploring her in return with a delicacy that belied his strength. He stroked her as if she was some fragile, priceless treasure.

"Neridia," he murmured into her hair, longing singing in his voice. "My mate. My mate."

Tears welled in her eyes at being so cherished. Even as her whole body turned to liquid pleasure, a bittersweet pain caught in her throat. He was choosing her, he had chosen her...but she knew what it would cost him.

I can't. I can't let him do this.

He went tense in her embrace, as if he'd sensed her sudden hesitance. His huge hands closed over her shoulders. She gasped as he tossed her back onto the bed. A rustle of fabric, and then he was on her, covering her body with his own.

Before, in the water, she hadn't truly been aware of just how massive he truly was. His solid weight pressed demandingly against her. She felt wonderfully small and fragile, utterly dominated by his strength.

His naked cock slid against her soft stomach, hard and slick with his desire. The feel of him burned away the last shreds of her self-control. No matter what the cost—or who would pay it—she *needed* him.

She cried out as he slid into her, wrapping her legs tight around his hips. He moved in her as powerfully as the sea, sweeping her away on waves of ecstasy. He was over her and in her, body and mind. She lost herself completely, willingly, dissolving into him even as he emptied himself into her.

Afterwards, they lay in a tangle of limbs, like driftwood washed up onto a beach. Neridia buried her face in his shoulder, breathing in his scent, trying to reassure herself that he was truly there. Even with his heavy, sweat-slick body pressing against hers, she couldn't shake a feeling that this was just a dream; that any moment, she would wake up, and he would be gone.

His rough fingers gently combed through her hair. She could feel his heart beating. Although her own was slowing, his was still fast. Despite the exhausted relaxation of his muscles, the mate bond betrayed his tension.

"I cannot bear to be parted from you," he whispered into her ear. "Please. Stay with me."

She stiffened underneath him, her own contentment popping like a soap bubble. "I thought...I thought this meant you'd chosen to stay with me."

"I cannot," he said, his voice the barest breath.

"Then what was this?" She pushed angrily at him, trying to shove him away, but he didn't move. "You broke your honor just to say goodbye?"

In the darkness, she felt more than saw the shake of his head. "I did not break my honor. I spoke with my Knight-Commander. He released me from my vow of chastity."

"What? Why?"

"I told him that we were in danger of losing you utterly. I told him of your fears, and how the Master Shark had preyed upon them. I told him...I begged him to allow me one last chance to convince you not to throw away your heritage. I asked permission to show you what it was that you were sacrificing."

A turmoil of emotions flooded her. Outrage at how he'd inadvertently misled her, relief that he truly hadn't sacrificed his honor, a surge of sheer annoyance at his arrogance, joy that he was still fighting for her, terror that she could still lose him...

She settled on annoyance. "Wow, you really do think highly of yourself, don't you?"

"I did not mean this." John traced the shape of her face, as though trying to read her expression with his fingertips. "Not just this, at least. I know…I know I am not sufficient inducement. But he did not only release me from my vow. He also gave me permission to show you the true reason you cannot turn your back on the sea. Even if you cannot shift, he will allow you to enter Atlantis."

She closed her eyes, knowing that she should move away from his gentle touch, unable to bring herself to do so. "John…"

"Please," he breathed, desperation weaving a staccato melody under his words. "Please, come. Let me show you your true home. I swear on my honor that I will protect you, from any foe, if you will but come. Please. Come to Atlantis."

She wanted to say no. But if she did…she didn't know what he'd say. What he'd do.

I cannot bear to be parted from you, he'd said.

But he was a sea dragon. She knew by now that he would face any challenge, any pain, if that was what his honor demanded.

She couldn't bear to be parted from him either. And she wasn't a sea dragon.

"Yes," she whispered. "I'll come."

"Oh my mate, my heart, my Empress. I swear to you, you will not regret this." His arms tightened around her, pulling her close. "You will understand, when you see Atlantis. And whatever happens, we will be together, like this, every night and day. All will be well, as long as we are together."

Neridia curled into her mate's embrace, listening to his soft words of relief and reassurance, surrounded by his strength and love. She had never felt so alone.

CHAPTER 22

You're sure this is the place? Dai's telepathic tone was dubious. His horned head dipped, his eyes narrowing as he peering down at the apparently featureless waves below. *I don't see anything.*

This is as far as you will be able to take us, kin-cousin, John sent back. *Atlantis is protected by powerful magics, which prevent either shifter or human from crossing the city's borders.*

Neridia straddled Dai's broad red-scaled neck in front of him. Overhearing their telepathic communication, she turned her head to catch his eye. She shouted something, but the wind whipped her words away.

John shook his head at her, gesturing between their foreheads. *Mindspeech, my mate. You must learn to become comfortable with it, since you do not yet know our spoken language.*

She grimaced, screwing up her face in concentration. Wobbly and ill-formed, her halting psychic projection brushed against the edge of his mind. *We're...getting...off?*

Yes, he replied. *We must make our own way from here.*

She swallowed hard, her face tight with apprehension. He tried to send her encouragement down the mate bond, but his silent reassurances washed around her without effect, like water swirling around a silent stone.

Last night, their bodies had been as close as it was possible to get. Today, he had the terrible sensation that her soul was further away from him than ever.

She is simply nervous, he told himself for the thousandth time. *When she is embraced by the sea, her fears will be swept away. All will be well.*

He tightened the straps across his chest, checking that both his sword and his pack were secure. He'd worn his armor, of course—there was no need for human clothes any more.

There would never be need for anything human, ever again.

He tapped Dai's scaled shoulder. **If you would oblige me by swooping low to the water, kin-cousin?**

Dai curved his head to look back at him. A dragon's face was not capable of expressing emotion like a human one, but John could tell the sorrow behind Dai's burning green eyes.

This is really goodbye, then? Dai asked.

John laid his palm flat on the red dragon's hot neck for a moment. **If all goes well, then yes. The Empress must stay in Atlantis, and I must stay by her side. We will not be free to leave the sea.**

And if all does not go well?

John shrugged one armored shoulder. **Then I will not be* alive *to leave the sea, kin-cousin.**

Dai blew smoke out of his nostrils in a long sigh. **Then, much as it pains me...I wish you the very best of luck.**

The red dragon swept his wings back, dropping into a dive. John swung a leg over Dai's broad neck, holding on with one hand to the curving spines running down the dragon's back. With his other, he gathered Neridia close.

"Hold your breath," he shouted into her ear, not trusting her erratic telepathic abilities. "Are you ready?"

Wide-eyed with fear, she nodded. She grabbed hold of the straps of his harness, clinging to his chest.

Dai's crimson wings flared. The dragon had managed to swoop so low to the ocean, the tip of his tail cut a furrow through the waves as he leveled out.

Holding tight to Neridia, John jumped.

He was shifting even as he hit the water. Exploding into his true form, he swirled in a tight coil around Neridia, bearing her back up to the surface. She spluttered, spitting out sea water as she scrabbled to sit astride his neck.

Dai's shadow swept over them. John sang a farewell in his own language, the notes shaking the water, and the red dragon dipped a wing in response. Then he was gone, beating his wings hard to spiral back up into the sky.

He couldn't see Neridia, perched as she was behind his head, but he could feel her shiver as the wind blew across her ocean-drenched clothes. She huddled against his scales, drawing her feet up out of reach of the waves.

Despite the salt water soaking her to the skin, she was as human as ever.

"Now what?" she asked out loud, looking around at the empty sea. "There's no one here."

John hid his disappointment, not allowing even the faintest tinge to taint his mental voice. *To human senses, perhaps. But not to mine.*

In the water, sound was a matter of touch, felt with the whole body. He stretched himself out to his full length, luxuriating in the sweet vibrations whispering along his scales. Only the need to keep Neridia above the surface stopped him from diving and rolling, wrapping himself in music.

Oh, I have missed this. I did not know how much.

A sea dragon song could carry around a quarter of the globe. This close to Atlantis, the entire ocean shook with their voices.

The martial chants of knights patrolling the border, the sweet piping calls of infants playing; the duets of lovers and the call-and-response of hunters; some singing for purpose and others simply for the pleasure of being alive. It all blended into one great tapestry of song, the song of his people.

He could not put his head under the water to add his own voice to the chorus, but his presence had not gone unnoticed. The nearest knights were several miles away, but they had seen Dai fly overhead, and heard the splash of their entry into the water. Their deep voices shook John's bones as they focused their songs on him in challenge.

"Identify yourself," one of the unseen border guard sang to him, in harsh notes as warning as a bared fang. "Who seeks to enter Atlantis in silence? Why do you not sing?"

"Peace, peace, honored Knight," sang a higher, much closer voice, in rippling melodies of delight. "They are known, they are expected, and oh, they are welcome!"

Air did not carry sound as well as water, but John called out anyway, his heart unable to contain his song. "Little sister!"

Her familiar, beloved head broke through the waves, sea water streaming from her indigo scales. "Little brother!"

He rumbled in delight at the old joke, curving his head down to rub his cheek along hers in greeting. Hatched from the same clutch of eggs, it had always been a matter of debate which of them was actually the eldest. She claimed to have cracked her shell first, while he had always countered that *he* had fully emerged before she had. In any event, he had not been "little" compared to her since their seventh year.

They had been inseparable as youngsters, and even though the tides of duty had carried them far apart since then, they would always share a bond deeper than words. He had missed her greatly.

"You have not changed," he said fondly. Her strong, graceful coils were as beautiful as ever, and her song still sparkled with her irrepressible zest for life.

She studied him for a moment, her turquoise eyes troubled. "You have."

Before he could ask what she meant, she lifted herself higher in the water, curving her neck. "Is this really her? Your mate?"

"Yes." John's chest swelled with pride as he bowed his head to display Neridia. "This is the Empress-in-Waiting. But we must use mindspeech. She does not yet fully understand our tongue."

"She is very small," his sister said doubtfully. "Smaller than I expected. How can someone so tiny truly be the Empress-in-Waiting?"

He was glad she hadn't said *that* in mindspeech. "There can be no doubt, my sister. The very sea proclaimed her status."

His sister gave him a rather dubious look, which was understandable given that the sea certainly wasn't doing so *now*. The waves rolled unconcernedly about their business, to all appearances utterly ignorant of the fact that their ruler perched above them. Had John not heard for himself the ocean's first greeting to Neridia yesterday, he too might have thought that she was nothing more than any other human from its current lack of reaction.

"The sea is wise," he said firmly, ignoring his inner human's uneasy silence. "It hides its devotion now, so as not to reveal Her Majesty's presence to unfriendly observers. It does not wish the Master Shark to find her. Once she takes her throne, her full glory will be revealed, I assure you."

His sister clicked her fangs, still looking less than convinced. "Well, if the Knight-Commander is willing to allow her into Atlantis, then I suppose she must be more than she seems."

Neridia flinched back into his neck-ruff as his sister bent to peer at her more closely. *What's she saying?* she asked him privately, down the mate bond.

It does not matter, he sent back. He widened the mental contact to include his sister. *Sister, you are being rude. I told you that we needed to use mind speech.*

I am sorry, his sister told Neridia, still inspecting her in fascination. *It is just that you are the first human-ah, that is, the first dry-lander I've ever met.*

Oh. John felt Neridia lean back a little, craning her neck up to examine his sister in return. *Well, you're only the second sea dragon I've ever met. I hope you don't mind me saying, but you're smaller than I expected.*

His sister's iridescent neck-ruff bristled with laughter. *And I hope you will not judge us all based on my brother's sole example. In brute size, or any other respect.*

Neridia laughed too, her nervous tension easing a little. *John didn't say which one of you was older, but I'm guessing you've got to be his big sister, right?*

His sister shot him a triumphant look. *I like her already.*

John bared a fang at her, though his own neck-ruff betrayed his amusement. *I did not summon you merely in order to disparage me to my mate. You are here to perform a duty, if you recall.*

She flicked water at him with the tip of her tail. *That's my brother. Always duty first. Especially if it allows him to avoid an embarrassing conversation.*

He growled, neck-ruff flattening in real irritation, as Neridia giggled. *I am not avoiding anything except sharks. It somewhat defeats the purpose of flying to Atlantis if we then bob about on the surface all day like foolish baby seals.*

Oh, very well. His sister blew a stream of bubbles impudently at him as she sank back down beneath the surface. *But don't think this is anything more than a temporary reprieve. Your mate and I are going to have a nice long chat once we're all safely in Atlantis. I have many stories to share with her. Many, many stories.*

Behind his head, Neridia chuckled. "I was nervous about meeting your sister," she said out loud, in human speech. "But now I think we're going to get along just fine."

And I was not nervous about you two meeting, John replied. *Now...I am not quite so sanguine.*

Still, at least his sister's jibes had lightened Neridia's mood. John would happily endure *days* worth of teasing for that. Which was just as well, seeing that he probably would have to. His sister had never been one to make idle threats.

Neridia giggled again as she sensed his resignation, patting his scaled neck in sympathy. Then she leaned over, looking down through the glittering waves. "What's she doing now?"

What I called her here to do. Even without being able to put his head underwater to track his sister's position, he could sense the swirling currents of her movements. *She is dancing.*

In a spray of sea foam, his sister broke the surface some way off.

Her body hung in a breathtaking arc for a moment, the tip of her tail coming clean out of the water with the force of her leap. Her webbed forefeet spread wide, as if she sought to gather the entire sky in her embrace.

With an ear-splitting crash, she dove back under the water again. Trails of silver bubbles rose in her wake. Twisting elegantly, she swirled her body around them, herding them together. Beneath the water's surface, a delicate, gleaming sphere of air started to form.

Leap by leap and twist by twist, she captured the sky and coaxed it under the sea. John sang his sister's name in admiration, saluting her artistry.

He could tell Neridia was equally impressed. "Oh, she's so beautiful. I'd never have imagined something so big could move so gracefully."

My sister is a master of her art, John sent, pride filling his mental tone. *This form of dance does not come naturally to most of our people, but she has always had an affinity for air.* His jaws parted a little in a wry smile. *Do not tell her this, but I sometimes think that she would have made a much better Walker-Above-Wave than I.*

His sister had finished trapping a glimmering sphere of air within her coils. Carefully, as if putting on a complicated necklace, she manipulated it so that it rested between her shoulders, at the base of her neck. She made a few experimental loops and turns, checking that it was secure, then looked back up at them both.

I'm ready, she called up mentally. *I'd normally draw down a much larger quantity if I was restocking Atlantis's air, but that would take too long. This will be enough to get us there, at least.*

Hold your breath, my mate, John told Neridia. *And keep a firm grip.*

She wound both hands into his neck-ruff, taking a deep breath. When he sensed that she was ready, he dove. He could still taste the panic rising in her throat as the ocean closed over them.

Only a moment, he reassured her.

Swimming as fast as he could without risking unseating Neridia, he joined his sister. There was a slightly awkward moment transferring Neridia from his neck to hers, but at last his mate was safely settled in the bubble of air.

Neridia gasped, drawing a huge, shaking breath. She said something, but the words stayed trapped in the air around her. From the relief pounding down the mate bond, John suspected it had been something she would not care to repeat telepathically.

"What approach are we taking?" his sister asked in song, once Neridia was secure. "The Pearl Gate?"

John shook his head, answering out loud since there was no need to include Neridia in this particular conversation. "Much as I would like to bring the Empress-in-Waiting home in glory, we must take a less visible route. The Knight-Commander does not want rumors of her existence to get out before she has been presented to the Sea Council."

"He'd better not hope to keep it secret much longer than that. The screams of outrage will be heard across the entire city." She flicked her tail, propelling herself through the water. "Let's take the Broken Road, then. It's usually only used by us dancers, and there are no air runs scheduled for today. It should be empty."

John hummed a note of agreement. Dropping back a little, he curved to bring one eye level with Neridia. *I must range ahead, and check that our path is clear. I may need to move out of your sight, but do not fear. I am always but a thought away.*

Neridia nodded, though her racing heartbeat pounded down the mate bond. The bubble of air surrounding her seemed very small and fragile. He could sense her fearful awareness of the cold water pressing down all around.

He wished that he could comfort her, but he had no words to do so. How could she find the ocean claustrophobic? To him, it was freedom.

Rolling away from her, he dove. And at last, at *last*, he could swim unhindered.

Chase and Dai had occasionally teased him about the way he had to be carried on their backs whenever Alpha Team had to race to the site of an emergency. The pegasus and red dragon could not help pitying anyone who could not fly as they did.

He'd always smiled, and said nothing. They were like children proudly hoarding a shiny piece of glass, having never seen a diamond.

Now, John flew with a freedom that his winged colleagues could not even imagine. No ungainly flapping, no constant fight against gravity; he moved as easily as thought. With the merest twist of his tail, the slightest flick of a webbed foot, he could stoop faster than a striking hawk, or hover more gracefully than any hummingbird.

The entire sea was his, and it was vaster than any sky.

He closed his nostrils, holding his last breath of air safe in his vast lungs, and spread his neck ruff to better taste the water through the hidden gills underneath. He had been forced to breathe the harsh air and chemical-filled waters near human cities for so long, he had almost forgotten how sweet the sea could be. The pure water was like a benediction through his gills, washing him clean of the reek of humanity.

But he could not allow himself to become distracted by the ecstasy of being home again. Alert for any danger, he probed into the dark depths with short, wordless notes. The echoes bounced back to him, allowing him to feel the shape of the unseen ocean floor as easily as if he ran his hands over it.

His echolocation revealed nothing larger than a tuna for half a mile around. The tumbled rocks of the sea bed hid no lurking sharks. Nonetheless, he stayed on high alert, circling under and around his sister and Neridia as they too descended.

Down the mate bond, he sensed Neridia's fear rise the deeper that his sister carried her. Although the ocean was fairly shallow around Atlantis, it was clear her human eyes were struggling to cope with the dim sunlight filtering down from the mirrored surface high overhead.

All is well, he reassured her yet again. *Look, I am here.*

He concentrated for a moment. A tingle ran over his scales as his phosphorescent patches lit. The glowing lines swirled over his shoulders and down his flank in twining spirals, more intricate than any human tattoo.

Oh! Neridia gasped.

Try to look impressed at how sparkly he is, his sister told her, dryly. *Males do so love to show off.*

I am not showing off. I merely thought to light the way. Nonetheless, he was unable to help feeling a certain masculine satisfaction at Neridia's reaction to his markings.

Schools of small fish swirled around him, drawn by the shimmering blue-green glow. Normally a knight on patrol would swim dark, so as not to alert enemies to his presence, but at the moment Neridia's fear was a greater threat than any hypothetical lurking shark. He could feel her imminent panic retreat a little as her eyes fixed on his luminous form.

Look. Seeking to distract her further, he curved down so that he swam only a few body-lengths above the sea floor. He brightened his glow as he twisted around a jagged, broken pillar of stone.

That looks carved. Neridia's mental tone was startled. *Is that writing?*

Yes. We are swimming over what was once a coastal village. John wove in and out of the ruins, the wake of his passing stirring the seaweed blanketing the shattered buildings. *All this was once part of Atlantis. When the island sank, our ancestors were able to keep the capital city intact, but the outer parts of the land had to be sacrificed.*

She stared at the irregular lumps and rocks of the sea bed with new eyes. *How long ago was this?*

Many thousands of years, as humans reckon time. I do not know the exact count.

Neridia was silent for a while, as his sister carried her over the ruins of millennia. *We have legends of Atlantis,* she said eventually. *Humans, I mean. A lost island, sunk by some ancient disaster.*

Your legends hide a kernel of truth, he sent back. *But it was no disaster. Our ancestors sank Atlantis deliberately.*

Why? she asked.

Fear, his sister said.

War, he corrected. *The Dragon Wars, remembered by humankind only as whispered legends of battling gods. The dragons of the land grew *jealous of our beauty, our wisdom, our treasures. They allied with humans and sought to invade our home. Our ancestors retreated beneath the waves rather than see all that they loved laid waste by flame.*

They chose to hide from the outside world instead of learning to live within it, his sister added, her mental tone sad. *And so they divided our people. Not all inhabitants of Atlantis were shifters. Our human kin were forced to flee to other lands, exiled from their own home.*

John shrugged, the motion making his light ripple over the sea bed. *They made new homes. Some of the greatest human civilizations owe a debt to sea dragon blood. It was a necessary sacrifice.*

His sister snorted, silver bubbles trickling from her flared nostrils. *I am sure that is what our honored ancestors told our unfortunate kin. Strange how the sacrifice is always judged necessary by the one who is not making it.*

Funny, that, Neridia agreed, a hint of bitterness darkening the thought.

There was not much John could say in response. With a sweep of his tail, he moved ahead again, scouting out the way.

The ruins around them became larger and more complex as they swam onward. John led his sister along the sea floor, so that the ancient structures hid them from any unfriendly eyes. He kept alert to the background murmur of sea dragon song, listening for any hint of warning from the knights patrolling Atlantis's borders.

None came. The knights' songs were routine, speaking only of passing fish and idle gossip. Much of this latter was speculation about their own presence. From what he could overhear, the Knight-Commander had not informed even the Order of the First Water that the Walker-Above-Wave was returning, let alone who he was bringing with him.

It felt wrong, all wrong. The Empress-in-Waiting should have been greeted with a sea-shaking chorus, every inhabitant of Atlantis calling out to bid her welcome. She should have been coming home in triumph and glory. Not like this, creeping through the mire like a crab scuttling into a hole.

John clamped his own jaws shut on the song that wanted to rise in his throat. The Knight-Commander knew the political currents of Atlantis better than he did. Much as it went against the whispers of his own heart, he was honor-bound to trust in his superior's judgment.

Still, he could at least try to make the moment more appropriate. Deliberately, John picked a route that followed ancient, twisting roads overhung by coral-encrusted ruins. The sunken land was starting to slope upward, the waters brightening as they became shallower.

Though they were not yet within sight of the city itself, the sea teemed with life. Fish scattered at their approach, darting into empty windows to hide from the greatest predators in the sea. A giant octopus shifted color to match the carved wall it clung to as they passed by, faded hieroglyphs rippling across its skin.

John sensed the delight rising in Neridia's heart, her innate joy in the wonders of nature overwhelming even her apprehension. *Oh,* she exclaimed, head swiveling as if trying to see everything at once.

"Don't think I don't know what you're doing," his sister sang to him privately, in laughing notes outside human hearing. "You always did have a taste for the dramatic."

He bristled his neck-ruff at her. "Do not spoil the surprise."

It's more beautiful than I could have imagined, Neridia said telepathically, oblivious to the exchange. She twisted round on his sister's back, following the flight of a brilliant school of fish as they swirled around a once-proud dragon statue now worn soft by time and tides. *Is this Atlantis?*

No. John rose, his sister following, allowing Neridia to at last see what lay ahead. *That is Atlantis.*

CHAPTER 23

Neridia could barely comprehend what she was seeing.
The broken grandeur of the ruins had been impressive enough. But this...this was no ruin.

A broad, stepped mountain rose from the rolling sea floor. Thousands of white buildings clustered on the wide tiers, gleaming like pearl in the shifting sunbeams filtering down from the half-seen surface far above. Elegant arches connected one level to the next, so light and airy that it hardly seemed possible that they could support their own weight.

It was like some impossibly huge, intricate wedding cake. Vast, glimmering bubbles of air encased some parts in crystal domes, but many of the towering buildings and elegant, spiraling roads lay open to the ocean.

And, through the sunken city, the sea dragons swam.

At this distance, they were as tiny as minnows, but there was no mistaking those sinuous forms. They soared around the towers and ziggurats as easily as birds through the sky. She could see the luminescent glow of the males, winking like fireflies through the white spires. There were the darker shapes of females too, and others that were too small to be sea dragons, too big to be mere fish.

Home, whispered her strange inner voice. *We are home.*

Neridia felt like she could stare for a week, and still barely take in a tenth of the city's wonders. Wide, curving streets opening out into column-lined plazas. Vast statues of dragons, ten times life size, carved into the living rock itself. A huge palace of soaring towers at the very top of the mountain, crowning the city with the unmistakable gleam of pure gold.

And *she* was supposed to rule it all.

The thought punctured her awestruck wonder as ruthlessly as a sword-thrust. The idea of an ordinary human—of *her*—put in charge of all this shining splendor was so ridiculous that Neridia didn't know whether to laugh or cry.

"I can't do this," she whispered, alone in her tiny bubble of air. "This is madness. I want to go home."

This is home, insisted her inner voice. *This is our domain. Claim it!*

Neridia shut her eyes tight, trying to shut out the city, to shut out that terrifyingly fearless voice. What was she thinking? What place was there for *her* in this magical underwater world?

My mate? John's mind brushed against hers as gently as a caress.

She opened her eyes to find him hanging in the water at her side, his luminous blue eyes anxiously studying her expression. Here in his natural element, he seemed even bigger than he did on land. The glowing spirals running down his scaled flanks emphasized his powerful bulk. Every slight movement of his finned tail, every idle flex of his ivory talons revealed his strength.

He belonged here. She didn't.

But she had come too far to turn back now.

She took a deep breath of the stale air, straightening her spine. **I'm okay.** It still felt weird to just *think* the words, and know that he heard them in his own head. **I was just...it's all just a bit overwhelming.**

His own mental tone lacked its usual deep, certain ring. **Perhaps I should not have sprung it on you all at once, without preparation. But I thought the sight would delight you more if it came unexpected.**

Underneath Neridia's thighs, John's sister heaved a deep, heartfelt sigh. *Please forgive my brother,* the sea dragon said privately, mind-to-mind. *He means well. But you have to remember, this is the male who once put a live and extremely angry vampire squid in my bed, because I idly remarked at dinner that nothing exciting had happened that day.*

Despite herself, Neridia had to smile. *I am really looking forward to hearing those stories you mentioned.*

Then by all means, let us get to Atlantis as swiftly as possible. John's sister broadened the mental conversation to include John. *Brother? Is it safe for us to proceed?*

John swung his horned head to scan the surroundings. Neridia didn't know how he could see anything in the murky depths, but after a moment he hummed in evident satisfaction.

The way ahead lies clear. Flicking his tail, he soared effortlessly up, leading the way. *We will enter by the-*

He broke off abruptly, his head snapping round as if he'd heard something. Underneath Neridia, every muscle in his sister's back went tense. Both sea dragons stared back the way they'd came.

What is it? Neridia turned to look back herself, but couldn't see anything in the dim light. *What's wrong?*

Go! John swirled back, every talon bared to the full extent as he stationed himself behind his sister. *Get her to Atlantis! Now!*

Neridia jolted back, nearly sliding out of her bubble of air as John's sister surged forward. She'd thought they had been swimming quickly enough before, but now it became obvious that they had been going at the sea dragon equivalent of a leisurely walking pace. She grabbed at the dragon's trailing mane, clinging on for dear life.

"What's going on?" she yelled.

One of the border guards just spoke to a comrade, John's sister responded, even though she'd forgotten to use mind speech. *Wondering why the Master Shark is in such a hurry to reach Atlantis.*

What? They let him through? Neridia's pulse spiked with fear. *Why didn't they challenge him?*

Because he is the Master Shark! The sea dragon's head wove through the water like a snake as she increased her speed still further.

And since the Knight-Commander hasn't seen fit to warn his knights about your existence, let alone that the Lord of Sharks is after you, they have no reason to deny him entry! And now he is here!

Neridia twisted, straining her eyes to try to see through the deep blue sea. John wasn't following. He'd spiraled up to hang halfway between the sea floor and the surface, facing away from them, his intricate markings blazing as bright as neon signs.

He was so huge, so fierce, that some of Neridia's panic eased at the sight. He was a sea dragon, a sea dragon *Knight*, born and trained for battle. He was armored in plated scales, and armed with teeth and claws and powerful magic. Surely no shark, not even the biggest great white, could get past him.

Then she looked past John's glowing form, and saw what he faced.

The Master Shark wasn't a great white shark. He could have swallowed a great white whole, in a single mouthful, without pausing.

In a flash, she understood the reason for the Master Shark's oddly-proportioned face in human form, with its prominent brow ridges and heavy jaw. It was a face from prehistoric times, echoing his true form. No wonder John had been so certain he had to be commanding the plesiosaur shifter assassins. Like them, he was a primitive throwback, a relic from another age.

An age of giants.

"*Megalodon*," Neridia breathed.

The biggest shark ever to swim the sea. Eighty feet of muscle and teeth and bottomless hunger.

And John hung motionless, right in his path.

Hands numb with shock, Neridia tugged at John's sister's mane to get her attention. *John isn't following us! He's planning to fight!*

What? Of course he's not- The sea dragon's mental voice cut off as she glanced over her shoulder. *What in the-BROTHER!*

Faintly, Neridia heard John sing something back in return. His sister hissed something that was very definitely a dragon swearword.

What did he say? Neridia asked, though she was pretty sure she knew the answer.

That he would cover our retreat, the sea dragon said grimly, swirling to a halt in the water.

Neridia shrieked as the sea dragon started fluking back toward her brother and the rapidly-approaching Master Shark at top speed. *What are you doing?*

I'll be dry-beached before I let my little brother hurl himself down the Master Shark's gullet just to slow him down! The sea dragon's teeth bared in a snarl. *You're meant to be the Empress-in-Waiting, so act like it! If anyone can stop the Master Shark, it's you!*

Me? Every muscle in her body was rigid with fear. *What do you expect me to be able to do?*

John's sister didn't get a chance to answer. Ahead of them, John himself spun around, the luminescent lines on his body blazing with fury.

GET BACK! His roar knocked his sister head-over-tail backward in the water. *I told you to get her into the city!*

The Master Shark hurtled toward them, growing larger every second. He was further away than Neridia had thought. She'd been deceived into thinking that he was nearly on top of them, just from how big he already looked.

Which meant...he was actually even bigger.

Please, John! Neridia pulled on the mate bond, desperate to get him to listen. *Not even you can fight that thing!*

His sister paddled upright again, matching John glare for glare. *I'm not leaving you. If you want to get your mate to safety, then you're going to have to come too!*

John snarled, but turned. To Neridia's relief, he started to swim, herding his sister before him.

Neridia flattened against John's sister's neck. The sea dragon's tail lashed through the water, fighting the drag of the dwindling air bubble. It was clear that she was tiring.

Neridia risked a backward glance. The Master Shark was catching up. His streamlined body was even more perfectly adapted for this environment than the sea dragons. He was close enough now that she could see his tiny, flat eyes. His jaws gaped wide enough to swallow the whole world.

Swim! John's teeth snapped at his sister's trailing fin. *For the sake of all the sea, SWIM!*

"JOHN!" Neridia shrieked as his fluid body doubled back on itself.

John flashed toward the Master Shark like a bolt of electric blue lightning, claws outstretched. The shark's triangular teeth clashed together like a portcullis descending, but John darted out of reach just in time. Fast as a snake, he whipped round, seeking to entangle the shark in his coils.

The Master Shark bucked like a bull trying to shake off a rider. John might match him in length, but the shark was at least five times his own mass. Even though the dragon clung on with every tooth and claw, he couldn't keep a secure grip on the writhing monster. His coiling tail slipped, coming within range of the shark's twisting mouth.

"No!" Neridia cried out, as the Master Shark's teeth cracked through John's scales, sinking deep into his flesh.

With a jerk, the shark flung the sea dragon aside. Without hesitation, John twisted round. Blood trailing behind him in a dark cloud, he threw himself straight into the shark's path again.

Her mate was going to get ripped to shreds.

Don't! Neridia aimed the thought at the Master Shark like a torpedo. *Please, stop! I'll surrender, I'll come with you, just don't hurt him!*

She had an odd sensation of her mental plea bouncing back unheard, as if she'd shouted at a brick wall. The shark didn't give any hint that he was even aware of her attempt to communicate. The sea dragon and the shark closed with each other again, and the sea turning red around them.

Do something, Neridia! John's sister pleaded. Despite her brother's command, she'd slowed again, clearly reluctant to leave him. *Fling him away on a tidal wave, command a whirlpool to swallow him, freeze the very blood in his veins! If you're the Empress, you have the power!*

"I don't, I'm not, I'm *not!*"

John tumbled out of the swirling cloud of blood again. This time, it took him a moment to right himself, his previously-fluid movements stiffened by pain. There were deep puncture wounds in his side, and one side of his tail-fin had been shredded. But despite his wounds, his scales glowed brighter than ever.

He wasn't going to give up. He'd fight for her to the last drop of blood in his body.

Neridia reached for him, praying to draw that indomitable will into her own frail soul. John's head jerked round, his eyes widening in surprise. She felt him reach back in return. Their souls met, joined, like clasping hands.

The mate bond blazed up between them, bright and fierce as John's markings. Neridia shook as if she'd stuck her fingers in an electric socket. She'd thought to draw strength from him...but instead he seemed to be taking it from her.

She knew how his pain was suddenly washed away, his strained muscles moving freely once more. She knew how the touch of her soul filled him with renewed resolve.

My mate, his voice whispered in her mind. And then, more strongly, *My mate!*

He swirled to face the Master Shark head-on, his great chest swelling. The shark lunged for him, maw gaping, but John didn't move.

Instead, opening his own jaws wide, he sang.

Neridia clapped her hands over her ears, deafened by the power of his voice. The music exploded outward like a shockwave, tumbling even the Master Shark's massive bulk backward in the water.

Neridia didn't understand the thundering melody, but in her soul she knew what John was saying:

This is my mate, mine, mine alone! You shall not take her!

The Master Shark was beaten back by the tearing maelstrom of notes. Every muscle in John's body was taut with effort of his song. Slowly, as if battling against some vast weight, he raised his front feet. His claws spread wide.

The sea parted.

At John's command, a deep chasm sliced through the ocean. From surface to sea bed, the water drew back, trapping the Master Shark on the opposite side of a dry, widening canyon.

Neridia trembled, and felt the sea dragon beneath her tremble as well. Half-seen across that impossible chasm of air, the Master Shark was just a dim, wavering silhouette.

Then the megalodon turned, and was gone.

CHAPTER 24

"I told you," the Knight-Commander said through gritted fangs, "to be discreet. If *that* is what you consider being discreet, then sea help us all if you ever take it into your head to be obvious."

Almost, John wished he was back facing the Master Shark. The megalodon's teeth were far less pointed than his superior's sarcasm. Fixing his eyes on a point somewhere above the Knight-Commander's scaled shoulder, he endured.

"I wanted you to bring your mate here quietly, without anyone noticing." The Knight-Commander swirled around the underwater audience chamber, his emerald eyes glowing with barely-contained anger. "And now all of Atlantis is in an uproar! Dragons are already composing poems about your poem! Everyone is agog to meet the female who inspired such a show of power! What in the sea possessed you?"

The harmonics made it clear it was a rhetorical question, so John held his tongue. Had his superior asked directly, he could have explained that it was not a matter of *what* had possessed him...but *who*.

It was her power, not mine. I merely provided the words to enact the Empress's will.

His neck-ruff raised slightly, despite his efforts to maintain an appropriately contrite and solemn expression. He still felt half-drunk from the incredible surge of her soul through his.

Oh, my mate, my heart, my Empress. In my arrogance I thought I understood your glory. Now I know I have barely begun to sound your depths.

The moment of connection had lasted only a brief moment, but it had been long enough for them to drive back the Master Shark. Now their souls were parted again, like their bodies.

The Knight-Commander had insisted that John report to him immediately, in the fortified ziggurat that housed the headquarters of the Order of the First Water. Neridia, meanwhile, had been taken to the golden towers of the Imperial Palace, as was only appropriate. With the increased distance between them, the mate bond had returned to its usual tenuous link.

John was not certain whether he was sorry or grateful for that. Experiencing her true power had been like swimming in the very sun itself.

"Are you smiling, Knight-Poet?" the Knight-Commander demanded.

John hastily flattened his neck-ruff again. "No, sir."

"Good, because there is nothing to smile about." The Knight-Commander paused, his own expression turning more thoughtful. "Except for the fact that the Master Shark did indeed attack you."

John blinked. "Sir?"

"Even though I cannot reveal the cause of his attack, I can still use it as leverage against him on the Sea Council." The Knight-Commander tilted his head at the unmistakable bite-wounds on John's flank. "It is good that you are clearly marked by his teeth. The Master Shark inexplicably flying into a murderous blood-frenzy, attacking the noble Walker-Above-Wave as he returned on a routine errand...yes, it is a story that the other Lords will find convincing. I will be able to oust the Master Shark from his seat on the Council at last."

"Would it not be simpler to tell the Sea Council the full truth?" John ventured. "They will learn it anyway, when the Empress-in-Waiting claims her rightful place."

The Knight-Commander gave him a long, penetrating look. "I am the Voice of the Emperor-in-Absence, Knight-Poet. I hold the safety of Atlantis in my claws. That means that I must plan for all eventualities. Including the possibility that your mate will not be able to take the Pearl Throne."

Despite himself, John's neck-ruff rippled again. "I assure you, sir, there is no risk of that."

The Knight-Commander blew out his breath, a trail of bubbles rising from his jaws. "That remains to be seen. She still has not shifted."

"I am confident that she will, sir. When she ascends the Pearl Throne, it will doubtless unlock her true form."

The Knight-Commander rumbled deep in his chest, still looking unconvinced. "We shall see. But not immediately. I must calm both the city and the Sea Council before flinging yet another shockwave at them."

John flexed his webbed feet, pushing himself off the mosaic floor. "As you command, sir. I shall ensure the Empress-in-Waiting remains out of sight."

"No," the Knight-Commander said firmly, blocking his path to the exit in the ceiling. "You shall keep *yourself* out of sight, Knight-Poet. If you go out into the city now, you will be mobbed."

"A crowd cannot tear words from my throat," John said, perhaps a shade too tartly. "I am capable of holding my silence, sir."

The Knight-Commander's eyes narrowed at his insolence. "I have seen no evidence of *that*, Knight-Poet. Need I remind you of your vow of obedience to me?"

John clenched his talons, fighting back the instincts that urged him to knock the other sea dragon aside and swim straight to his mate. "No, Knight-Commander. But-"

"Then you will remain here, in Order's headquarters, until you can show your scales again without causing a riot."

The Knight-Commander's harsh, forceful notes brooked no argument. Though his blood seethed at being separated from Neridia, John's honor prevented him from arguing further. He forced himself to bow his head respectfully.

The Knight-Commander's melody smoothed a little at the show of deference. "I sympathize with your impatience, Knight-Poet. But this is for the best. Your mate must stay in the air-locked parts of the city, and your own wounds will heal faster in salt water. Stay, rest, and you will be ready to resume your duties as her bodyguard all the sooner."

"May I ask who will guard the Empress-in-Waiting in my absence, sir?"

"You need not fear." The Knight-Commander flowed up toward the door. "I shall deal with her personally."

CHAPTER 25

Where's John?

Neridia leaned out the tower window, feeling rather like Rapunzel. She couldn't guess which of the distant, gleaming buildings far below currently housed her mate. There was no-one to ask, either. The two silent, towering knights who'd escorted them to the opulent tower top room had remained outside the door. When Neridia had tried the handle, she'd discovered that it was locked.

Still, if she couldn't get out, at least no one would be able to get in. Although the tower windows were glassless, the sheer golden walls would be impossible for even a ninja to climb.

No one could swim in, either. An enormous air bubble covered the building, from base to pointed spire. John's sister had told Neridia that this wing of the palace was used to house high-ranking whale and seal shifters who couldn't spend all their time underwater like the dragons and sharks could.

She was safe in Atlantis at last. But she didn't *feel* safe.

She hadn't forgotten the Master Shark's warning about an unknown, powerful enemy lurking in Atlantis. Although after the shark lord's attack on John, she was no longer quite so sure that he'd been telling the truth. If he really was on her side, surely he wouldn't have tried to kill her mate. Maybe the Master Shark *had* been behind the attacks on both her and her father after all.

But he'd sounded so sincere when he'd spoken of his oath-brother...

Neridia didn't know what to think. The only thing that she knew for certain was that she needed John at her side. He was the only person in Atlantis she could trust completely.

Well, nearly the only person.

"Look at this inlay!" John's sister ran an admiring hand over a intricate end table carved from coral and set with precious gems. "See how the slices of opal catch the light. And these mosaics! Have you ever seen such pearls?"

In human form, John's sister stood only a few inches shorter than Neridia herself. She wore the briefest of bikini tops and a short, green-and-blue patterned sarong, exposing the lush curves of her body without a hint of self-consciousness. Her long, braided hair was exactly the same deep indigo hue as her brother's.

Even though her coloring and features echoed John's, she couldn't have been more different from her sibling. Instead of John's solemn reserve, his sister bubbled over with enthusiasm and energy. She was in constant movement, practically dancing around the room as she tried to see everything at once.

"Oh, the palace is more splendid than I could have ever imagined." John's sister spun on the spot, arms opening as if she wanted to embrace the entire building. "I could spend all day just in this one room."

"Just as well," Neridia muttered. "Since it's looking like we're going to. We must have been here for hours."

Where's John? What's taking him so long?

Part of her wanted to reach for him down the mate bond...but she didn't dare. Not after what had happened last time.

He parted the whole sea.

The vast rush of energy between them had been as terrifying as a tsunami. Neridia was scared that if it happened again, she'd be swept away entirely.

She could still feel him somewhat, at the back of her mind. She knew that he wanted to come to her, but was prevented from doing so. Whatever the reason, he wasn't worried or angry about it. Still, his frustration and impatience vibrated down the mate bond, setting her own teeth on edge.

Neridia sighed, turning away from the window. "I wish John would get back. I don't see why he couldn't have reported to the Knight-Commander here."

"From what I've heard, the Knight-Commander hates wearing human form," John's sister replied absently, busy admiring the intricate mosaics covering the walls. "He only shifts for two reasons: duels, and talking to non-dragons. If he could, he'd probably spend all his time in the sea."

Neridia leaned back against the windowsill, though she really wanted to be pacing around the room. Seeking to distract herself from her irrational nerves, she asked, "Is that why you all speak English so well? You learn it in order to communicate with other types of shifter?"

John's sister nodded. "We cannot speak each other's languages in our true forms. A shark cannot sing like a whale, nor a dragon bark like a seal. And most shifters can only communicate telepathically with those of the same type. If we wish to speak to each other, we must do so in a human tongue."

"So do you have a human nickname, like John does?" Neridia asked hopefully. "He said I wouldn't be able to pronounce your real one, but it seems rude to keep thinking of you just as 'John's sister.'"

The sea dragon shrugged one shoulder. "My duties mean I don't have need to meet with other types of shifter all that often," she said, sounding a little regretful. "When I do, people just tend to refer to me by the literal translation of my name. Third Dancer of the Mirrored Void."

"Um," Neridia said, cautiously. "Is there a short form of that?"

Third Dancer of the Mirrored Void laughed. "That *is* the short form. My full name is rather longer." Her turquoise eyes brightened. "But you could give me an air name!"

"Me? Why me? Can't you just pick one for yourself?"

"Oh, no." The sea dragon looked shocked at the suggestion. "Names have to be given, not taken. And air-names can only be given by land-dwellers. I was terribly jealous of my little brother when he won his. Ever since I was a little hatchling listening to fairy tales, I always dreamed of walking the fantastical lands above the waves."

"Why didn't you?" Neridia asked.

"It is not permitted. The Sea Council says we can't risk too much interaction with the dry-landers, for fear of another Dragon War. Very few of us ever walk the land." She clasped her hands together, fixing Neridia with entreating eyes. "I never thought I'd have the chance to win an air name. Please, please give me one!"

"Well...okay." Neridia quailed at the thought of trying to come up with a name worthy of the strong, vibrant woman. "Um, do you have a preference?"

The sea dragon's forehead furrowed seriously. "I would like something that matches my brother's, so that everyone will be able to tell that we are family. Is there a female form of his name?"

"Jane Doe, I guess," Neridia said dubiously. "But I'm not sure it really-"

"Jane Doe," the sea dragon said, with great satisfaction. "How exotic. Yes. I shall be Jane."

Neridia rubbed her forehead, biting back a groan.

I just named a fifty-foot-long sea dragon Jane.

Oh well. At least she seems happy about it.

"I cannot wait to tell my little brother that I have my own air name now." Jane danced over to Neridia's side, peering out the window herself. She sighed. "Though I suppose I will have to wait awhile yet. No doubt all the knights of every Order will have their jaws full quelling *this* pandemonium."

Neridia stared from the sea dragon to the peaceful city below, and back again. "What pandemonium?"

Jane looked at her in surprise. "I am sorry, I didn't realize human eyesight was so much poorer than ours. Can you not make out the hordes thronging the Sun Plaza?"

Neridia followed the dragon's pointing finger. The air bubble surrounding the tower also covered a wide circular area just outside the palace gates, about the twice the area of a football pitch. There was no doubt that it was the Sun Plaza—thousands of golden tiles set into the gleaming white paving formed a huge circle with intricate, spiraling rays.

It was quite easy to make out the design, given that the vast space was mostly empty. There *were* quite a few scattered groups of people milling around, but it was hardly what she'd call a scene of pandemonium. The plaza could easily have accommodated a crowd ten times the size.

"You mean those people down there?" Neridia asked Jane, wondering if maybe she *was* missing something.

"Yes! Have you ever seen such a crowd? If there are this many in the Sun Plaza alone, most of the city must be out in the streets!"

Neridia did a quick head count and estimate, just in case she was being misled by the size of the plaza. But she still couldn't come up with more than a couple hundred people, at the very most.

She looked back at Jane. "You've lived in Atlantis all your life, right?"

"Yes. Many sea shifters prefer to reside in the deeps, saying that the city is much too crowded and busy for comfort, but I like being where everything happens."

"And…how many people live here?"

"Oh, a great many," Jane said earnestly. "Though most divide their time between the city and the open ocean. There are sometimes as many as three thousand people residing here!"

There were three thousand residents just in Neridia's tiny home village. Inverness, the nearest city, had *forty* thousand people, and she knew that Londoners considered it to be a rural backwater.

Neridia stared out at the crowded tiers of buildings dropping away to the distant sea floor. "There are only three thousand sea dragons in this *entire city*?"

Jane looked startled. "No, of course not. Most of the residents are other types of shifter, of course." She sighed. "We are not as numerous as we once were."

"Why not?"

"Not enough of us find true mates, these days. Unmated pairs can still attempt to breed, of course, but they tend to produce only one or two eggs at most." Her melodic voice hushed, as though speaking of something taboo. "And sometimes...sometimes the young are not even shifters."

Though Neridia wouldn't wish her own misfortune on anyone else, her heart still skipped a beat at the news that there were others like her. "Really? They can't turn into dragons either?"

Jane gave her an odd look. "No. They cannot turn into humans."

"Oh." Neridia frowned as something struck her. "You say that like it's a bad thing. But, if you don't mind me saying, I thought your people kind of looked down on humans."

Jane made a wry face. "Many do, I am sorry to say. There are those who would claim that we should have no connection to them. But even the staunchest traditionalists cannot escape the inconvenient fact that we are only fertile in human form. That is another reason why we keep parts of Atlantis under air."

"So you live in water, but have to breed in air? Like frogs, only backward?"

The sea dragon lifted an indigo eyebrow at her, a smile tugging at her full lips. "I suggest you don't say that in the hearing of one of our males. I am not sure they would take kindly to the comparison. But yes, that is essentially the case."

Neridia nodded as the problem became clear. "So those of you who can't shift…"

"Can never have young of their own. They are dead ends." Jane's turquoise eyes darkened with sorrow. "And so our people slowly dwindle."

"Hmm. Speaking as a conservationist, it sounds like your gene pool is too small."

Jane's forehead wrinkled. "You think that we should mate in pools?"

"No, I mean, your breeding population is too small to be viable. You need fresh blood."

"Ah, I understand now." Jane made a graceful, sinuous shrug. "I agree, but where is it to come from? Every sea dragon in the entire ocean is known and named. If we sing for our mate, and he does not answer, there is nothing we can do."

From the sad, minor key of her musical voice, Neridia was certain that Jane was speaking from personal experience. "Well, John found me on land. Maybe that's where you should be looking too."

Jane's eyes widened. "You—you think I too might have a human mate? Me?"

"Why not? John did. My father did. Why not you?"

"I might have a mate," Jane breathed, looking thunderstruck. "I might have a *mate*." She seized Neridia's hands, swinging her around in a dance of joy. "I might have a mate!"

"Don't get too excited," Neridia laughed, trying to keep up with the sea dragon's exuberance. "I have to warn you, finding him might not be easy. There are, um, a few more humans than there are sea dragons."

"I don't care if I have to spend *years* searching. For my mate, I would go anywhere, do anything—oh." Jane stopped dancing, as suddenly as she'd started. "But I won't have the chance. The Sea Council would never allow me to walk above the wave."

"They let John go, didn't he?"

"Yes, but that was a special case. The Knight-Commander sent him to investigate rumors of the lost Emperor. It was a matter of the utmost importance."

"Well, saving the species is of the utmost importance too," Neridia pointed out. Then she hesitated. "Though maybe I'm wrong. I'm not exactly a good advertisement for sea dragon-human cross-breeds."

Jane looked at her sidelong, biting her lip. Then her mouth firmed. "My brother is convinced that you will shift. Will *you* give me permission to look for my mate on land, when you become Empress?"

"Um. Sure, of course." Neridia's own mouth twisted. "But don't hold your breath on that one."

At Jane's blank expression, she realized that the expression probably didn't mean much to a creature with gills. But before she could explain what she meant, the door swung open.

Jane gasped, quickly dropping her gaze to the floor. "Honored Knight-Commander of the First Water, Voice of the Emperor-in-Absence."

The huge man in the doorway didn't even glance at the sea dragon woman. Neridia flinched as his gaze fixed on her. Even with his face hidden behind his elaborate dragon-faced helmet, she felt the intensity of that stare like a hot iron.

"You are the human?" His deep voice vibrated her bones.

Dry-mouthed, Neridia could only nod, silently. He was as tall as John, and seemed even more superhumanly massive thanks to his dazzling diamond-encrusted armor. The hilts of two swords protruded over his hulking shoulders. One had a pommel set with a fist-sized, pure white pearl; the other bore a pearl of deepest midnight.

The Knight-Commander studied her for a moment. Whatever he was thinking was hidden behind his jeweled helm.

He turned, gesturing with one gauntleted hand. "You will come with me."

CHAPTER 26

Wake up. John's inner human prodded him insistently. *Something's wrong.*

John lifted his head from his coils. He hadn't intended to doze, but the currents gently circulating through his sleeping-chamber had been too soothing for his weary body to resist. Shifter-fast healing required a great deal of energy.

Nonetheless, he shook himself, forcing his stiff body into a state of readiness. His wounds were already starting to close up. Blinking bleary eyes, he cast around for whatever had disturbed his inner human.

Nothing immediately seemed awry. Evening had fallen while he slept. The strip of sea visible through the small window-slit in the ceiling had darkened from brilliant turquoise to a deep indigo. The sleeping-chamber was dim and peaceful, lit only by the soft glow of a single uncovered light-pearl.

He flared his gills, tasting the water, but couldn't detect any sign of an intruder. He couldn't hear anything either. The thick stone walls of the Order's headquarters muffled all sounds of the city outside.

Perhaps it was the very silence that woke me? John wondered. He'd become accustomed to sleeping in human cities, after all, surrounded by their unending din. He suspected his instincts had become warped by his long stint on land.

No, his inner human insisted. *It's our mate. She called out to us. We have to go to her, now!*

John concentrated on the mate bond. It was pale and nebulous, as though Neridia was distracted, or veiling her thoughts from him. But surely if she was in any great distress, he would sense it.

Of course she isn't distressed. She is home at last, safe in the heart of the sea. What harm could come to her in Atlantis?

His inner human promptly filled his mind with a flurry of pointed, vivid images. Sharks hunting her through the streets at their Master's bidding. Assassins secreting poisoned sea urchin spines in her royal bed. Disdainful aristocrats making hurtful remarks. Feral moray eels. Deadly jellyfish. Fire.

"Fire?" John said out loud to himself. "Really?"

All right, so maybe that last one was a little far-fetched, his inner human grudgingly conceded. *But we can't just sit on our ass, blindly trusting that others will protect her in our place. She is* our *mate! We have to be at her side!*

John stirred uneasily, his own instincts in full agreement. But the Knight-Commander had ordered him to remain here. He was honor-bound to obey.

"She will be fine," he said, as much to reassure himself as his agitated human. "The Knight-Commander promised to guard her personally."

His inner human rolled its eyes. *And we all know what a kind, thoughtful, and sensitive person he* is. *And how much he loves humans. Yep, I see no way this could* possibly *go wrong.*

That was far too close to being a treasonous thought, let alone a dishonorable one. The Knight-Commander was the Voice of the Emperor-in-Absence. To criticize him was only one step removed from insulting the Pearl Throne itself.

John crushed his inner human back down into the depths of his mind, resolving not to listen to its baseless fears any further. Circling round a few times, he tried to make himself comfortable again.

But not even the gentle rocking of the sleeping-chamber currents could relax his taut muscles. A deep unease gnawed at his soul.

No matter how he tried to tell himself that his inner human was being ridiculous...he couldn't shake the feeling that Neridia was in danger.

CHAPTER 27

"Where are you taking me?" Neridia asked, yet again.

Just like all the other times, the Knight-Commander made no sign that he'd even heard her words. He strode on through the maze of corridors, never so much as glancing back to check that she was still following. Even with her long legs, Neridia was hard-pressed to keep up with him.

Despite his intimidating appearance, Neridia was starting to get annoyed.

"Look," she said, panting a little. "I know you don't like me, but there's no reason to be rude."

"I neither like nor dislike you," the Knight-Commander said, without looking around. "You are a human. I have no more of an opinion on you than I would have on the personality of a particular sea slug."

Neridia scowled at his muscled back. She stopped dead in the middle of the corridor, folding her arms. "Well, I don't like *you*. I'm not taking another step until you tell me where we're going."

She immediately regretted her unwise show of defiance. She couldn't help shrinking back as the towering sea dragon turned on his heel, his armored body dwarfing hers.

"We are going to find out for once and for all whether you are truly a sea dragon." His powerful shoulders shifted a little, the pearl pommels of the swords strapped across his back glinting in the light. "Or would you prefer for me to simply assume that you are not?"

Neridia gulped, wishing with all her heart that John was by her side. "How—how are you planning to find out if I can shift?"

His foot tapped on the mosaic floor. "If you stop wasting time asking pointless questions, you'll find out."

Every instinct screamed at Neridia to turn back, to run and find her mate...but even if she knew where he was, she'd be caught before she went two steps. The Knight-Commander was fully capable of flinging her over his shoulder like a sack of potatoes, and she had a nasty suspicion that he wouldn't think twice about doing so if she didn't obey him.

The Master Shark's cold grey eyes and warning words rose from her memory. *You must not go to Atlantis,* he'd said. *A powerful enemy awaits you there.*

Neridia stared up at the diamond-covered, dragon-faced helmet sneering down at her, and wondered if she was face to face with her true enemy at last.

John, John, where are you?

"Your mate is recovering from his wounds," the Knight-Commander said, as if he'd read her mind. "He was gravely injured, in *your* defense. If you want him to recover, you must not disturb his healing trance."

When she still hesitated, the Knight-Commander heaved an irritated sigh. "You don't need to look at me like that, human. I am not going to eat you. I give you my word, all I am trying to do is discover whether you are capable of claiming your birthright. There is one final test that will settle the matter for once and for all."

The Knight-Commander might be rude, but he was still a knight, sworn to the same vows as John. From what she knew of sea dragon honor, Neridia couldn't believe that any knight would tell a flat-out lie.

It can't be him. He didn't want me to come to Atlantis at all, until John forced his hand. And anyway, it wouldn't make sense. He can't have been responsible for my father's assassination. He would hardly have sent John up onto land to search for the missing Emperor if he knew that he was already dead.

Neridia squared her shoulders, squashing down her instinctive fear of the intimidating warrior. "Okay then. If this will determine whether I can shift...I'll come."

"I did not require your agreement, or your permission." The Knight-Commander turned away again. "Keep up. And stop broadcasting that irritating whimper. You will disturb your mate."

Guiltily, Neridia withdrew from the mate bond. The Knight-Commander was right. If John thought she was in trouble, he'd race to her side even if he had to do so on four broken legs. She couldn't let him sense her irrational bad feeling.

The Knight-Commander led her deeper into the palace complex, the corridors becoming ever grander. They were still in air rather than underwater, but the architecture had definitely been designed with dragons in mind. Even John could have walked down the grand, arched passageways without having to dip his horned head.

Yet despite the ornate stonework and lavish mosaics, there was a sense of mustiness in the air. There was no dust, but Neridia had a feeling that this part of the palace hadn't been used for many years. Maybe even decades.

Maybe not since my father left the sea...

A huge, closed door blocked the way ahead. It was formed from carved planks of coral—Neridia hadn't seen a single thing made from wood in the entire city so far—inset with gold in curling, abstract wave patterns. A single massive pearl the size of Neridia's head shone from the exact center.

"The first test." The Knight-Commander gestured at the door, light glittering from his diamond-encrusted gauntlets. "Only those of royal blood can open the way."

There was no sign of a lock or keyhole. Tentatively, Neridia put her hand flat against the carved coral surface, pushing. She might as well have tried to open solid stone.

She glanced at the Knight-Commander, but the visor of his dragon-faced helmet just stared back at her impassively. It was clear he wasn't going to give her any hints.

This is the Pearl Door, her inner voice whispered. *And we are the Pearl Empress.*

Neridia looked up at the huge pearl inset into the door. She stretched up on her toes, straining her arm as far as she could. Even with her height, she could only just reach it.

The moment her fingertips brushed the smooth surface, the pearl lit up with a soft, silvery glow. Neridia nearly fell flat on her face as the door swung inward under her hand, dividing in half. Without a sound, it opened.

Behind her, the Knight-Commander said something...but Neridia wasn't listening. All of her attention was fixed on the Pearl Throne.

There was no mistaking it. Though the audience chamber was vast enough to hold a hundred dragons, the Throne still dominated the room. It stood eight feet above the floor, on a plinth formed from seven concentric circles that echoed the seven tiers of Atlantis itself. The edges of the circles were etched with images of the city. The lowest three tiers were carved from coral; the next three were gleaming silver; and the top dais, supporting the Throne itself, was pure gold.

And the Throne, oh, the Throne...

The Pearl Throne rose from the dais like a cresting wave. It was unmistakably designed for a shifter. A human could sit in the heart of the wave, shadowed by the great curving canopy, or a dragon could curl around the flowing form, resting its head and forefeet on the top. In either form, whoever sat on that throne would command utter respect.

It shone like the full moon at midnight. It couldn't possibly have been carved from a single pearl—not unless the oyster had been the size of a whale—but the smooth iridescent surface was utterly flawless, without hint of join or crack.

Though on first glance it appeared perfectly white, as she drew closer she began to see the secret, shifting hues gleaming where the light struck the polished curves. All the colors of the ocean lay hidden in those translucent depths. The warm turquoise of a tropical lagoon and the dark indigo of ice-covered seas; the golden glitter of sunlight on the surface and the electric green flash of phosphorescence in the deepest abyss.

Our Throne! her inner voice sang out, like a whole orchestra playing a single bone-shaking note of triumph. *At last, at last, our Throne!*

"Are you going to stand and gape like a codfish all day?" Neridia stumbled as the Knight-Commander's shoved her roughly forward. "Go on. Sit."

Neridia had been so mesmerized by the sight of the Pearl Throne, she'd entirely forgotten what they were here to do. Now all her doubts and fears came rushing back like a tsunami. How could *she* possibly plant her fat backside on that gleaming treasure?

It is ours, ours by birth and blood, her inner voice insisted. *Claim it!*

"I-I'm not ready," she stuttered. "I need more time."

The Knight-Commander made an impatient sound under his breath. Seizing her wrist, he started dragging her up the dais.

"No! I'm not ready, not yet!" Neridia twisted futilely, his steel gauntlet biting into her skin.

"You claim to be the Empress-in-Waiting?" he snarled. "Then prove it. This is the Pearl Throne, the seat of the Empire, the very heart of the sea! If you have a drop of power in your body, then this will call it out."

"Please, let's wait until John's better," she begged. "I can't do this without him. And he'd want to be here."

"I cannot allow the Knight-Poet to witness this moment." Unceremoniously, the Knight-Commander dumped her onto the human-sized seat. "Now. Show me if you are truly a dragon."

Instinctively, Neridia cringed back from the cold touch of the gleaming Throne. Surely she would be struck by lightning for daring to defile it with her mere human presence. She expected it to crack in half under her weight, for an earthquake to shake the palace, for Atlantis itself to come crashing down…

Instead, nothing happened.

Cautiously, Neridia uncurled. Now that she was sitting on it, she could feel the shallow depression worn into the ancient seat by long-dead Emperors and Empresses. Her hands rested where their hands had rested; her curves fit perfectly into the Throne's, as though it had been carved for her personally.

And yet still, nothing happened.

No great rush of power; no dragon surging up from her soul. Just the hard Throne underneath her, slowly warming with her own body heat.

She had failed.

Her head jerked up at a loud, repeated metallic crash. The Knight-Commander was clapping, slowly and ironically.

"Well done," he said. "Very well done indeed. You are absolutely, unmistakably, and utterly human. Nothing more."

Dismay fought with relief in her heart. "So I'm not the Empress-in-Waiting?"

"Absolutely not." To her astonishment, he went down on one knee. "You are the Empress."

Neridia stared at him. Despite his posture, he didn't look at all humbled. Every line of his body shouted triumph.

"I shall back your claim personally." The Knight-Commander rose again, looming over her even though she sat on the Throne. "With the Master Shark gone, no one on the Sea Council will dare oppose me. We shall announce the good news to the whole city tomorrow. Though we should delay the coronation and your formal presentation until I have coached you—"

"Why?" Neridia interrupted.

She couldn't see his eyes through the narrow slits in his helmet, but she was certain that he was shooting her a withering glare. "So that you don't make an utter flounder of yourself in front of the entire city. We must convince them that you are appropriately Imperial, regardless of the fact that you cannot shift. The Crown Jewels will help, of course, but I must teach you how to comport yourself appropriately."

"No, I mean, why are you helping me?" Neridia was half-certain this was all some elaborate trick, that he was just toying with her like a cat with a mouse. "I'm human! You can't possibly want a human Empress."

"On the contrary, a human Empress is *precisely* what I want." His chest swelled with triumph. "A helpless human Empress, unable to wield the sea's power. Unable to wield *any* power."

"You want a puppet," Neridia whispered.

"Come now. Let us put it more politely. A ceremonial figurehead to appease the sentimental masses who are still enamored by royalty. The one thing I needed to make my rule here absolute. You will sit on the Throne, but *I* will stand behind it."

Neridia sat frozen, mute with shock. She wanted to protest, to say that she would defy him, that he couldn't force her to do his bidding... but they both knew that he could. He was the most powerful shifter in Atlantis.

And she was only human.

His deep chuckle echoed around the vast audience chamber. "Ironic, really. All that time and effort I wasted on ploys to keep you from reaching the Throne, when all along I had nothing to fear."

Neridia gasped, his words hitting her like ice water in the face. "It *was* you! You sent the assassins after me! You've been my enemy, all along!"

"What a terrible accusation." The Knight-Commander chuckled again, not sounding the slightest bit alarmed. "I would have to challenge you to a duel, should you repeat it in public."

"I don't care!" Neridia pushed herself up from the Throne, anger driving away her previous paralysis. "Did you order the assassination of my father too? How far back does your treachery go?"

The Knight-Commander's shoulders bunched under his armor, his air of amusement falling away. "I am no traitor," he spat. "Everything I have done, I have done for the good of the Empire. Atlantis needs a strong leader. Honor dictates that I must do whatever it takes to ensure that it has one."

"You *did* kill him," Neridia breathed. Her fists clenched. "You can threaten me all you want. I'm going to tell everyone what you did!"

He took one swift, angry step toward her, his armored body crowding against hers. She cried out as he seized her chin in one gauntleted hand, forcing her up onto her toes.

"If you do," he hissed, right into her face, "then I *will* challenge you. I will demand a duel, as is our custom, to settle the slight to my honor. Who do you think will be your Champion?"

"John," she spat back, as best she could around his crushing grip. "John will believe me. He'll call you out."

This close, she could see his shadowed eyes. She could make out the cruel curve of his mouth underneath his helmet.

She could see him smile.

"Yes," he said softly. "The Knight-Poet would be your Champion. He is young and raw, so lacking in accomplishment that he still considers *Firefighter* to be a name worthy of pride. I am the Knight-Commander, Voice of the Emperor-in-Absence, First Seer of the Water's Eye, and no-one has ever come close to defeating me in a duel. How long do you think *he* would last?"

He released her, casting her back down onto the Throne as carelessly as if tossing a too-small fish back into the sea. "I admit, he has potential. He is the only knight other than myself to have skill in the magical arts. I sent him on his fool's quest in order to ensure he would not become a rival in the future. He was supposed to perish quietly and conveniently in some blaze or accident. It never crossed my mind that he would *find* something, for I did not learn of your existence until you removed that infernal pearl of hiding. No matter. As he is now, he is no match for me. I would cut him to ribbons and feed him to the sharks."

Neridia huddled on the Throne, her defiance melting away in the face of his utter confidence.

I can't tell John. If he knew, he'd challenge the Knight-Commander, no matter what the odds.

And the Knight-Commander would kill him.

"That's better," the Knight-Commander said. She didn't know if he was reading her body language or her mind. "Your life here can be quite comfortable, if you submit to my will. You may live as an Empress, with every jewel and luxury your heart could desire, free from the trouble of decision-making and responsibilities. You may have the Knight-Poet at your side, as long as you do not trouble him with the details of our arrangement."

The huge, dragon-sized hall closed around her like a cage. She was acutely aware of the unseen weight of water above her head. The air was stale and thick in her lungs.

"You may even have children," the Knight-Commander continued, uncaring of her distress. "In fact, I insist upon it. Together we will found a dynasty—oh, not like *that*," he'd caught her gasp of horror, and his own tone twisted. "What a revolting thought. I could never debase myself with a human. But I am certain the Knight-Poet will oblige."

John, John! With her entire soul, she wanted to cry out to him, to call him to her side.

But that would be to pull him into certain death. She clenched her fists, her fingernails digging into her palms. She made herself breathe slowly and deeply, forcing down her panic. She couldn't, she *wouldn't* let her mate sense her fear.

"Your children will not be of my blood, of course, but they will be mine nonetheless. I will raise them to carry on my work. We will cut all ties with dry-landers, so that our noble people are no longer tainted by their filthy dirt." The Knight-Commander's voice softened. "We will make Atlantis great again. Future generations will revere me as the founder of a new Golden Age."

He fell silent, gazing into space at some glorious vision that only he could see. Neridia gripped the armrest of the Throne for support. She closed her other hand around her father's pearl pendant.

She prayed for his strength. More than she ever had before in her life, she needed it now.

Her pearl warmed against her skin…and so did the Pearl Throne. Her fingers fit so perfectly into the grooves worn by past Emperors, it felt as if her ancestors were holding her hand.

A sense of calm spread through her. It was like the comfort she usually took from her pearl, but magnified a hundredfold. The strength of generations of Imperial dragons filled her, lending her their courage.

She knew that she could do what she had to do.

"You said I could live like an Empress, if I obeyed you," she said. She was careful to keep her eyes downcast, fixing her gaze on the Knight-Commander's glittering boots as if she was too scared to look him in the eye. "I know I can't bring friends from the surface here, but can John's sister stay with me? I like her."

The Knight-Commander started a little, interrupted from his contemplation of immortal glory. "Why should I care who you pick for your ladies-in-waiting? You may form your retinue as you please. I'll have her attend you in your chambers. The Knight-Poet, too."

Neridia's heart thumped against her ribs. "I thought you said he needed to rest in order to recover."

"Did I? Well, I'm certain he's better now." The Knight-Commander gave her a long, assessing stare, his eyes hidden behind his helmet. "I will send him to you. Consider it a test of your obedience and discretion. And remember what will happen to him if you fail, and he uncovers the truth."

Neridia nodded silently. Her hand tightened on her father's pearl.

I can do this.

I have to.

"I can see we're going to get along very nicely." The Knight-Commander tossed her a mocking salute. "My Empress."

CHAPTER 28

"Oh, my mate, my heart." John went to one knee in the doorway, but couldn't tear his eyes away from her long enough to bow his head as etiquette demanded. "I am overjoyed to see you properly honored at last."

Finally, she was surrounded by the luxury she deserved. The Imperial apartments had obviously been hastily re-opened and prepared for her; only a few pieces of furniture had as yet been recovered from storage and returned to their proper places. But the lapis lazuli and turquoise floor was mirror-bright from frantic polishing, and embroidered drapes of the finest cerulean silk had been hung over the carved coral bed. Fresh light-pearls had been fitted into the wall sconces, casting out the gentle silver radiance of the full moon.

Amidst all this splendor, Neridia herself shone like a black pearl in an exquisite jewelry box. She'd changed out of her bedraggled human garments into a soft, simple robe, the white silk flowing over her curves like water. Bands of tiny seed-pearls formed intricate designs of curling waves around the neckline and hem.

Sat at the gilded vanity table, straight-backed, hands folded in her lap, she looked every inch the Empress she was. Beautiful. Composed. Regal.

Remote, his inner human muttered uneasily.

His human was right. She was breathtaking, but it was a distant sort of beauty, like the moon behind clouds. No matter how he reached out to her down the mate bond, she slipped through his fingers, untouchable as fog.

"Something is bothering you," he said, concerned. "What is it? What has happened?"

Neridia didn't look at him. Given that she was contemplating a selection of the Crown Jewels, set out on the vanity table for her pleasure, John could hardly blame her preoccupation. Still, his unease grew.

He mentally shook himself, chastising himself for his own arrogance. *Of course I cannot presume to be so familiar with her anymore. Not now that she has claimed her rightful place at last.*

The Knight-Commander had told him the good news personally. Neridia had been able to enter the Throne room, and the Pearl Throne itself had responded to her touch. True, she still had not yet shifted, but now even the Knight-Commander could not deny that she was indeed the rightful Empress.

Even now, the Knight-Commander was in conclave with the Sea Council. John had no doubt that his superior would be able to persuade the other sea lords to accept Neridia as the heir to the Throne. Soon, all of Atlantis would echo with songs of rejoicing.

She is the Pearl Empress. And now...now she truly understands what that means.

John forced himself to fix his gaze to the floor as her station demanded. "My Empress–"

"Don't call me that."

John's head jerked up in surprise at the bitter note in her voice. She'd picked up the crown of the Empress-in-Waiting. She turned the heavy gold circlet round in her hands, as though examining the pearls and sapphires that adorned it. Still, John had a strange certainty that she wasn't even seeing the wondrous gems.

Abandoning formality, John rose. A little stiff from his half-healed wounds, he crossed the room to her side. She still didn't look up at him.

"My mate." John crouched again—not in any sort of formal bow, just in order to put their faces level with each other. "Please tell me what is wrong."

Neridia let out her breath, carefully putting the crown back down onto the vanity unit. "John, if I told you that someone had…if I told you that someone had upset me, what would you do?"

"Someone has upset you?" John's hand instinctively flew to his sword-hilt. "Who? Who has dared to insult you?"

Neridia's hand covered his, stopping him from drawing the blade. "It's just a hypothetical question. If someone insulted me, you'd challenge them to a duel, right?"

"Of course," John said, rather confused. "How could you doubt it? Has someone been insulting *my* honor, by implying otherwise?"

Neridia's mouth twisted a little. "No. Quite the reverse. Someone told me that you'd be my champion even if you knew that you couldn't win. Even if it was absolutely certain that your opponent was a better swordsman than you."

"Yes," he said, taking her hands. "I swear on my honor, I will always fight for you."

She met his eyes at last. "What if I asked you not to?"

"You may command anything of me." He held her gaze steadily. "Except to ask me to leave you in pain. If someone caused you distress, I would challenge them. No matter who they were, or what the odds. In this one thing, my Empress, you cannot command me."

Her shoulders dropped in a long sigh. "That's what I thought."

"I assure you, I will do everything in my power to ensure that an unfortunate situation does not occur." Her hands were cold. He wrapped his fingers around hers, trying to warm them. "I am your weapon, my mate. I take that duty seriously. It is my responsibility to ensure that I am fit to meet any threat. Now, will you tell me why you are suddenly so troubled by the thought of duels?"

Neridia shook her head. "It doesn't matter. Just something that came up today when I was talking to someone. I wanted to make sure I understood your customs correctly."

He ran his hands lightly up her bare forearms. "I know how overwhelming it is to be immersed in a strange new place. But remember that you are not alone. I am here, at your side, always."

He thought he saw tears start to well in her eyes—but before he could be sure, she'd leaned forward, pressing her mouth to his. There was something desperate about her kiss, as if she wasn't really certain he was truly there.

He returned her frantic caress more gently, his mouth steady under hers. He claimed her lips, her tongue, making her slow down. Cupping her face, he turned the kiss more lingering, his lips moving against hers in silent promise.

I am here, my mate. I will always be here.

He gathered her close in his arms, so that she would be able to feel his solid strength encircling her. With long, gentle caresses, he soothed the tension in her spine and shoulders. Wordlessly, he showed her that she could lean on him. She could rely on him.

With a sigh, she relaxed against his chest at last. Her own hand explored the edges of his shoulder pauldrons, where leather straps held the gleaming armor tight against his body.

"I've still never seen you naked," she murmured against his mouth. "Not properly."

He nipped lightly at her lower lip. "Shall I take that as an Imperial command?"

She smiled, but his attempted playfulness sparked no answering merriment in her eyes. She still looked so solemn, as if they were performing some momentous ritual.

I suppose it is, for that matter. Her first night in Atlantis.

John fervently vowed to make it a memorable one.

With one last kiss, he drew back from her. More slowly than was strictly necessary, he worked free the buckles securing his pauldrons. To his satisfaction, Neridia's eyes went wide and dark as he shrugged off the heavy plates.

Equally unhurriedly, he unfastened his vambraces, sliding them down off his forearms. He stripped away the wrappings beneath, unwinding the soft leather strips with languid, teasing movements.

Then he hesitated.

"Don't stop there." Neridia's voice trembled with desire.

"I will not, I promise." Candor compelled him to admit, "I was merely trying to work out a dignified way of removing my boots."

That won him a true smile at last, though it was brief and fleeting. "At this point, I'll take speed over spectacle. Take them off, John."

He obeyed, though as he had feared it was not entirely a graceful process. Still, Neridia did not seem to mind. He could sense her heat rising through the mate bond.

He was already so painfully erect, it was a relief to finally unfasten his trousers. Neridia's soft gasp as he revealed himself was so delicious, it was all he could do to keep his movements unhurried. He clenched his jaw, forcing himself not to rush.

"Now," he said huskily, when he stood before her naked at last. "It is your turn."

Her beautiful full lips were moist and parted, and he knew that the hidden folds were equally flushed. Nonetheless, she shook her head.

"Not yet." She rose from her chair, stepping close. "Let me look at you first. Just once, I want to look at you."

Distantly, it crossed his mind that this was a rather strange thing for her to say—but then she ran her hand across his chest, and all thought was consumed in the fire of her touch. It took all of his discipline not to push her up against the gleaming wall then and there.

Control, control! He knotted his fists, forcing himself to hold still as she circled him. Her fingertips ran down his side, over his hip, up the broad curve of his back. She explored him with an exquisitely agonizing slowness, as if seeking to memorize every inch of his body.

He caught her wrist as she ventured lower. "Even a Knight's discipline is not *that* good, my mate. If you do not wish this to speed up somewhat…"

In answer, she kissed him, her hand closing around his hard length. He groaned into her mouth as she stroked him. There was no longer any possibility of restraint.

Never breaking the kiss, he unfastened the ties of her robe, jerking the fabric down off her body impatiently. At last, at last her exquisite curves were fully exposed to him. He buried himself in them, pressing his whole body against her, wanting to possess and claim every glorious inch.

Neridia's hand stilled. She pulled back from his mouth, far enough that she could look into his eyes. Her own were dark with desire, yet still they held that strange solemnity.

"I want this to be special for you," she said, as if it could ever be anything else. "I want—I want this to be a night that you remember, always. Is there anything I could do? Something you'd particularly like?"

You, was his immediate thought…but the gravity of her manner made him pause. Pulling back a little himself, he forced himself to give the matter more serious consideration.

Not that he had to think for more than a second.

"There is something. And since the means are at hand…" He gestured at the vanity unit, and the glittering treasures arrayed there. "I would very much like to adorn you. I would like to see you properly crowned."

Something flashed across her eyes, too fast for him to interpret. His sense of her down the mate bond weakened, as if she'd retreated into a shell.

"Not that," she said. She glanced at the waiting crown, and a shiver shook her. "I'm sorry. Anything else, but not that."

On second thought, he supposed it wouldn't be entirely proper to use the Crown Jewels in such a fashion. A pity. Perhaps another evening they could pay a private visit to the Imperial hoard…

"Then I will make a different request." Gently, he drew her over to the vast bed, laying her down on the silken sheets. "I want to take *my* time."

And he did.

With his mouth, his hands, his body, he treasured her. He could spend a lifetime exploring her depths, and never grow tired of her wonders.

When she was undone by pleasure, crying out his name in need, he could hold himself back no longer. She welcomed him in like the sea itself, closing around him as strong and sweet as the tides.

At last he was truly home…and so, he thought, was she.

But in the morning she was gone.

CHAPTER 29

Neridia clung to Jane's branching horns, salt spray whipping her face. They'd discovered that it was quicker for the sea dragon to swim along the surface rather than dragging an air bubble under the water. Faster than any ship, they raced across the ocean.

Neridia could only pray that it would be fast enough.

Jane's rhythm faltered, and Neridia felt a shiver pass through the sea dragon's scaled skin. "What is it?" Neridia shouted into Jane's ear.

The Knights of the First Water are singing to each other behind us. Jane picked up her pace again. *They have discovered your departure. They're coming after us.*

"Do they know where we are?"

They're led by the Knight-Commander himself. Fear colored Jane's mental tone. *He is the most powerful Seer in generations. The entire ocean is his eye.*

Neridia touched her pearl pendant, wishing with all her heart that she had the Master Shark's one as well. She was hidden from the Knight-Commander's magical gaze, but Jane wasn't.

She'd hoped that it would take the Knight-Commander longer to work out who had to be accompanying her. But it seemed that hope was futile. Now, their only chance lay in their head start.

Neridia shaded her eyes against the wind, scanning the horizon. The sea stretched out in every direction, featureless and empty. She couldn't see any hint of land yet.

"How much further?" she asked Jane.

The currents are in our favor, but it's a long swim yet until we reach the shore. Jane's powerful finned tail churned the water behind them to froth, her head weaving through the waves. *You are certain we can find help in the human city of Brighton?*

Fire Commander Ash's calm, powerful eyes flashed through her mind. If anyone could stand against the Knight-Commander, it would be the Phoenix.

"John's friends will help us," she said to Jane. "John asked them to protect me, when he couldn't. If we can only get there-"

She broke off, nearly unseated as Jane shied like a skittish horse. The reason was immediately apparent. A vast, triangular fin broke through the sea's surface in front of them, rising higher than a yacht's sail.

"Master Shark," Neridia breathed.

The fin's shadow swept over them as the shark circled. Neridia felt Jane tremble beneath her. The megalodon's half-seen bulk under the water dwarfed the female sea dragon.

Neridia patted Jane's scales, trying to project a confidence that she didn't entirely feel herself. "It's all right. He's on our side."

I hope, she added silently to herself, as the megalodon rose alongside the sea dragon. He rolled a little in the water, staring up at her. His eye looked tiny in proportion to his vast jaw...yet it was still bigger than Neridia's entire head.

Neridia met that cold grey gaze. "You were right," she said, hoping that the shark could hear her. "It was the Knight-Commander. He's the one who had my father assassinated. He wanted me dead too, until he realized I don't have any power to threaten him. Now he wants to use me as his puppet."

The megalodon's jaw worked, exposing triple rows of serrated teeth. Each one was longer than Neridia's forearm.

Jane sang an urgent, agonized chord as the megalodon started to sink out of sight again. *Neridia, my brother swims at the Knight-Commander's side!*

"Wait!" Neridia yelled. To her relief, the shark paused, looking back up at her.

"John doesn't know any of this." Her voice shook, despite her best effort to control it. "I couldn't tell him. He's innocent. Please, whatever you do, don't hurt him."

Without making any response, the megalodon disappeared beneath the sea. Neridia could just make out a ripple cutting against waves, arrowing back the way they'd came.

He is calling his people, Jane reported, her mental tone uneasy. *I can feel the sharks rising to follow him...Neridia, he is calling them to war. Will my brother truly be safe?*

"He'll be safer than if he knew the truth." Neridia wound her hands into the sea dragon's mane again, flattening herself against the indigo scales. "Swim."

CHAPTER 30

"Oh, the sea will sing of this day!" The Knight-Commander was a blaze of green and gold in the water, his eyes alight with battle-rage. "Destroy the traitors utterly, my knights! Let this be the hour that the sharks are finally hurled back into the abyss, outcast from the Empire for once and for all!"

The Knights of the First Water roared back their approval, the entire ocean trembling with their gathered wrath. Sea dragons met sharks, upraised claws matched against tearing teeth. Scales of every hue flashed in brilliant contrast to the sharks' dull greys.

Amidst the sea-shaking thunder of battle-song, John was the only silent voice. Though his fellow knights were filled with the righteous delight of testing their strength against worthy opponents, he could not join in their chorus of joy. He had no heart for it.

His heart was gone, fled across the sea.

Why, my mate, my Empress, why? He called out for her down the mate bond, but only silence met his anguished plea. *Why do you run? What do you fear? Why do you not trust me to help you?*

He had told her that he would face any danger for her, confront any challenge. He had thought that she had believed him. And yet still she had fled. She had thought his *little sister* a more worthy protector than him.

Oh my mate, my heart, have I failed you so badly?

There was only one thing he could do. He would follow her, and find her, and win back her trust. Whatever it was that she feared, he would show her that he was strong enough to face it with her.

John extended his claws, his markings glowing with new resolve. He dove at the nearest swirl of combat. He would fight his way to his mate's side, even if it meant swimming through an ocean of blood.

A dozen sharks scattered at his charge, abandoning the knight that they had been harassing. John was surprised by the pack's cowardice. A single shark was no match for a sea dragon, but in numbers the sharks' superior speed and maneuverability made them deadly foes. It was not like them to retreat from confrontation so readily.

"My thanks, Knight-Poet," his fellow knight sang. Despite his wounds, he laughed, bloodlust lighting his eyes. "It seems even the sharks have heard of your great poem! See how they fear your power!"

John left him to pursue the fleeing sharks, turning instead to help another knight who was beset by foes. As before, the sharks immediately broke off at his approach. No matter how he chased them, they refused to turn and give fight.

This is very odd.

John curved his body in an arc, bringing himself to a halt. His futile pursuit had brought him close to the surface. Hovering in the water like a hawk in the sky, he surveyed the battle below.

He was the only knight not engaged in bitter combat. Every other sea dragon was mobbed by sharks, wheeling and darting around them. So far, the sea dragons' superior discipline was holding the sharks at bay, but more were arriving by the minute.

Now's our chance! his inner human urged. *Go, while everyone else is busy! Run to our mate!*

John hesitated, torn. Honor demanded that he fight alongside his brother-knights until the foe was vanquished...but his inner human had a point. What if this attack was but a diversionary tactic? What if even now, another force of sharks was hunting down the Empress-in-Waiting?

Below, the vast shape of the Master Shark loomed out of the depths. Jaws agape, he hurtled straight up toward the Knight-Commander, who was preoccupied fighting a pack of great whites.

Without thought, John dove down to defend his superior. There was no time for subtlety or poetry now. Claws extended, he flashed past the Knight-Commander, ready to meet the Master Shark head-on.

The megalodon saw him coming...and the great maw snapped closed. The shark turned, aborting its attack. John was so startled, he aborted his as well, fanning out his webbed feet to halt his dive.

The megalodon circled away, one cold eye fixed on him. With a sharp movement of its tail, it sought to rush past him, but John blocked its path to the Knight-Commander with his own body.

"Brethren!" he sang, keeping his claws raised and ready. "Defend the Knight-Commander!"

Three knights sang back in answer, flashing through the water towards them. The Master Shark turned to meet their charge, jaws opening once again. The megalodon seemed to have no hesitation about attacking *these* challengers.

John gathered himself to join the assault—but found his own way blocked by a green-and-gold finned tail.

"Wait," the Knight-Commander said, eyes narrowing. Thin ribbons of blood spiraled around his reddened claws, slowly dispersing. "Did the Master Shark just *flee* from you?"

"I cannot explain it, sir. No shark seems willing to face me. A brother-knight suggested that perhaps they fear that I might part the sea again."

"Perhaps," the Knight-Commander said slowly, harmonies of doubt clear in his tone. His assessing gaze flicked from John to the battling Master Shark, and back again. His song turned more thoughtful. "Or perhaps they have been ordered to turn aside from you..."

John rippled his length in a shrug, dismissing the mystery. There were more urgent matters at hand now. "Sir, we must not lose sight of our greater purpose here. Where is the Empress-in-Waiting? Is she too in danger of ambush?"

The Knight-Commander hesitated, turning his head to stare into an empty patch of water. The green glow of his eyes turned to pure, brilliant gold. John knew that he was using his powers as a Seer to scry out Neridia's location.

The Knight-Commander blinked, his eyes returning to their normal hue. "I can still see your sister, although her rider is hidden from my sight. There are no sharks near them. You need not fear for your mate, Knight-Poet."

"Nonetheless, sir, I must go to her," John said, in a stern melody that bordered on being an outright command. "I must stop her from this inexplicable, disastrous flight. I swear that I will do whatever it takes to bring her home."

The Knight-Commander stared at him for a long moment, a still point in the maelstrom of battle raging all around. John had the distinct impression that his superior was engaged in furious mental calculation.

"You are quite correct, Knight-Poet," he said, his tone still thoughtful. "We must not lose sight of our true purpose."

John let out his breath in relief, bubbles trickling from his nostrils. "Then I have your permission to quit the field of battle, sir?"

"We shall *both* go." The Knight-Commander swirled, heading for the open sea. "Come, Knight-Poet. And stay close by my side."

CHAPTER 31

They are right behind us! Jane's mental voice came in panting gasps, matching her labored breathing. *Neridia, it's the Knight-Commander and my brother! They'll be within sight of us any second now!*

"Just a little further!" Neridia shouted back. "Look! There's land!"

The south coast of England was a dark smudge on the horizon. Despite Jane's obvious exhaustion, the sight seemed to hearten the sea dragon. She redoubled her efforts, fairly flying over the sea.

Neridia could make out the lights of Brighton now, glittering through the twilight like stars that had fallen to earth. Neridia fixed her eyes on the rapidly-approaching city, her heart rising. They were so close now…they were going to make it…

Jane shrieked like a hundred off-key flutes, recoiling from the sea as if the water was suddenly burning hot. Or, as Neridia discovered as spray dashed against her legs, burning *cold*. Between one breath and the next, the sea had turned icy.

Literally icy.

Neridia swallowed freezing sea water as Jane frantically back-finned away from an iceberg that hadn't been there a second ago. Spluttering and coughing, Neridia gaped as the sheet of ice grew thicker right before their eyes. It raced out to either side of them, forming a wide crescent blocking their path.

"How-?" Neridia began—but even as she spoke, she already knew the answer.

There is ice in my brother's heart. Jane paddled back to the white wall, which loomed a good ten feet above sea level now. *Enough to freeze half the sea. It's too thick to dive under, you'd drown before we got to the other side.*

"We're trapped!" Neridia's pulse raced. "You go, Jane, leave me here. You can still get to safety-"

And abandon my Empress? Not likely! Jane dug her claws into the ice. *Hold on!*

Neridia grabbed onto the sea dragon's mane as she pulled herself up, seawater streaming from her scales. Breath hissing between her fangs with the effort, the sea dragon climbed the sheer wall of ice.

The iceberg's surface was unnaturally flat, level as a table. Jane lay still for a moment, panting, then painfully hauled herself to her feet. She tested the ice gingerly with one webbed foot.

It'll be faster to cross this on two feet, she said, ducking her head to allow Neridia to slide off her back. *Sea dragons aren't built for walking.*

Neridia hastened to support Jane as the sea dragon resumed human form, glad to finally be able to do something to help her. "Just a little farther," she said encouragingly. "Come on!"

She'd feared that the ice would be slick, but the flash-frozen sea water was gritty with trapped particulates. It crunched under Neridia's shoes as she half-pulled, half-carried Jane across the iceberg.

Just a little farther...just a little farther...

Indigo scales erupted from the ocean ahead. The entire iceberg tilted as John's enormous bulk landed on the far edge. Neridia was knocked off her feet, sharp ice crystals cutting into her palms as she fell.

The iceberg rocked again. Neridia clung onto the ice for dear life as it bobbed like a cork on the sea.

Slowly, the wild, bouncing movement lessened. The iceberg stilled again, floating calmly once more. Heart hammering, hair across her face, Neridia looked up.

John stood in her path, sword drawn.

He was fully armored, his dragon-faced helm hiding his face. She couldn't make out his expression, couldn't even see his eyes. The mate bond was as cold as the ice underneath her.

Jane's sob of terror made Neridia glance back. The sea dragon wasn't looking at her brother, but at another towering figure, standing behind them. Light blazed around his diamond-encrusted armor as he sauntered forward.

"Empress-in-Waiting." The Knight-Commander sketched the briefest bow. "Going somewhere?"

Slowly, Neridia got to her feet. Backing away from the Knight-Commander, she turned instead to her mate.

"Please, John," she whispered. "Please let us go."

He didn't move. He might have been a statue of a knight, carved from granite. He held his sword two-handed, like a cross, the point resting on the ground between his braced feet.

"Come now, Empress-in-Waiting." The Knight-Commander stepped over the huddled Jane, not even sparing her a downward glance. "You have claimed the Pearl Throne! The Sea Council accepts you as the Heir! You cannot try to back-fin away now."

Neridia put a hand on John's bare arm, between the plates of his armor. His muscles were as hard as the metal.

"Please." She tightened her grip. "I don't want to go back."

His helmet tilted, very slightly. The snarling dragon of his visor looked down at her.

"Why?" His voice was so quiet, she could barely hear him.

"I can't explain." She was acutely aware of the Knight-Commander's stare boring into her back. "I'm sorry, John, I just *can't*. Please, trust me. Let me go."

"Your Imperial Majesty, I beg you, master your human fears. Consider what you have to lose, should you continue to pursue this action," the Knight-Commander said. "Would you break your mate's heart? I fear he would not have long to live, if you abandon him like this."

The Knight-Commander's tone dripped with honeyed concern. Only she could hear the sting in his words.

Even if I somehow got past them both, even if he couldn't catch me...he'd take his revenge on John.

Neridia took a deep breath. Squaring her shoulders, she reached up to hold her pearl pendant tight in her hand.

I'm sorry, Dad. You sacrificed so much to try to prevent this. I'm sorry.

But I can't abandon my mate.

She met the Knight-Commander's triumphant eyes. "All right," she said, dully. "You win. I'll come back. I'll be your Empress."

The Knight-Commander let out a long-suffering sigh. "Well, *finally.*" Striding forward, he reached for her arm. "Come, Empress-in-Waiting. I will take you back where you-"

He stopped dead.

"With the greatest respect, sir." John's outstretched sword barred the Knight-Commander's way. "I cannot allow you to do that."

CHAPTER 32

The Knight-Commander stared at him, shock and outrage clear even though his face was hidden behind his helm. "Have you gone utterly mad?"

"Brother, no," John's sister called weakly, so exhausted she could not even rise from the ice. "Do not throw your life away."

"Stand down, John!" Neridia tugged at his arm. "As your Empress, I order you to stand down!"

John's sword never wavered. "My mate, I told you that the one thing you could not command me to do was to leave you in pain."

"It's okay, really," Neridia insisted, though the mate bond put the lie to her words. "I'm choosing to go back willingly. You don't have to do this."

John shook his head gently, never taking his eyes off his seething opponent. "I do not know why, but the thought of returning to Atlantis makes your soul cry out in anguish. I will not allow you to be dragged back there."

The Knight-Commander tried to press forward, but John angled his hand slightly, making the razor-sharp edge of his blade glint in warning. His superior was forced to stop, his eyes flashing as angrily as the steel.

"I will have you executed for this," the Knight-Commander spat. "This is treason!"

"No, sir." John shifted to a two-handed grip, setting his feet. "This is a challenge."

Well, finally! His inner human cheered. *Skewer the fucker!*

"Knight-Commander, you would force the Empress-in-Waiting back to her Throne, in the name of honor and duty." John carefully picked the most respectful harmonies he could manage in human form. "I contest that the Throne is the Empress-in-Waiting's, to do with as she pleases. That includes the right to relinquish it. In all honor, we cannot stand in her way."

"She must return! I have already forced the Sea Council to accept her!" The Knight-Commander's gauntleted fists clenched. "Would you have me made a laughingstock? Already the other lords grow arrogant, seeking to challenge sea dragon rule. The politics-"

"Are irrelevant," John interrupted, his tone hardening. "This is a matter of honor. I accuse you of acting dishonorably, sir. Will you answer the challenge…or yield?"

The Knight-Commander answered with a wordless snarl of rage. In a single fluid movement, he drew his own swords.

"No!" Neridia grabbed a strap of John's armor, trying to haul him back. "Don't, John! He'll cut you to pieces!"

Catching the Knight-Commander's eye, John lowered the tip of his sword. "A moment, sir. Then we may begin."

"By all means," the Knight-Commander sneered. "Make sure to kiss your mate goodbye."

John pulled off his helmet, casting it aside. By tradition a formal duel was fought bare-headed, face to face with one's opponent without concealment. The Knight-Commander made no move to follow suit. Instead, he flicked his blades through a complex sequence of dizzying, flashing figures, loosening his wrists and shoulders.

He made that look easy, his inner human muttered. *You sure we can't just stab him now, while his back is turned?*

From Neridia's expression, she was having much the same

thought. "Please, John, don't go through with this. I'd rather live with you in Atlantis than see you die here."

John cupped her cheek in his gauntleted hand. Without speaking, he bent down, gently pressing his mouth to hers. Her lips were cold, but they still ignited a fire in his blood. He closed his eyes, feeling that warmth fill him with strength.

She was his mate. He would protect her.

He would win her freedom…even if it meant losing her himself.

"Do not fear for me." With one last kiss, he drew back, tightening his grasp on his sword. "I have honor on my side."

Neridia took a deep breath, closing her eyes. When she opened them again, their sky-blue depths were resolute. Her mouth set in a determined line.

"Yes," she said, her tone so clear and commanding that the very waves seemed to fall still to hear her. "You do. If you would challenge the Knight-Commander, do it for the right reason."

"Yes!" John's sister called, her own tone fierce. "Tell him, Neridia!"

The Knight-Commander wheeled on his heel to confront Neridia, muscles bunching in rage. "Don't you dare-!"

Neridia faced him down without a trace of fear, her spine straight and her head up. "You sent assassins to kill my father, the Pearl Emperor. You tried to kill me too, and when you could not, you sought instead to force me to do your will by threatening my mate. You are an honorless traitor, and at last you will pay for your crimes."

Now, *now* he understood why she had fled, what she had not been able to tell him. The mate bond opened wide, showing him her whole soul.

He had thought to protect her…but she had been protecting him.

"Oh my mate, my heart," he whispered. "My Empress."

Words failed him. He could only open his heart to her in return, showing her all that he felt. His sorrow at the burden she had been forced to carry alone. His fierce, awestruck pride at her courage. His love for her, wider and deeper than the ocean itself.

The sea wind blew her hair back from her face as she turned to him. She stood proud as a queen, as an Empress, as a very goddess.

"My Champion." With steady hands, she removed her pearl pendant. "Take this as a mark of my favor. Punish the traitor. Avenge the Emperor. Uphold my honor."

"Vile lies," the Knight-Commander snarled, as John knelt so that Neridia could fasten the chain around his own neck. "I deny them all. Make what accusations you will, human. It will make no difference. I will wash my honor clean in your Champion's blood."

John rose. The Emperor's pearl rested in the hollow of his throat, warm from the heat of Neridia's skin. Setting his feet, he looked levelly across at the Knight-Commander.

"You may try." He swept his blade up to a guard position, deliberately forgoing the customary salute to an honorable opponent. "Traitor."

The Knight-Commander leaped forward with a fierce sequence of strikes. John did not even try to follow the dazzling flicker of the twin blades. Instead, he concentrated on the Knight-Commander's eyes, half-hidden as they were beneath his helm. He let himself flow as easily as water, without thought.

The power of the Knight-Commander's blows vibrated down John's blade and through his bones...but he blocked every one. The Knight-Commander hesitated for a moment, as though surprised that his first assault had failed. His left blade dropped fractionally.

Suspecting that it was a trick to lure him out, John firmed his own stance. Though he had seen the Knight-Commander duel many times —and even sparred with him, during his own training—it was all several years in the past.

He will have mastered new techniques unknown to me, while I was away on land. I cannot rely on my memory. I must bide my time, until I have learned his style.

Until I can find a weakness.

"You will be waiting a long time, Knight-Poet," the Knight-Commander taunted. "Drop your guard, and I will at least allow you a swift death."

As a powerful Seer, the Knight-Commander could read thoughts directly from the tides of a person's blood. It was another of the things that made him such a dangerous opponent. John tightened his own mental walls, and waited.

The Knight-Commander sighed. "And to think that I once thought you might become a worthy opponent, in time. How disappointing."

He attacked again, faster this time. His swords spun in interlocking patterns. John caught and deflected the right blade, but the left was already darting in to strike at his exposed side.

On pure instinct, John pivoted. The Knight-Commander's sword missed him by a hair, passing so close that he felt the whisper of it against his skin. Distantly, he thought he heard his sister stifle a shriek of fear, but he could not spare her a glance. All of his attention had to be fixed on his opponent.

He didn't *need* to spare a glance for Neridia. He felt her presence at his back like the heat of the sun. Her courage filled him, more powerful than the tides.

The Knight-Commander pressed his attack, seeking to catch him off-balance. John danced away on the balls of his feet, his own sword a blur as he parried. He still had yet to venture an attack of his own… but a deep, calm certainty was forming in his mind.

Sea dragon duels were always in human form, with blades. The vast majority of duels—unlike *this* one—were only fought to first blood, and a dragon's natural form was too powerful, too deadly, to allow safe combat. Thus, all sea dragon knights trained scrupulously with the sword. Serious duelists might spend as much as two hours a day in human form, practicing.

But John had lived two *years* as a human.

He knew the reach of his human limbs as instinctively as the span of his talons. He moved as easily on two feet as he could through the sea. He had worn this form for so long, its instincts had become his own.

The Knight-Commander was a master of the blade, winner of countless challenges. He was hailed as the most skilled duelist in the entire Order of the First Water.

And John…was *better* than him.

The Knight-Commander realized it at the same moment as John himself. His aggressive storm of blows faltered.

Now John struck, taking advantage of the longer reach of his own greatsword. For the first time, the Knight-Commander was forced to raise his blades in defense rather than attack. He crossed his swords, only barely managing to catch John's between them.

Their hilts locked, and the contest became one of strength rather than finesse. John dug his feet into the gritty ice for purchase, his biceps straining as he struggled to keep both the Knight-Commander's blades trapped. They were so close that John could see the Knight-Commander's rictus snarl beneath his helmet...and the fear in his eyes.

The Knight-Commander had the powerful arms and shoulders of a swordsman. But long shifts hauling heavy hoses and firefighting equipment had honed every muscle in John's body. His own strength came from more than just endless practice drills and polite, formal combat.

He drove forward with that strength now, bringing to bear all the coiled power of his legs and back. His heavier blade smashed through his opponent's guard.

Only the Knight-Commander's diamond-studded armor saved him from being sliced in half from shoulder to hip. John's sword screeched off the edge of one pauldron, striking sparks. It gave the Knight-Commander enough time to leap backward—but not before the tip of John's blade scored a thin red line across his chest.

"First blood!" John's sister called, exultant. She and Neridia had drawn back to a safe distance, clutching each other's hands. "First blood to you, my brother!"

"First blood?" The Knight-Commander sounded positively indignant, as if he could barely believe the outrageous affront of it. "To *him?*"

"Yes." John resettled his grip on his sword hilt. "And I will claim the last, too."

He powered forward again, his leaping blade as swift and eager as a dolphin. The Knight-Commander fought back furiously, defending with one sword even as he struck with the other. John twisted aside from some attacks; caught others on his armored forearms and shoulders.

His sword tasted the Knight-Commander's blood twice more, and still he himself was uninjured.

The Knight-Commander broke off, retreating a few paces. He circled, keeping his blades warily upraised. His ragged breath hung in the freezing air. He cast a quick glance around, as though searching for an escape route.

"There is no fleeing from dishonor, traitor." John's muscles burned with effort, but his own chest still rose and fell evenly. "You cannot escape. And you cannot win."

The Knight-Commander's shoulders set. His blazing green eyes glared at John from behind his visor, filled with hate.

"I might not win," he spat. "But neither will you."

The Knight-Commander reversed his grip on his left sword, raising the weapon to shoulder-height with the blade sticking straight out in front of him. It was such a bizarre stance, John instinctively angled his own sword across his body, ready to defend himself from any possible attack.

Which meant he was caught completely unprepared.

In a swift, vicious movement, the Knight-Commander hurled his sword straight at Neridia.

CHAPTER 33

"He's going to win." Jane's hand crushed Neridia's. "My brother's going to win!"

Neridia was no expert at judging sword fights, but even she could see that the Knight-Commander was flagging. Though he still cut and lunged with ferocious speed, his movements didn't flow together quite as smoothly as they had at the start at the fight. Crimson drops speckled the surface of the ice around him.

John's torso was sheened with sweat, but still unmarked by the Knight-Commander's blades. He moved with the unconscious, fluid grace of a hunting predator, wielding his heavy sword as if it was an extension of his own body. His calm, steady eyes never left his opponent's.

Neridia could feel his intent focus down the mate bond. All of him —mind, body, and soul—was utterly concentrated on destroying the threat to her.

All she could do was send back her shining faith in him. Her utter certainty that he would always, always protect her.

My mate. My heart. My Champion.

Then, in an eye blink, everything changed.

One moment, the Knight-Commander and John were circling

each other, swords raised defensively. The next, John was spinning away from his opponent, hurling himself straight at Neridia. His sword swept round in a great, desperate arc.

There was a loud *clang* of steel against steel. Neridia found herself staring at one of the Knight-Commander's swords, point embedded deep in the ice just a few feet away from her. It was so unexpected, for a heartbeat she was at a complete loss as to how it had come to be there.

The Knight-Commander threw it...at me?

Wrenching her eyes from the quivering blade, she looked up at John. He'd had to move so fast to deflect the sword, he'd skidded to a halt close enough for her to touch. His own sword was still outstretched, point low to the ground. The mate bond vibrated with his shock.

Four inches of reddened steel protruded from the center of his chest.

Behind him, the Knight-Commander wrenched his blade free. Very slowly, his eyes never leaving hers, John sank to his knees.

"No," Neridia whispered—and then, more loudly, echoing the scream of her inner voice, "*No!*"

Her former hesitation, her doubts—all were utterly washed away by the sight of her mate's lifeblood staining the ice.

Power rose in her, unstoppable as the tide. She embraced the surging torrent, stretching out her arms, welcoming it as it filled her. She expanded, her body reshaping to match the surge of her soul.

"*NO!*" she roared, in a thundering chord that flattened the waves.

The Knight-Commander's blade dropped from his hand, clattering on the ice. He turned to flee, but Neridia whipped her tail round, catching him across his back. The blow knocked him clean off the iceberg.

But not into the sea.

A huge, gaping maw surged from the water, opening wide as the gates of Hell. The Knight-Commander didn't have time to scream, let alone shift.

The megalodon's jaws swallowed him whole. Not so much as a drop of the traitor's blood tainted the ocean.

"*Stop!*" Neridia shouted—not at the Master Shark, but at the sea dragons racing toward him.

She knew their exact positions, as she knew the exact position of every creature in the sea for miles around. She *was* the sea. She knew every wave and every current, as naturally as she knew her own body.

The sea dragons' war-songs turned into discordant chords of astonishment as they broke the surface, catching sight of her. The sharks who'd been pursuing them broke off too, their bloodlust forgotten. Sea dragon and shark alike stared up at her.

"Empress."

"The Pearl Empress."

"The Pearl Empress!"

One by one, the sea dragons took up the whispered melody. The rising chorus strengthened, awe swelling into full-throated adulation. Beneath the sea dragons, the sharks swept in spirals of silent ecstasy.

"THE PEARL EMPRESS!" the sea dragons roared, and the whole ocean echoed their joy.

Neridia was barely aware of the deafening chorus. All she could hear was the terrible silence of John's heart.

He'd fallen to his back, his crimson blood pooling around him. Jane, sobbing, knelt beside him, futilely trying to stem the tide with her bare hands.

We are the Pearl Empress, her inner dragon said in her soul—no longer a whisper, but a mighty voice that left no room for self-doubt. *All tides must obey our will.*

Nudging Jane aside, Neridia spread her claws over John's still form. He was a sea dragon, with the sea in his veins. He was as much a part of the ocean as the waves and the tides.

He was hers to command.

Focusing her power, Neridia drew together the disrupted currents of his blood. She stopped it from spilling out onto the ice, despite the gaping rent in his chest. She forced it to move through its usual channels. She was his heart, keeping life flowing through his body.

His grey pallor warmed...but he still lay motionless, deeply unconscious. Though she could hold his death at bay, she couldn't heal the fatal wound in his chest.

But she knew someone who could.

She reared up, turning her great horned head in the direction of the glittering lights of Brighton. Her mind quested out, rushing over the city like a tsunami.

HUGH! she cried out, with all the power of the sea. *Come, come now! John needs you!*

His soul touched hers, a pure brightness like silver moonlight on fresh-fallen snow. Other minds rose in answer too. Dai, a swirl of smoke and sparks; Chase, swift and unstoppable as a storm; Ash, a veiled power equal to her own, the sun to her sea. They heard her call.

They were firefighters. They knew how to respond to an emergency.

In mere minutes, Chase's black hooves touched down beside her. Hugh slid off his back, his white hair brighter than the ice. Both the pegasus and the paramedic did a double-take at Neridia's new form, but quickly turned their attention to John.

"Oh, you have got to be kidding me." Hugh let out a groan as he saw John's wound. "You bloody overgrown fish, can't you even get *injured* like a normal human being?"

Neridia put out a claw to restrain Jane, as the sea dragon instinctively tried to block Hugh from her unconscious brother. *You can heal him, can't you?*

"I can heal anything short of decapitation." Hugh scowled irritably, his long-fingered hands already probing John's chest. "And I swear to God, one of these days someone is going to put even that to the test. Now shut up and let me work."

A brilliant silver glow spread out from the paramedic's hands. It ran over John's still form, covering him like a blanket woven out of pure moonlight.

A clean, clear scent filled the air, like lilacs, and rain, and the first leaves of spring. Despite everything, a sense of peace settled over

Neridia. She had a sudden deep, powerful certainty that all would be well.

"Come on, you bastard," Hugh muttered under his breath. "If you make me shift in front of all these people, I'll kill you myself..."

Jaw clenching, Hugh bowed his head as if in deepest prayer. For the briefest instant, an even brighter light flared, like a star set into his forehead. Neridia had to close her eyes against the dazzling flash.

When she opened them again, she found herself looking into John's.

She very nearly squashed poor Hugh flat, forgetting her current size and strength in her haste to reach her mate. He was still flat on his back, the ice red around him, but his wound was completely healed. Only an old, pale scar marked where it had been.

He stretched one hand up to her. She bent her head to meet him, feeling the sweet fire of his touch even through her armored hide. His spread fingers barely spanned a single one of her scales.

Pure joy filled his blue eyes. He smiled up at her.

"My Empress," he said.

EPILOGUE

John would never tire of watching Neridia swim.

No one would ever be able to tell that she had not been born to the form that she now wore. She curved through the water more gracefully than the finest Dancer, and more powerfully than the strongest Knight. She moved like the sea itself.

She was the rarest of all sea dragon colors—a true, deep black, the exact same shade as her hair in human form. As she swam, iridescent highlights gleamed from her sinuous flanks; flashes of darkest blues and purples, like distant nebulas hidden in the depths of her midnight scales.

As the Empress's mate and bodyguard, he had the honor of swimming closest to her. He took secret delight in trying to perfectly echo every graceful movement of her ebony body. When she dove, he rose; when she spiraled one way, he went the other, arcing around her in precise counterpoint.

Now, however, duty required him to break off his private game. They had crossed from the cold Atlantic into the narrow, shallower waters of the English Channel, and were rapidly approaching the shore. Even though an entire honor-guard of knights flanked them, John trusted his mate's safety to no one other than himself.

Rising closer to the surface, he propelled himself forward with a powerful stroke of his tail...and laughed out loud as, below, Neridia perfectly matched his increased speed. It seemed that his secret game was not as secret as he had thought.

Her sky-blue eyes gleamed mischievously at him through the dim water. "Trying to out-swim me, my Champion?"

"Never, my heart," he sang back. "But you must allow me to precede you for a little while. It is a matter of security."

"You do realize that nothing in the sea can harm me, right?" she teased...but the subtle harmonies she wove around the melody told him that she understood his need to protect her, and loved him for it.

That was another thing he would never tire of—the rich, glorious symphony of her voice. Sea dragons usually learned their native tongue while they lay dreaming in the egg, from listening to their parents. Neridia was the only person who'd ever had to master it as an adult, yet she'd become perfectly fluent in a matter of weeks. It was like she'd already known it, somewhere deep in her soul, and had merely had to be reminded.

"We are leaving the sea, Your Majesty," he sang. "I am responsible for your safety, and I take that duty seriously. It is a matter of personal honor."

"Then I am safe indeed." She looked up at him fondly. "Go on then, my Royal Consort, Imperial Champion, Knight-Poet of the First Water, and Firefighter for the East Sussex Fire and Rescue Service."

And there was the third thing he would never tire of—his new name. Even the short form of it sent a thrill through his very bones. No matter how long he lived or what deeds he accomplished, there would never be a greater honor than the first few notes of his name.

Royal Consort.

Pride swelling his chest, he increased his speed, rising toward the surface again. This time, she let him go. Leaving the Imperial retinue behind, he quickly caught up with the two knights he'd assigned to the role of advance guard.

To his surprise, he found them stationary in the water. They were so close to the shore now that the sea was barely deep enough to support a sea dragon's bulk. Both knights had flattened their bodies along the rocky sea bed as though trying to hide, peering anxiously up at the glimmering surface just over their heads.

"Is there a problem?" John inquired, swimming up to them.

"Imperial Champion," the first knight gasped, looking immensely relieved. "You have come to lead us in the charge!"

"Charge?" John said sharply. "Against what foe?"

"A great force of dry-landers is arrayed against us, sir," the second knight said, his crimson eyes wide. "They are flying battle-flags and singing dire songs of war."

John cautiously raised his head a few inches above sea level...and his neck-ruff bristled in amusement.

"Ah," he said, sinking back down again. "Yes. Perhaps it would be best if *I* emerged first."

The first knight extended his claws. "We shall be at your side, sir! We shall drive back this army!"

"No, no." John waved them back down again. "I believe I can handle this on my own."

Leaving them whispering anxiously behind him, he clambered up the sloping shore. As he emerged from the ocean, he shifted into human form.

"Sword-brother Chase," he called. "Perhaps it would be better if you turned off the music. It is being...somewhat misconstrued."

Chase obligingly pressed a button on the sound system. The thumping bass and screeching notes fell thankfully silent.

"I told you sea dragons wouldn't like Beyoncé," Griff murmured.

"Shut up. Everyone likes Beyoncé." Elbowing Griff aside, Chase threw his arms wide open, grinning broadly. "Surprise!"

John's mouth quirked as he took in the scene. "Yes. This is definitely a surprise."

Colorful bunting hung from striped parasols. Shifter children—Griff's son Danny among them—ran shrieking with joy, splashing in the shallow surf. Their parents watched indulgently from scattered beach towels. Other shifters wandered about, chatting and laughing in the sun.

A little way down the beach, Dai and his mate Virginia were roundly thrashing a couple of wolves from the local pack at some sort of game that involved punching a ball over a net. Hugh watched over their daughter while they played, an uncharacteristic smile on his face as he bounced the giggling infant on his knees. Nearby, Rose was dispensing chilled beverages from a cooler. Ash stood at her side, calmly flipping burgers over a barbecue.

John turned back to his friends. "Is this another one of your strange human customs?"

"Aye." Griff clapped him on the shoulder. "The custom of throwing a party to welcome back a friend. We've missed you, these past few months."

"And I you." John breathed deeply, tasting the familiar scent of smoke on the air. "I never thought I would say this, but it is good to be back on land."

"Good enough that we can tempt you to stay permanently?" Chase teased.

John shook his head, smiling. "Atlantis will always be my home. But truly, I belong to two worlds. All of us sea dragons do. Hopefully more of us will realize that, now that the Empress has decreed that she will be spending six months of each year on land."

"Good thing she decided to pick Brighton as the site of her new sea dragon embassy," Griff said, grinning. "You wouldn't happen to have had anything to do with that, would you?"

"It was a sound political decision," John said mildly. "We needed a human city on the sea, after all, with a large shifter population. And if there may have been a few personal reasons for the choice…there *are* some privileges to being close to the Pearl Throne."

Griff laughed. "Think you'll find time to fit in some firefighting amidst all those Imperial duties?"

John raised an eyebrow. "Why do you think I didn't allow them to make me Knight-Commander in addition to everything else?"

John. Neridia's mental voice held an undercurrent of laughter. *There are a couple of knights here who are very worried about the fact that you're currently taking on an entire army of land-shifters single-handed. Should I send in reinforcements?*

John chuckled under his breath. *Hold for a moment, my heart. Let me ensure we do not accidentally start a war.*

Catching Griff and Chase's curious looks, he explained, "The Empress approaches, along with the rest of our group. My brothers, I am overwhelmed by your, ah, enthusiasm, but I fear that the other sea dragons may find it a little *too* overwhelming. This is the first time any of them have ever ventured on land, and the first time they have met dry-landers."

"Don't worry, everyone's been briefed to keep their distance." Chase gestured at the assembled crowd. "But pretty much every shifter in Brighton is dying of curiosity. None of us have ever met any other sea dragons, after all. Are they all like you?"

"Wait for a moment." John turned, taking a few steps back into the surf. "And you will be able to judge for yourself."

All is in readiness, my heart, he sent to Neridia. He hesitated, glancing back at the crowd. *But...there are a great many people here. Do you wish me to send them away?*

No, it's fine. He could tell that she was touched by his concern, but unruffled herself. *I am the Pearl Empress. It's natural that they want to see me.*

Her sleek head broke through the waters, rising high into the air. Voices stilled all along the beach, every shifter turning in her direction. Neridia met their stares calmly, allowing them to look their fill.

Someone started to clap. The applause speed like fire through the crowd. Neridia dipped her regal head in acknowledgement, accepting the acclaim as her due. Then she shimmered, shrinking down into human form.

"They're still clapping," Neridia murmured in his ear, as she smiled and waved at the crowd.

"You are still the Empress," he replied, taking her hand. "Come. Our friends are waiting to welcome us."

Tucking her hand through his arm, he escorted her up the beach. Somewhat to his own relief, the applause faded after a few moments, shifters going back to enjoying the party. He was used to dry-landers staring at him...but not cheering while they did so.

"Chase! Griff!" Neridia greeted them with hugs, laughing. "What *is* all of this?"

"You're royalty now. You have to expect people to break out the bunting when you appear." Chase hugged her back. "Is this proper protocol? Shouldn't we be bowing?"

"That was one of the first things I banned. I hate people staring at my feet when I'm trying to talk to them." Neridia hesitated, glancing back at the ocean. "John, I think everyone else is too scared to come out. Can you go give them some encouragement?"

John bowed in acknowledgement. "As you command, my Empress."

"*He* still bows," he heard Griff say, as he headed down the beach.

"He's John," Neridia replied wryly. "The sea itself can't change his course..."

Smiling to himself, John waded back into the water. A couple of the Empress's escort had worked up the nerve to take human form, though they were still chin-deep in the sea. Shading his eyes, John picked out his sister's indigo hair, half-hidden amidst the waves.

"Frightened, little sister?" he called. "I thought you were eager to finally walk on land."

As he had hoped, his brotherly taunt drew her out of the waves. Jane strode out with chin up and shoulders squared, the wet silk of her formal sarong clinging to her legs. Despite her bold posture, her turquoise eyes darted over the crowd nervously.

"There are so many people here!" she whispered, taking his hand. "Why has the entire city turned out to greet us?"

"I am afraid this is just a small gathering, my sister." John tightened his fingers on hers reassuringly. "I was overwhelmed too, when I first walked on land and realized how numerous the dry-landers truly are. Do not be intimidated. I will be here to help you adjust."

A few more sea dragons were taking tentative steps up the beach, following Jane's example. Griff, who seemed to have volunteered for the role of ambassador, went to meet them. John relaxed, knowing that he could trust in his oath-brother's combination of eagle perception and lion charisma to make the nervous sea dragons feel at home.

"Let us go up to the house," John said, indicating the large villa overlooking the private cove. "All should be in readiness. You can rest. You don't have to plunge into the human world all at once."

Jane took a deep breath, throwing back her shoulders. Some of the usual sparkle returned to her eyes. "Thank you, little brother, but no. I'm not going to waste a single day. I've come onto land to find my mate, and that's what I'm going to do."

She let go of his hand, clearly intent on starting the search right there and then. John let out his breath in a long-suffering sigh.

"Jane," he said, as patiently as he could. "You have not yet quite grasped exactly how many people there are on land. The chance of you finding your mate here is-"

He realized his sister wasn't listening. As if in a dream, she was walking away from him, eyes locked on someone in the crowd.

"What's up with her?" Neridia asked curiously, coming up to his side along with Chase.

John stared after his sister, barely able to believe what he was seeing. "Apparently, my sister has just found her mate."

Oh, for fuck's sake. His inner human buried its face in its hands with a groan. *It took us two years, and she does it in* two minutes?

"Your sister? That's your sister?" Chase's black eyes widened. "Bloody hell, is she heading for Hugh?"

She wasn't. Jane pushed straight past the startled paramedic. In all the crowd, she only had eyes for…

John abruptly felt as if he'd just been sucked down by an undertow.

"Him?" he spluttered. "My sister's mate is, is…*him?*"

A little distance away, Reiner Ljonsson was walking towards Jane with a stunned, wide-eyed expression.

"No," John said, as the pair joined hands. His own fist clenched. "No. No. No. Absolutely not. This is-"

"None of your business," Neridia said firmly.

"But-"

"This is your Empress speaking, John." She poked him in the side. "What's wrong with him, anyway?"

"Oh boy." Chase let out a low whistle, shaking his head. "Now *there's* a long story. Ask Griff about it sometime."

"Well, given that he was at Griff's wedding, it must have worked out all right in the end." Neridia folded her arms, glaring up at John. "You will *not* interfere with your sister's happiness. Understand?"

John stared morosely at his sister. Even from this distance, it was obvious that she was practically radiant with joy. Reiner was gazing at her as if she was a priceless diamond. His usual scowl had been wiped away, replaced by pure wonder.

John sighed. "They are true mates," he said reluctantly. "And whatever Reiner did in the past, it is true that my oath-brother trusts him now. It is not my place to stand in their way."

Chase glanced at him, eyebrows rising. "You *have* changed."

"And if he is not worthy of her," John added, "I shall personally skin him and wear his mane as a hat."

"Though not that much," Chase concluded. He brightened. "I just thought of something. She's a sea dragon, right? And he's a lion shifter."

"Oh, is that what he is?" Neridia narrowed her eyes at Chase. "Why are you smirking like that?"

"Think about it," Chase urged, his evil grin spreading wider. "Sea dragon. Lion. So their kids will be...?"

They both looked at him blankly.

"Sea lions!" Chase yelled, and collapsed into helpless laughter.

∽

There was such a thing, Neridia decided as she poked through her dressing-room for something to wear, as having too many pearls.

No there isn't, her inner dragon said promptly. *One either has all the pearls, or one does not. And we do* not *have all the pearls.*

Neridia grinned to herself at her dragon's reproachful tone. It was still miffed at her for having sold a few of the smaller pieces from the royal hoard to finance the purchase of this house. The sea dragons in her entourage had been even more shocked.

"No one needs a literal mountain of treasure," she said to her inner dragon now, as she'd told the other dragons then. "And it's not like we don't have plenty left over."

She pointedly looked around her dressing room, which would perhaps be more accurately described as a treasure room. Her human clothes were vastly outnumbered by ornate caskets, each one overflowing with gold and jewels. And this wasn't even a *hundredth* of her personal hoard.

That is a good point, her inner dragon conceded. It settled down again in the depths of her mind. *Tomorrow, we must send word back to Atlantis. The Voice of the Empress can send us more of our treasures.*

Neridia chuckled under her breath, shaking her head at her dragon's unabashed avarice. "The Master Shark is quite busy enough without distracting him with your whims, greedy beast."

The Sea Council had not taken well to her appointment of the Master Shark as her Voice while she was away on land. Nonetheless, Neridia had great confidence in the megalodon shifter's ability to bring the fractious sea nobles to heel. He could, after all, make them all fall silent merely by looking slightly hungry.

"You'll have to be content with what we brought," Neridia said to her dragon, smiling. "And our greatest treasure is already here, you know."

Her dragon blinked its luminous eyes in contentment. *Yes. He is.*

John ducked through the doorway. Despite his caution, he still managed to catch his broad shoulders on the frame. Grimacing, he straightened—only to bash his head against the light fitting.

"This I have *not* missed about life on land," he grumbled, catching hold of the swinging shade. "How small everything is."

Neridia was somewhat regretting encouraging her knights to swap their helmets and armor for human clothes. Quite a few of her entourage already sported bruises across their foreheads, and it was still only their first day on land.

Though, she thought as she looked at her mate, *there is definitely something to be said for human clothes.*

John was already dressed for the evening's formal dinner. The fine white fabric of his dress shirt clung to the powerful curves of his shoulders. She'd grown so accustomed to seeing him bare-chested in Atlantis, there was something erotic about his torso being covered.

Neridia found her gaze drifting lower, past the black cummerbund emphasizing the flatness of his abdomen. She regretfully tore her eyes away before she got too distracted. *She* still had to get ready, after all.

"Did you find out what all that shouting was about?" she asked John, as she went back to searching through her jewelry caskets.

"Ah." He tilted his head, making the charms in his hair catch the light. "I fear that I have good news, and bad news."

"What's the good news?"

"The good news is that Fifth Knight of the Third Water has successfully defeated the unnatural creature lurking in our utility room."

"What?" Neridia turned to stare at him.

His mouth quirked. "The bad news is that we need a new washing machine. Ideally one that does not make *quite* such an alarming growling noise when it starts."

Neridia let out her breath in amusement. "Oh dear."

"She was so proud at having saved her Empress from such a dire threat, I have not yet had the heart to explain the truth of the matter." John sighed. "I have left her trying to work out how to dismember her kill. I think she plans to offer you its head as a trophy."

"I'll have a word with her later." Neridia held a twisted rope of multi-colored pearls up to her neck, examining the effect in her mirror. "Any other casualties?"

"Seventh Artist of the Coalescing Tide has twisted his ankle. He absent-mindedly tried to swim off the deck. I have taken the opportunity to remind everyone about the concept of gravity." John frowned, his tone shading darker with disapproval. "And it seems that Chase has introduced several of my knights to the concept of beer."

"Don't be too hard on them. It was their first human party, after all."

"I shall not dispense any formal punishments." John's blue eyes glinted wickedly. "But I believe that I shall hold a full sword-drill tomorrow. At five in the morning."

"A dead washing machine, a twisted ankle, and some hangovers. Our first day on land is going better than I expected." Neridia tried on a simple circlet of gold, set with a pearl the size of a walnut. "Hmm. Is this too much?"

Even without looking at him, Neridia could feel John's appreciative gaze sweeping down her silk-clad body. "Too much for what?"

"For the dinner tonight." Neridia straightened the circlet, frowning at herself in the mirror. "It's just local dignitaries, like the mayor and the regional representatives for the Parliament of Shifters. I don't want to overdress for the occasion."

Gently but firmly, John took the circlet from her head. "You are the Pearl Empress. It is impossible for you to be overdressed. You *are* the occasion."

"John!" Neridia protested as he picked up one of her most elaborate crowns, a golden confection that blazed with diamonds and black pearls. "I can't wear that!"

"But it is the one that becomes you the most." He settled the crown on her head. "And besides, it is my favorite."

"Well..." Neridia met his eyes in the mirror, smiling. "In that case, of course I'll wear it."

"You should wear this, too." He reclaimed the necklace she'd tried and discarded earlier. "There will be dragon shifters there. They measure status by the value of hoards. They must be left in no doubt as to your rank."

His calloused fingertips trailed over the curve of her neck, lightly, sending delicious shivers through her. "All right," she said, a little breathlessly. "If you think it's a good idea."

"I do." He sank to one knee, capturing her wrists in his huge hands. "And you need bracelets too. Sapphires, I think."

"John, I really don't-" Neridia caught her breath, her protest dying away half-formed as he swept his thumb over her inner wrist.

"Sapphires," he breathed, pressing a kiss to the sensitive skin.

"Many sapphires."

Neridia could only submit as he fastened wide golden bracelets around her forearms. The gleaming sapphires caught in the fine filigree nets precisely matched the deep indigo of his intent, hungry eyes.

His hand ran over the intricate metalwork, and then, more slowly, up over the soft curves of her upper arms. Neridia's lips parted as he leaned in close…but rather than claim her mouth, he tilted his head to place a light, teasing kiss just behind her ear.

"Earrings," he whispered, his breath warm against her skin.

Neridia gasped as he gently nipped at her lobe. Withdrawing again, John selected a pair of pearl and diamond drops from a casket. With infinite care, he fastened them to her ears.

"There," he said, his voice husky. Placing his hands on her shoulders, he gently turned her to face the mirror. "See."

Neridia looked at herself. Her eyes were as large and dark as the black pearls of her crown. The gleaming jewels around her neck emphasized the heightened color of her skin. Diamonds dripped from her ears like falling drops of rain.

"Okay," she said, laughter mingling with desire. "Now that really *is* too much, John."

He made a deep, thoughtful rumble, low in his throat, as he drew her up to her feet. "Perhaps you are right."

His hand ran up her spine. Before she'd realized his intent, he'd undone the fastenings of her ball gown.

"John!" she protested, as he slipped the indigo silk over her shoulders, leaving her only in her panties.

He stifled her objection with his mouth. His hard body pressed her back against the wall of the dressing-room. The crisp linen of his shirt rubbed against her bared breasts, sending jolts of pleasure through her hardening nipples.

His fingers slipped under the waistband of her panties. "Still too much," he murmured against her mouth.

Stepping back, he drew her panties down, slowly. Neridia trembled, a wash of heat pulsing between her thighs as his hands caressed the soft curves of her legs from hips to ankles.

"There," he said, rising again. He took a step back, gazing at her as if she were some priceless work of art. "Now that is just right."

She shook her head at him, pursing her lips in a mock-pout. "Wrong. Now this is not enough."

He started to turn to the treasure-hoard, but she caught his hand. Lacing her fingers through his, she pulled him out of the dressing-room and into the bedroom.

He let her guide him so that he was sitting on the bed. Straddling his lap, Neridia kissed him deeply, unfastening the tiny buttons of his shirt as she did so. Never breaking the kiss, she ran her hands over the planes of his chest.

Her fingers found the pale, smooth scar over his heart. The feel of it made her kiss him even more fervently, winding her other hand into his braided hair. She had come so close to losing him...

He kissed her back with equal hunger. His hands tightened on her back. His hot mouth, the press of his bare skin against hers, the solid strength of his arms around her...they were all a silent, unspoken promise.

A promise that he would always be there. That nothing would ever part them again.

His hard length pressed against her wet sex, demanding even through the layers of fabric separating them. She moaned into his mouth as he flexed his hips, rubbing against her in just the right way.

"Still not enough," she gasped.

He answered with a hungry growl, biting at her lip. His hands jerked impatiently at his belt. Raising herself up on her knees, she helped him free his eager cock.

He seized her hips, stopping her from lowering herself down again. She squirmed, her core clenching in anticipation at the tantalizing feel of his thick head just parting her folds.

"Enough?" he murmured into her ear.

"No!" No matter how she writhed, his strength kept her in place. "Please, John, please!"

Slowly, teasingly, he slid her down a few inches. "Enough?"

Desperate with desire, she tightened around him in answer. He gasped, and the surge of his need swept her over the edge. Abandoning his teasing at last, he drove into the pulsing waves of her ecstasy.

She dug her fingernails into the rock-hard muscles of his back, locking her legs around his waist. Her climax surged higher and higher, drawn out by every thrust of his body, until she couldn't tell the difference between her pleasure and his.

His sweat-slick torso pressed against hers as he arced up. Body to body, soul to soul, they came together, and were one.

Breathing hard, Neridia collapsed against John's chest. He held her tight, rolling back himself so that they spooned together on the bed. She closed her eyes, wrapped in his arms, drifting in perfect contentment.

Only for a moment, though.

With a sigh, she opened her eyes again. "We're going to be late."

"Mmm." John pressed his face into the back of her neck, inhaling deeply. "It appears so."

"John." She pushed at his arm, which had no effect whatsoever. "*John.* We have to get up."

"It occurs to me," he said, his voice a deep, lazy rumble, "that if one is going to be late, one might as well be *very* late."

She let out her breath, half-amused, half-exasperated—and then caught it again, as he started kissing the side of her neck.

We are *the Pearl Empress,* her inner dragon pointed out. *Others can wait on our pleasure.*

With a laugh, Neridia surrendered to temptation. Rolling onto her back, she wrapped her arms around her mate.

"This isn't setting a very good example, you know," she teased, drawing him down for another kiss. "You're the Imperial Champion. Aren't you supposed to put duty before everything else?"

"Probably." He smiled down at her, his blue eyes shining like sunlight on the sea. "But I'm only human."

Printed in Great Britain
by Amazon